Taryn is the author of *The Harper Effect* and currently lives on the Sunshine Coast with a family that includes teen children and a highly strung dog. Taryn's lived on four continents, meaning her job experience has been varied: an advertising sales rep, a ski chalet chef, a late-night newsreader and the CEO of an internet company, but writing and Australia are her true loves. Taryn is currently working on her PhD in Creative Writing while tutoring undergraduates and writing more novels. When she's not writing or teaching, she's training for triathlons in the hope they will compensate for the fact she spends ten hours a day sitting at her computer.

Also by Taryn Bashford

The Harper Effect

the Astrid Notes

TARYN BASHFORD

PAN

First published 2019 in Pan by Pan Macmillan Australia Pty Ltd
1 Market Street, Sydney, New South Wales, Australia, 2000

A catalogue record for this
book is available from the
National Library of Australia

Typeset in 11/16 pt Minion by Post Pre-press Group
Printed by McPherson's Printing Group

The paper in this book is FSC® certified.
FSC® promotes environmentally responsible,
socially beneficial and economically viable
management of the world's forests.

For Mum, Ella and Eric . . .

I'm no songwriter, so this book's my song for you.

'To thine own self be true'

William Shakespeare

1

Jacob

The hotel air conditioner blasts arctic air so my goosebumps sprout goose-babies of their own. We've lost the air-con remote. Mad Dog tells a joke and Callum laughs so hard Coke spews out of his mouth and nose.

'Who's hidden the frigging remote?' I kick at the clothes and shoes on the floor in case it's been buried. We've yet to open a wardrobe on this tour. Why would we? The floor is the biggest shelf in any hotel room.

My phone pings and vibrates in my pocket. I can tell by the ring tone and the way it pulses that it's a text from my ex. Harper.

Her text reads, *Good luck for tomorrow.* And two little pink hearts. I don't deserve the big red heart anymore.

Even though Harper has a boyfriend and is playing a tennis tournament in China right now, she's remembered to text me. Tomorrow's the biggest gig we've booked. It could get us an agent, a recording contract – our dream of being as big as the Arctic Monkeys folds through me like heady sweet smoke.

Thanks, Harps. Our fanbase is exploding even after only

being on the road two months. How's my favourite girl? I leave out the hearts.

I search for the remote behind cushions, inside Emery's two-foot-high pile of dirty laundry, which he calls a modern art sculpture, and in the toilet – I wouldn't put anything past them. The fridge only contains vodka and sour-smelling milk.

'A little help, guys,' I complain. But JW's on his nightly call with his mum, Emery's combing his hair into the perfect flick, and the other three are somehow sharing one tiny sink in the bathroom to shave. Everyone's getting charged up for a big night out.

The hotel phone on the bedside table vibrates. Its grating ring cuts through the boys' whoops as they tease Skittles. He's going through what Mad Dog calls his 'time traveller' phase. At last night's gig he wore a white belted–jacket and tonight he's wearing gold trousers.

'You could steal the sun and replace it with those trousers,' I joke, and decide not to answer the phone – anybody I want to talk to is right here in this room. And Harper would call my mobile. *Oof.* Even though she's been gone for months, each memory of her feels like a wooden drumstick stabbing a hole in my heart.

The phone stops ringing. Mad Dog shoves Callum, but Callum's a big lad and doesn't budge. 'You're so Lilliputian,' he says. A smirk pushes out his stout cheeks.

'You calling me small?' All of Mad Dog's skinny-arse six-foot-two frame towers over Callum.

Callum straightens and nods, hands folded in front of him. '*And* unimportant.' Callum has an inflated sense of his own importance. He wrote 'Boldly Meekly' when he was fourteen. I'll never be as good at songwriting. Even back then, when the six of us started jamming together, just casual kids' stuff, he was a talented writer. Now that it's our biggest hit, he thinks he's gold.

The phone starts ringing again. It's this old-fashioned ring that climbs inside you and rattles your bones. I snatch it up. 'Yeah?'

'Jacob. Is that any way to answer a phone?'

I stiffen. 'I'm used to my mobile, Dad. Why don't you call that?' But we both know it's because I screen his calls.

'Another wrong answer,' he says.

Gripping the phone harder, I wait for his reason for calling. It's never good. The sound of Sydney traffic in the background means Dad's just leaving his law firm.

'I'm calling to remind you to visit my sister. You have one more performance tomorrow, don't you? And then you're moving on.'

Performance? Guess that's one way to describe the biggest gig of our lives. I turn to face the boys, patting the air to tell them to hush up, and step in the wet patch of Coke, courtesy of Callum. 'But we're celebrating tonight. Aunt Jane will understand.'

'You're out every night. I'll text her and say you'll be over by 8.30 pm. She has a parent-teacher night, but she's still going to cook you dinner because she wants to see you. It's been three years. I'll text you her number and address. No doubt you've lost them.'

'But Dad, we're . . .'

'I won't be argued with, Jacob.'

Jeez, don't I know it. When did I ever win an argument with him? 'Yeah. Whatever.' I slump onto the bed.

'And remember your manners.' He hangs up. No 'good luck'. No 'we miss you'.

I unclench my jaw, shove the phone into its cradle. After I explain I can't go out tonight, I lie down and drown out the ribbing the boys dish with a pillow over my head.

On their way out, JW waves a bottle of hair dye at me. 'When you get back put this on your hair like I showed you. Christina Aguilera blond suits lead singers better than dirty carpet blond.'

Mad Dog flicks his long hennaed hair like a girl and says, 'No-one's going to remember the dude with hair the colour of hotel carpets.'

'With you MIA, there'll be more ladies for us.' Skittles punches my arm. I picture him drumming a rhythm on the bar, reeling in the girls with his wide smile. His hair's shaved up the back and sides but long on top, and he likes to let his stupid flick cover his eyes so he can peer out mysteriously. That's his MO. Gets him lots of girls. Mentioning we're an indie-pop band never hurts either. I usually get a lot of attention, being the lead singer, but I never take anyone back to the Purple Daze van because my heart is still stuck full of drumsticks.

'Joke's on you mate.' I chuck Skittles the van keys. 'You just became designated driver for the night.'

♫

A line of light spills under the hotel room door providing a dim glow. I flick on the bedside lamp beside me, wait until the bulb flash disappears from my retinas. My head throbs from too much cheap wine with Aunt Jane. Grunting, I swing my legs off the bed, pull open the bedside drawer. It contains the hotel Bible, Callum's fake ID, a strip of Advil. I fumble for two painkillers. They slip down my leg onto the carpet and I shove the drawer shut with my foot. A whiff of cheesy socks drifts by when I grope around for the lost Advil, then dry swallow them.

It's fricking cold in here. I didn't find the air-con remote before I left, and I was bone tired when Aunt Jane dropped me back. I shuffle toward the table in the corner to resume the search, but the hard object under a dirty T-shirt turns out to be the bottle of hair dye.

Shivering like a plucked guitar string, I give up on the remote and open the doors onto the balcony. Despite it being late July, it's hotter outside than in. Warmth spills all over my skin. Far below, the city of the Gold Coast gleams, a cobweb of shimmering lights. To the left a narrow strip of moonlight beams across a black ocean. It's as if I'm looking down on two different worlds.

Even though I'm warmer now, a shiver passes through me.

Back inside, the clock radio reads 4 am. *Where the hell is everyone?*

After texting them on the group chat and getting no response, I call their mobiles. They ring out. That gives me a bad vibe – they've been known to party too hard. Unsure what else to do, I hit the sack and only wake when the door rattles with several pounding blows. The brightness of the room tells me it's morning, yet the other beds haven't been slept in.

I sit up. Even with the balcony doors open, it's freezing.

From behind the door, a man's weighty voice says, 'Jacob Skalicky. Of the band Purple Haze?'

'Purple *Daze*,' I yell back. The name thing annoys me. '*Daze.*'

'This is Senior Constable Cox. Could you open the door please?'

'*Cox?*' I snort-laugh. 'That's the best you can do? Who is that – JW? Mad Dog. It's Mad Dog, isn't it?'

'This isn't a hoax, Mr Skalicky.'

I check the clock. 8.05 am.

The voice adds, 'There's been an accident.'

'Shit. Seriously?' It's probably a Mad Dog adrenaline-rush stunt gone wrong – falling off the moving van roof or losing his balance off someone's balcony. I pull on some shorts, search around for a shirt so the cops don't think I'm a punk-ass. But every shirt I own stinks or has food spill stains.

'Officer. Constable. I'll be right there.' I snap up JW's white T-shirt, the only stain being a spot of tomato sauce from the spaghetti he ate for lunch yesterday, and tug on a pair of Mad Dog's socks before realising I don't need socks to answer the door.

I yank open the door. Two uniformed coppers loom.

'Jeez, we've got a gig tonight,' I say. 'They better not have broken anything vital.'

A wave of annoyance hits me. What stunt did they pull this time? Dad'll go off if they've damaged the van.

♫

Five hearses.

Five shiny cockroaches, all in a line.

Callum's dad, a big guy like his son, shuffles over. 'Morning.' He dips his double chin. Dad stands on my other side. 'Bit worried about Riley,' continues Callum's dad. 'Not sure he can manage carrying the coffin.' Riley is Callum's thirteen-year-old brother. 'Reckon you could step in?'

My stomach jerks with nausea. 'I don't think – no. I just – can't.'

'Doing your duty will bring you comfort,' Dad states, no doubt seeing my refusal as further evidence of another major flaw in my character or a dereliction of my duty as a man. But how can I choose Callum over the others? The six of us have been more than friends; when you're in a band you become brothers, and when you're a band on tour you're blood brothers. They were my makeshift family to cover for the one I was born into. How could I choose one coffin over another?

'S'okay, son,' says Callum's dad. 'I understand.' He smacks a palm on my bicep, then moves away. Dad follows him, head bowed.

In slo-mo each coffin is unloaded from its hearse. My fists ball. My vision smears. I attempt to breathe, but the air is no longer oxygen – more of a poison; with each gasp I want to vomit. I'm wearing Dad's polished, black leather work shoes – apparently Vans are inappropriate for a day of burying friends – and use their heels and toe caps to rake and dig at the dirt as though I'm excavating a hole to drop into.

'Jacob.' Mum beckons me. 'Come inside the chapel now.' But I'm not ready to say goodbye, and don't plan to go anywhere near inside. And I can't deal with the way the boys' parentals looked at me when they arrived. Their faces flared with something like sympathy. Only not. A question hangs in the air that no-one dares ask. 'Why our sons and not you?'

JW's coffin fronts the line. Overhead, trees ten times his age shift and hover under the stale winter sky. The faces of his pallbearers are red and glisten with tears, their shoulders hunched against the weight of his body. Gazes lowered as they pass, they kick up dust. The last time I saw JW, he'd chucked a bottle of hair dye at me.

I focus on the hole I'm digging with Dad's shoe as Emery and Mad Dog float past in their wooden boxes. The sob that's strangling me gushes out. Shocked by the strange sound, I check no-one heard and catch sight of Skittles's dad leaning against a tree by the entrance, downing a bottle of rum. That'd be right.

In the end, Callum chooses me to carry his coffin anyway. Thanks to liking his chips large and fatty with a couple of burgers on the side, by the time Callum passes me – *Christ, he's inside that box* – the six pallbearers sweat and adjust their grips, knees buckling. At the back his brother stumbles. Assuming he'll recover, I throw out a limp arm to steady him. But the back of the coffin tilts dangerously. Suddenly I'm there, my fingers slipping against the sweating wood where Riley's hands were.

I'm carrying a dead body. Callum's dead body.

The last time I saw him he laughed so hard Coke spewed out of his nose. He'll never play the keyboard again. He's eaten his last plate of chips. My throat prickles. Reality hits me in the chest and stomach simultaneously, like a freak breaker at the beach. The air gets knocked out of me. The coffin almost goes down again. I yell at myself. *You will not let him fall. You will* not *let him down today.*

I grind my teeth. Pain shoots up my jaw and behind my eyeballs, but my legs straighten, along with my back, and Callum's dignity is restored.

Inside the chapel, the stale air rubs against the back of

my throat. After we lower Callum's coffin, I search for a seat. Sorrow is folded into each mourner's expression, scrunched against sobs. In the front row a woman cries into another woman's neck. I clamp my arms to my sides and sit in the aisle seat Mum's patting with her hand.

A woman starts speaking. A eulogy. She stops when Skittles's dad stumbles into the chapel, scraping his feet on the floor and slumping into one of the extra rows of metal chairs they set up at the back. The chair screeches. Mum tuts him. Is Skittles's dad sorry for all the arguments he had with his son? Maybe he's sorry for the times he smacked Skittles around.

The eulogy continues.

I can't listen.

Top three Arctic Monkey singles. 'A Certain Romance', for sure.

A void expands in my skull.

I grip the sides of the seat and rock myself.

'Warm-hearted yet shy, and extremely clever and talented, we'll never forget you, JW.' Miss Eulogy sits down. JW's coffin retreats on some sort of conveyance, the curtain closing on it. One down, four to go.

Someone nudges me from behind. 'They're probably wearing a suit inside those coffins.' I turn to find Riley behind me. He leans in closer. 'Callum's first and last suit.'

'Perhaps they're wearing stupid pointy leather shiny shoes too,' I say.

Mum prods me and frowns. Someone stands and shuffles to the lectern up front. My tongue sweeps across furry teeth. I can't remember the last time I brushed them.

'Did you go to Josh Mayor's funeral last year?' whispers Riley, clearly preferring to talk than listen.

'Nope.' Josh, a boy from one of the schools round here, fell from a balcony at schoolies week, with a helping hand from Mr Jack Daniels.

'Funny how no-one mentions Josh anymore.'

A life forgotten.

Six months and three days ago, when I ran a red light and rode a Harley-Davidson into a brick wall, people said I was lucky. I said I was destined for a forgettable life; Harper, the only girl I will ever love, chose someone else – and I failed my audition for a place at the Sydney Conservatorium. At the time, dying tragically and memorably seemed a good idea.

If I had died, would I already be forgotten?

'How long will it take for people to stop mentioning Callum?' Riley adds. Mum turns to him, a stern finger to her lips.

Sadness muscles through me. The band was meant to become our legacy, with people singing our songs for decades, like Elvis or The Beach Boys – because being forgettable is worse than never having lived at all.

Mad Dog. Mad Dog? What was his real name?

I can't remember.

My head has a fire inside it; beads of moisture dribble down my back.

A man's voice shouts, 'How come you got all the luck, Jacob Skalicky?'

Along with everyone else, I swivel toward the voice at the back of the chapel. Skittles's dad sprawls across two chairs, beaming. As if there's something to laugh about. I can't stay here and charge for the exit, tripping on one of the spare metal chairs. I pick up the chair and throw it at the back wall, then launch myself outside and down the steps.

With each step Mad Dog's socks, still on my feet, glower at me.

The socks get to stay.

What was the last song Mad Dog heard? His profile pic on Instagram rattles my brain, with his sly sideways glance that shows off his square jaw. Will someone delete his account or will he beam at the world, the number of followers logged at 921, forever? How long will it take for people to stop searching for his name – six months? Six years?

He'll never get past the bum-fluff stage, and it doesn't matter that Skittles did.

My rib cage clenches against the howl trapped inside me. My fist punches my open palm. I'm overwhelmed by the urge to fling myself on the ground, grind my face into the dirt, and pound my fists into the earth. But my father's curt call stops me. We watch each other. *I saved your life.* The words sit in his eyes like magnets.

'If I hadn't insisted you visit Aunt Jane, that'd be you in a box,' he says. 'Be grateful you have a second chance.'

Bet he's been dying to say that for days. 'It's not that simple,' I spit out. 'It should've been me.' And if I'd been there, I wouldn't have driven while drunk.

Dad pats his ginger-blond hair, meticulously combed back and smoothed, tucks his trilby hat under his arm, and returns to the chapel service. Parenting is the only thing he and Mum have ever failed at.

I fumble with the buttons on my formal shirt, touch the spot of spilled sauce on JW's T-shirt beneath. It seems to throb on my belly. He ate spaghetti *a few days ago*.

'I will never wash this shirt. Ever. Okay, JW?'

I still can't accept that if I call their mobiles they won't be on the other end. They'll never pick up again. Where are their phones now? Had the coppers logged and zip-locked them with their belongings, ready for a parent to claim? Along with the bodies of their sons.

They're all gone. Harper's gone. She has a whole new life on the professional tennis circuit and she's in love with someone who isn't me.

I'm alone again. And without the band, forgettable.

I tug off my jacket and formal shirt, dump them on the ground, and go in search of my motorbike.

2

Astrid

After my sister died, I did everything I could to follow her.

Trying to die was easier when I was five; I didn't understand there's no coming back. The other pull heaven had on me was that it had already taken our mum, so Savannah would discover the big secret of how she died as Maestro had refused to tell us until we were eighteen, and old enough to understand such things.

I turn the page of the book on the music stand and sing, '*Sempre tua per la vita*.' Sighing, I glare at the alphabetised opera scores on the shelves above the row of music stands Maestro sets up every morning. Each score waits to be learnt. Each one wants a piece of me. I slam shut the arrangement for *La Bohème*, feeling as though I need to scratch an itch. Except it's so deep inside me it can't be reached.

An afternoon breeze lifts my hair and tickles my cheeks. I slump into the window seat and scan the Sydney skyline in the distance. A hint of the salty ocean fills my nostrils, along with the scent of the eucalyptus trees on Honeycomb Avenue where my younger self once stepped off the curbside into oncoming traffic – on purpose. Maestro, who was simply

Dad back then, virtually pulled my arm out of its socket to save me.

I was nine years old the day we decided I would become a famous opera singer – like Maestro and Mum were, and my sister had dreamt of being. That day I woke knowing I was one day older than Savannah would ever be. I needed a hug from my ever-silent father and snuck downstairs to the music room to find him.

Maestro was standing in the open French windows watching the sky, a beautiful canvas of greys and blacks networked with lightning. He swirled brown liquid in a crystal glass, his back to me. On his record player, '*Pie Jesu*' played. I sensed he needed to be comforted, but I didn't have the words. So I sang. I concentrated more than ever on all he'd taught me, and tried to express how sad I felt, and that he wasn't alone.

At first, his shoulders slumped, then his head. I thought he was crying. But when I finished, he looked toward me, and it seemed as if my singing had breathed life back into him. His eyes roared with delight. His lips curled into a giant smile. After the meningitis had taken Savannah, he had disappeared inside himself. He had become as automated as a metronome, ticking through each task of each day with the exact same precision and blank-faced expression. So the energy pouring from him in that moment was a miracle.

Shaking his head, he said, 'Your singing is –' His voice cracked. 'Heavenly.' He opened his arms for me to run into.

'Speaking as an ex-opera singer and a voice coach, not your dad. I have goosebumps all over.'

Grateful for my miracle, I hugged him.

'Tell me, Astrid. What do you wish to do with your voice?'

There was hope in his features, and it was clear that without my singing he'd ghost through life forever. Suddenly, I needed to sing more than I needed to die. 'I'd like to follow in Mummy's footsteps. I want to be a famous soprano.'

It was the right answer. He'd been a faded black and white version of himself, but my singing resurrected him in technicolour. I suppose you could say my singing saved his life.

And now that makes us even – because clearly it's *my* fault Mum died.

Why else won't he tell me the truth until I'm eighteen? Mums die. All the time. They have cancer or heart attacks or car accidents; I'm seventeen and a half – why would Maestro think I couldn't cope with knowing what happened? Unless it's something truly terrible, but that would've made the newspapers. Google reported my mother withdrew from public life after giving birth to her second child. Maestro said it was a publicity strategy used to stop her funeral and our lives turning into a media circus. Therefore the truth must point the finger at me, and given she died right after I was born, I'm guessing my birth caused her death.

I reach for my maths notebook, except it doesn't contain complicated equations or geometry. Instead, it's chock-full of lyrics and snippets of music I've written. I scan over the pop song I'm working on, humming happily to myself. The phrasing in the last line needs to match the melody better.

'Have you finished rehearsing, Astrid?'

I startle as Maestro enters the music room. I slap shut the book and shove it behind me. He peers around the vase of calla lilies on the black grand piano. Although he's only fifty, his hair is so bushy and white-grey, his vocal students nicknamed him Dr Who because he resembles the original doctor, Jon Pertwee. That was before Savannah died, before he retreated from the music world. Then about five years ago, he began to teach again and insisted on reverting to Dr Bell. I assume he thought the nickname inappropriate.

Some of his braver students from the Con gave him a new nickname: Maestro. That one he appeared to prefer – perhaps it matched his suddenly more serious demeanour, and it worked with the Dracula-style cloak he'd taken to wearing in colder weather. Somewhere along the line, normally on the days he drove me to sing for longer and longer hours, I began to call him Maestro, too.

'*Zut, alors.* It's the weekend,' I reply, using the phrase I picked up in Paris earlier in the year. When he leans over to shut the piano, I shove the notebook under some cushions and tug my hair into a messy ponytail. 'It's been a long week. I'm exhausted.'

Maestro pretends a deep frown. His face is loose and animated, as if made from liquid clay; it has the power to express a thousand facades. Perfect for opera. 'You're always exhausted. Too many late nights.'

'I go to bed at 10 pm every night. No partying, no drinking –'

'Don't think I can't see the light in your room at midnight, young lady.' He retrieves the sheet music from the music stands, playfully swipes them across my arm. 'Reading silly romance novels, no doubt.' He beams, the love he has for me in plain sight. 'Instead of learning your music.'

He's wrong, but I don't correct him because what I'm actually doing is, in his view, more wasteful than reading romances. And because I love him too much to disappoint him.

Maestro places the music in a neat pile on the piano. 'Are you too exhausted to go out?' He's still dressed in his work clothes – a dark grey suit, white shirt and sky-blue tie. 'I've booked Bernados and ordered the soufflé in advance. It's quiet there. You needn't shout to be heard across –'

'I know, I know. Protect my voice. Are we going to the Opera House?'

'I have tickets for Janacek's *From the House of the Dead*. It's Czech.'

I give an exaggerated grimace. 'That'll be a cheery opera.'

Maestro origamis his face into a 'death throes' expression. But he knows I'll listen to anything. Besides, we rarely go out; cool night air is bad for my throat; shouting in loud places is bad for my throat; late nights are bad for my throat.

'Wear a pretty dress,' he adds, glancing at my leggings and over-size jumper. 'We're sharing a box with some of the benefactors of the Music Conservatorium.'

'*The Con*. Say the Con. Everyone else does.'

He checks his vintage watch, the kind that needs winding every day. 'You've got fifty minutes.'

'Maestro, did you ever sing in Czech?'

His features kink into a frown. 'I did.' He glances at the painting of Mum above the fireplace. Her pose is almost haughty, like the Mona Lisa, but there's a feisty gleam in her eyes. 'As did your mother.'

I shift the cushions in the window seat to make room for him, careful to keep the notebook hidden. 'Tell me about how you met Mum at the Opera House in Vienna again.'

'We don't have time now.'

'It was a stormy, icy night, the day before Christmas Eve . . .' I reach for him, knowing he can't resist when I ask about Mum.

He sigh-smiles and perches beside me. '. . . and I was running late for a performance.' I nestle into his bear-like chest. 'The stairs were slippery as marble and as I mounted them, two at a time, I skidded and twisted my ankle. I hopped up the final step and clung to the big brass handles of the double doors, catching my breath, when a woman's voice said from behind me, "You certainly know how to make an entrance, Sean Bell. Let's hope you don't repeat that onstage." And I swung around and saw an angel. I wondered if I'd hit my head when I slipped, then died and gone to heaven. Even her voice sounded angelic.'

'What was she wearing?'

'She shimmered, all in white – her dress and cape flowed to the floor in soft layers, and diamantes glittered from the edging around the bust line. But none of them were as bright as her smile or as sparkly as her grey eyes.'

'Eyes the same as me and Savannah. And what did you say back?' I snuggle closer.

'I said, "I see you came dressed for our wedding. You accept my proposal then?" And she laughed this tinkling, captivating laugh, making my legs, already unsteady from the fall, more or less give way. She helped me inside and called for ice –'

'You forgot the bit about her saying, "Who do you think you are, Cary Grant?"'

'Yes, she said that. And we talked awhile about Vienna and opera and her home in London and how she had a ticket in the first row for my performance.'

'And after the performance?'

'She sent her ticket to my changing room with the words, *My proposal is we meet at Higgins' tomorrow at 9am. Do you accept?*'

'And you did.'

'And the rest is history – now come along.' Maestro stands and smooths the creases in his suit trousers.

'But what did she wear the next morning?'

'You must get dressed, Astrid.' He moves away and straightens the already straight line of music stands. He points at the music to *La Bohème*. 'Tomorrow we must continue with that. Come, come.' And he disappears from the room.

I'm usually ecstatic to leave the house, to take a break from striving to become, as the newspapers reported of Mum, 'the most outstanding vocalist of her generation'. But today something's niggling me. I toe one of the music stands harder than I intend. They become dominoes; the row of stands clatters to the floor and *La Bohème* flies across the room.

3

Jacob

Why would you name your house after an opera that's about torture, murder and suicide?

Dr Bell's house appears ancient from the outside. Huge slabs of stone, mapped with moss and lichen, make up the surrounding wall. A terracotta-tiled roof emerges at the bottom of a long gravel driveway. Compared to our house, made of box-like shapes of glass and steel arranged on top of each other, this home has history. And heart. Except they've gone and called it Tosca.

My phone beeps. A text from Dad. *Going into court. Don't miss that lesson.*

Two days ago, a month after the funerals, Dad paid me a visit. He and Mum work at lawyering fourteen hours a day and they rarely come into my music studio. Dad picked his way through the dirty dishes and instruments on the floor – if I hadn't been so goddamn sad I'd have laughed at how he inspected the business suit he wore, afraid he had something sticky clinging to it.

'You're eighteen and no further forward than you were this time last year,' he said, his critical eyes pale to the point of being translucent. Then he dropped his bombshell: 'You need a goal. Your mum and I have decided you will audition for the Sydney Music Conservatorium at the end of November again. You have three months to get your act together. But this is your last chance at a music career. If you fail again, given you didn't make the grades for university, you choose a career, and start working your way up from the bottom rung. I refuse to fund your drop-out lifestyle any longer.'

This time last year I had a real chance of making it into the Con. My ex-girlfriend Aria and I had practised our instruments in her kitchen every day, but we broke up, and I got distracted by her sister, Harper.

'I don't need an effing certificate to tell me I'm a musician,' I spat back at him. 'Keep donating wads of cash to the Con – that'll impress your friends and clients enough.'

Because *I* will never be enough.

As always, I lost that argument. Should've kept my mouth shut because I probably made everything worse. Like the main character in a *Step Up* movie, I either pass this audition or my music dreams are over, and apparently Dr Bell is the man who can make my dreams come true. He comes highly recommended by one of Dad's cronies at the Opera House. If I fail, I leave home and join the work force. No studio. No time or money for music. A forgettable life laid out for me.

Dad knows he's won this clash because we've been here before. I left home for a week once. That's when I figured out I wasn't qualified for anything – a waiter's salary wouldn't cover the rent, never mind a guitar or a tour van. Or food. My music dreams would stay on hold, possibly forever. I came crawling back to all the advantages I have, tail between my legs. Leaving again now would be an overreaction that wouldn't solve a thing. But it's more than that: I'm kind of afraid the world might chew me up and spit me out: a forgettable nobody.

I knock back the last of my beer and crush the empty, hide it in a hedge, then trek down the driveway carrying my music in the new leather case Mum bought me. The gold plate by the latch lock is engraved with my name and the dot over the 'I' in Skalicky is a diamond. For Mum, there's nothing that can't be solved with presents. Especially of the leather or jewelled variety.

A playful piano intro floats through the open windows of a room to the right. It's joined by a woman's voice. Opera's not my thing but doesn't mean I can't recognise talent when I hear it. My crunching footsteps in the gravel seem rude; I stop to listen. The song's from an opera I can't name and she's singing in Italian. When the song ends she begins another – this one I've heard Yolanda Gustav sing. I don't know every opera star, but she's my favourite female – Aria liked dragging me to the Opera House every chance she got.

A magpie lands on the birdbath beside me, cocks its head, seeming to listen. The woman's voice is mesmerising; it releases some of the tension inside me. When she begins a third song, I decide I need to interrupt – Dr Bell *is* expecting me. I skulk to the entrance.

The huge front door has an old-fashioned knocker. Its beat of brass against wood is jarring and makes me wince for intruding. The singing stops. The door swings open. There, framed by the door, is a well-dressed Dr Who. The original one, with the bush of thick grey hair. I peer over his shoulder for the TARDIS but find a grandfather clock instead.

'You're late,' he says, adjusting the knot on his tie and buttoning his suit jacket. 'I don't tolerate tardiness.'

I smirk. TARDIS. Tardiness. 'Um. Sorry. I wasn't. I was listening –'

'Come in.' He pivots and disappears stage right. That's a personal record – three seconds to make a bad impression.

We walk through a dining room wallpapered in beige candy stripe. The space is classy, with antique furniture and a tiled fireplace. The crystal chandelier could've been lifted from the Queen of England's palace.

Dr Bell's Armani-looking shoes clunk on the floorboards. I match his quick footsteps so mine don't clatter. We enter the room where the woman must've been singing because in the centre is a black grand piano and several music stands supporting sheet music. I search the bright room for her, taking in the crackling fire, the enormous oil painting above the fireplace, the cream curtains that reach the floor, the patterned rugs and vase-based lamps. Instead, I find the expectant expression on Dr Bell's face.

'Take a seat.' He gestures toward a beige sofa against one of the walls; its curtain of tassels around the base swings and sweeps the floor when my feet approach. 'I hear you're a pianist, but additionally play the guitar, flute, double bass, violin – quite the talented young man. And you sang in a band – for about two months.'

With his last words it's as if a truck ploughs into me.

He makes it sound trivial. We may have toured for a short time, but we'd been jamming together for years.

'With three months to go to the audition for the Conservatorium,' he continues, 'I understand you've decided to work on one instrument. Probably wise. Which instrument have you chosen?'

'Piano.' My voice sounds like the crack of ice. I swallow the frozen chips and don't elaborate.

The good doctor scans me, assessing. My fingers thread through themselves and my left leg bounces. Harper hated that habit, but it's just energy needing to be released.

'Let's see what you can do, Jacob, before we make any decisions. We can start on piano though. Did you bring your music?'

Before I can answer, a petite girl, maybe sixteen or seventeen, enters the room carrying a tray of glasses and a jug of something yellow. She dresses like my mother on weekends: pale peach jumper, grey trousers. Her gaze stays on the jug till she reaches the circular table beside me. Then she glances my way from under long lashes. She's low-key attractive – long wavy brown hair to her elbows and the sunlight catches strands of red, light freckles over her nose, grey eyes. But it's the full lips that snag my attention. I pocket the thought.

'Pineapple juice,' says Dr Bell, indicating toward the jug. 'Good for the throat. Like anything that helps you salivate, because salivation lubricates the gullet. Have you tried it before you sing, Jacob?'

'Nope. But olives help – and there are usually olives in bars.'

'Yes, of course. Both are preferable to water or tea. But best not to drink the juice ice cold. This is my daughter Astrid, by the way.'

She gives me a curt smile.

'Was that you singing – before?' I ask. Her flush before she nods matches my red T-shirt.

She's shoeless. I've never noticed a girl's feet before, but hers belong in a magazine – pale and dainty, and as if they had never been squashed into a pair of bad-fitting shoes or climbed trees or the rocks on the beach.

She circles back to her father. 'I'll be upstairs.' She leaves without looking back.

'Play me something.' The doc performs a flourish with his hands toward the piano stool. As I position myself and my music, I'm shaking a little. I play something classical, more the Con and less indie pop. I'm grateful to focus on the notes and lose myself in the melody; my nerves evaporate.

The doc stands off to the side. When I stop he nods. 'Good. Another.'

He lets me play and I gradually relax. Then he asks me to demonstrate my flute skills, followed by violin. We stop there because he doesn't teach any other instruments.

'Your skills are highly accomplished,' says the doc, stroking his neck with a faraway expression. 'With whom have you studied?'

I tell him about the different tutors over the years, each one impressive, each one expensive, but leave out the voice coach. The infamous and respected Dr Sofia Adessi spent four years grappling with my voice as though it was a naughty child, until she had it exactly where she – and Dad – wanted it. But the child grew up and after failing the Con audition, chose an indie-pop band instead of classical jazz solos and popera, a decision she would not accept. She abandoned me on the spot.

'Right.' The doc claps his hands once. 'Now let's try the instrument God blessed you with.'

I play dumb and scowl at the giant vase of lilies on the piano, the same flowers as at the funerals. I haven't sung since – since the universe disbanded Purple Daze a month ago. To sing without them is like saying I can live without them – like I don't need them. I clutch the neck of the violin, then return it to its case. 'I don't sing anymore.'

Dr Bell raises an elastic eyebrow. He has the kind of supple face that could express a hundred different emotions, yet I haven't made it smile once.

'So, do you agree I should play the piano?' I ask, perching back on the piano stool. 'For the Con audition.'

'You've been drinking. Beer? I can smell it on you.'

I shrug and stare through one of several over-size windows toward the harbour and freedom. Harper and I used to jump out of her parents' dining room window when we were little, because we believed ghosts lived in that room. We dared each other to circle the table twice, but we never made it all the way around before leaping out the window. Now I'd give anything to jump out the doc's windows. Strike that. I'd give anything to bump into the ghosts of Purple Daze.

'Jacob, it's eleven in the morning.'

'Yeah, Doc. I can tell time.'

'Not Doc. It's Maestro or Dr Bell.'

Maestro? I hide a smirk. 'I'm not drunk though.' Just escaping a little.

'I won't tolerate it –'

'It doesn't affect my playing.'

'If you come here smelling of alcohol again –'

I slam both hands on the keyboard. The jarring chords stop his words. 'What does it matter, so long as it doesn't affect my playing?' I yell, expecting him to walk away, like Dad does when I lose it.

'It's a matter of discipline, Jacob. Of respect. Of focus. It tells me your head's in the wrong space.'

'Yeah? You'd be about right there.' I stand so fast the stool falls backwards. 'Five of my mates, guys I've known for six years, just *died*. I'd be a pretty weird person if my head was in the right space, don't you think?'

The doctor's mouth clamps shut. He spins round, his back to me. I'm grateful because my face crumples, my throat tightens. I breathe through the sensation.

After a few minutes Dr Bell pulls in a breath, lets it out again. 'Is that why you don't sing anymore?' he asks, without turning around. I swear he's upset.

'Pretty much.'

He moves toward a side table, arranges some sheet music into two piles. 'I've heard you sing before. You have an amazing tone. I judged part of the auditions at the Conservatorium last year.'

'I wasn't good enough though.'

He keeps staring at the sheet music. 'The way you sang that day. We could hear your heart wasn't in it. You didn't want to be there enough. And you seemed distracted, as if you'd rather have been anywhere but there. That's why you didn't make it in. It wasn't your voice.'

'Still not singing,' I say to his back. Coming here was so not a good idea. 'I'll have to get better at the piano.'

'How does giving up singing help? Does it help you forget your friends?'

'I will *never* forget them,' I bellow.

Dr Bell straightens and spins round. 'Well then, *remember* them. Honour them,' he says, in an explosion of words. 'Through your singing.' He's not going to butter me up. He's not going to dismiss me or walk out. 'I doubt your friends would want you to give up on *their* account.'

I seize my music. The sheets scrunch when I shove them into the leather case. I march toward the exit as Astrid appears. Embarrassed, I push past her, hurrying into the sunshine where there's no chance of me thumping my ex-music teacher.

4

Astrid

When Maestro's student pushes past me he's all untamed animal dashing for freedom. His blue eyes are wild, his blond hair covering half his features. But the scowl on his face is like a bruise.

'What happened?' I ask, rushing further into the music room.

Maestro slumps into the armchair, slapping his thighs. 'The boy's having some issues. Jacob Skalicky.'

'You mentioned him before. The surfing singer who was in a band?' Maestro's students are normally pimpled teen girls or shy academic boys. Even before he arrived, Jacob Skalicky didn't fit into Maestro's neat and elegant music room. 'What happened to make him run off? He seemed upset.'

'The problem isn't what happened here. He needs grief counselling after a recent loss. In addition, his father said there was a girl, a break-up some months back that left him broken-hearted.'

'Is he the one you said failed the Con audition last year?'

'Don't let this distract you, Astrid. Get back to your geography homework and then start on the new score – Czech will be a challenge for you. No downloading romance novels, Buttercup.'

'*Zut, alors*,' I reply, instead of explaining I've never read a romance in my life. But how do I explain that when I write chart music it's like escaping inside a bubble where my dead sister and Mum don't exist? And it's a relief. When I'm doing everything Maestro asks, it's like I'm a spinning top, whirling through my life but bumping into things, getting up again to swivel and reel like performing an exhausting, never-ending dance. But when I write music I'm inside that moment when the spinning top stops jerking sideways, when its tip spins on a precise point, centred and serene.

Upstairs in my bedroom, for the first time ever, I can't settle back into the song I was writing; I spotted my own grief in Jacob, and now it's haunting me. He looked like he wouldn't survive his emotions. And because I've been there too, I feel connected to him. Perhaps one of his parents died, or a sister. Both. My whole body hums with the possibility that maybe we're the same – maybe he's the one person who could comprehend what I've lived through.

I slap shut my maths/songwriting book and open my atlas to do some homework. I could put a pin in almost every continent on the map, but even though I've travelled the world, my father escorted me from luxury hotel to concert hall, from art museum to renowned restaurant. I'm betting Jacob's surfed some beaches abroad, stayed in hip hostels, eaten in cafés where the ambient music isn't classical. Although we're clearly similar in age, he seems much older. If not older, then worldly.

I believe everyone embodies a soundtrack, but I hope we get to change the soundtrack because mine is Adele's 'Million Years Ago'; because of the guilt of causing Mum's death, I wish I could live a freer life. Expand my horizons. Right now, Jacob's is a mash up of Bruno Mars' 'When I Was Your Man' – the haunting 'should haves' that led to losing his girl, and Pink's 'Beam Me Up'. The way his grief evaporates off him pulls at my heartstrings.

There's something else too – a wildness about him. Maybe it's his long hair, or the intensity in his manner, or the fact he was in a band. His horizons are unlimited. We're the same in that we both grieve the people we lost every day, yet we're total opposites; I'm caged songbird to his roaming lion.

As I take stock of the view through the same window I've stood in front of all my life, the itch I can't reach prickles, then morphs into a gnawing ache. It's as if Jacob opened the songbird's cage door, and even though I could fly into the blue sky – want to even – somehow, I can't.

5

Jacob

I kick at the plates of half-eaten toast and glasses stuck with juice pulp, then fling drumsticks at the walls of my studio and launch the drum kit into the cymbals. They crash to the ground with a satisfying blast of sound. The grief Dr Bell's words ignited sweeps through me like a bush fire and the only way not to get burnt alive is to destroy everything in my way.

All my life I've traded with my parents – I'll learn the flute if they pay for guitar lessons; I'll behave at school if I can have a drum kit; I'll audition for the Con instead of forming a touring band if they build a music studio at the bottom of the garden. When I failed the Con audition last year, I figured Dad would tear down the studio. Reckon I got in first with the Harley drama. For about a month they actually paid attention to me – spent some time at home. We even watched a black and white movie as a family. I didn't like the subtitles though.

What will we trade this time?

'I *won't* sing again. No trade,' I shout.

Steve. Mad Dog's name was Steve. I remember. 'Same as

Skittles.' I whoop and throw a glass against the wall. It bounces instead of breaking and I turn to find new targets.

Skittles was designated driver. I picture him perching on the drum stool – his throne – the one place he said felt like home. Home. Funny how that word is so important. Funny how home has always been next door, at Harper's house.

I kick the throne, rip sheets of music in half, fling them in the air, boot over the music stands, snag one of the guitars and strike it against the wall of the studio. It's only when I'm left holding the neck of the guitar, now separated from the body, that I stop. I've owned the Gibson Hummingbird with its maple fingerboard since I was ten. I look to the door, half hoping someone will come in and calm me down. Even my parents would do. I realise I actually want my dad to grab me, pin my arms to my side, and hug me until the feeling of wanting to destroy everything around me passes. But no one's coming.

Needing Harper, I race outside and with one step on the pool box, I vault over the wall that divides us from the Hunters' garden. Tom and Annie aren't home much these days, but instead follow their daughters around the globe. When we became neighbours, it didn't take long for the Hunters to become my adopted family. As children, Harper, Aria and I would play in the Purple Woods at the bottom of their garden for hours; we loved spring the most, when the lilac blossoms provided a secret world to hide in.

I stumble toward the woods, but it's late August and winter has stripped the jacaranda branches bare so that they resemble hundreds of old crooked wizard fingers. After reaching the Mother Tree by the river, I climb it as though I'm being chased by ghosts.

When my muscles burn from pulling myself through the boughs, I straddle a branch and lean against the trunk. Below, yellow leaves litter the ground. Eventually the wind will sweep them away.

'Like someone swept away Emery,' I tell the Mother Tree. 'They took down his Instagram profile.' The one he created for his fans. We each had one. The messages of condolence slowed to a trickle and then stopped altogether, and next thing his page disappeared. I wanted to add a new message every week, but how many times can you say the same thing?

My life for yours.

'Did dying hurt?' I ask the breeze.

The branch between my legs smudges; I blink until it comes back into focus.

Harper named the Mother Tree when we were small – something about it being the biggest because even when the three of us linked hands we couldn't surround the circumference. Using the thumbnail I keep long for picking on guitar or violin or double bass strings, I lift pieces of bark from the branch and discard them. They sail haphazardly toward the ground, one then another, and another. A fall from this height would kill me if it was a straight plunge, but there are loads of branches to hit along the way. I'd probably just break a few bones.

Lifting my chin to the weak winter sun, I face heaven. I face *them*.

'I miss it,' I yell. 'When we performed, it felt surreal.' The music became the air we needed to breathe and the bond that held us together. We were – my family. 'We were supposed to become famous and stay in glamorous hotels.' I'm shouting so loud now my head hurts. 'We were supposed to get chased by hordes of fans and have bodyguards on tap.' My voice crackles with tears.

The future I once imagined is like the fading chords of a melody that will be forever lost.

'There's nothing left for me here,' I croak. My chest heaving, I punch the branch three times before I hear the crack of a bone.

Cradling my fist, I slump against the trunk, exhausted. Maybe I'll fall asleep . . .

I'm thinking about dropping out of this tree. How can I live inside the same skin as the boy who chased Harper's paper boats down the river or who climbed the Mother Tree in his pyjamas so we could spot shooting stars? How can I have the same reflection in the river as the boy who named his band after the Purple Woods?

My thoughts tumble away at the sound of a cracking twig. Leaves rustle under shuffling footsteps. I shrink against the tree and freeze. Someone starts to sing. The voice is smooth and modulated, smoky in a guy sense. He's singing a Justin Bieber song – about as well as the man himself.

I glance around and suck in my breath. A boy is headed for the Mother Tree. His singing gets louder the deeper into the woods he strays. He's flashing a torch on and off, even though it's lunch time. He gets to the river and stands on a rock, launches into another JB song. That's when I recognise him; our housekeeper Maria's kid. When he was a little, Maria used to bring him with her when he was sick. He'd sit and snuffle on the couch and hog the TV, so I'd go hang with Harper and Aria. I'm ashamed to say I don't remember his name. All I know is now he's fifteen and he's been secretly helping Maria with the housework for the last six months. She's sick or old or something and she's terrified the parentals will find out. I think he even skips school to help some days. In exchange for keeping my mouth shut, Maria's agreed not to clean my studio. I hate people touching my stuff.

I work out it's not a torch he's flashing – it's fire. He's doing something with a closed fist, then opening his hand to reveal a flash of fire in his palm, like a magic trick.

'Hey,' I yell. 'Whatchadoing? You could burn the woods down.'

He stops, mid-note. We eyeball each other. I raise a hand in a short salute, hoping he'll go away.

'What you doing all the way up there?' He flicks flame from a lighter and then slips the lighter into his jeans pocket.

'Thinking and stuff.'

He keeps staring but doesn't respond. I add, 'Do the Hunters know you come here?'

'Sure. Me and Mrs H go way back – as far as me swimming in their pool this summer. I was hot after vacuuming your mansion and the water was this mind-blowing blue. She wasn't mad though. Said I could come by anytime.'

'Don't s'pose she knows you play with fire in her woods.' I want to ask him how he held fire without burning himself. But I want him to leave more.

He rubs the back of his neck, studies the tree, then rubs his palms on his T-shirt. He reaches for the first branch and swings his legs up easily. He's tall for fifteen.

I hide my injured hand in my lap when he perches on a limb to the side of me. He has a strong jaw and his dark hair flicks up in a coif. He looks at me sideways; his expression somehow says, 'I didn't do it', and I wonder if he gets in trouble a lot. How bad can he be when he helps his mum clean our house?

He gestures to my hair. 'You let it grow out again.'

After the accident on the Harley the surgeon shaved half my head so he could stitch me back together. I glance down at the one visible scar left – a shiny blemish the length of my calf.

Changing the subject, I say, 'Your voice slays. How'd you learn to sing like that?'

'Church.'

'A good Catholic boy then.'

He snorts. 'Tell my mamma that. She thinks pop songs are the devil's making. Her brother's some sort of bishop back in Italy. It's like if I sing pop, he won't make Pope or something.'

'What's your name?'

'Dexter De Brun.'

'No shit. Seriously?'

'Seriously. My dad was Dutch and a Dexter Gordon fanatic – saxophonist. Not exactly the name of a pop star. But De Brun means Brown. And I go by Dex. Unless I'm in earshot of my mamma, then I'm Dexter.'

'Got it.' The kid makes me laugh without forcing it. 'So where'd you live?'

'Naremburn. All my life.' He fiddles with the stud he's wearing in one ear.

'You go to school there?'

'Yep. Then a bus to get here to iron your carpets and clean up after your ass.'

'Hey, I hardly set foot in that house.'

'I noticed. I had to come next door to meet you.' He pulls at a twig and aims it at a distant branch. 'You're always in your studio or touring with your band – I mean –' He quickly looks away. 'Were. Used to.'

His words stab me and it's as if a hole opens and my insides are pouring out of it. He breaks off another twig, snaps that into smaller pieces, and lets each one fall. We watch them hitting branches on their way down.

'What you doing up here? Crap day?' he asks. He studies my cradled wrist, the blood on my knuckles. The pain scales eleven out of ten now.

'You could say that.'

'What the coif? I didn't think trust-fund kids had bad days.'

'What the what?'

He pats his own neatly combed coif. 'I'm a good Catholic boy and don't swear. Much. How can you have a bad day when you get to sing all day in that studio? The shower's my studio and I can't sing if Mamma's around.'

I feel for the kid. 'Money don't buy happiness though.'

'We'll swap then. You go to death-of-brain school all day then come clean some rich dude's house, then cook dinner for your sick mamma.'

I consider his logic. But he's only seeing what's on the outside. 'You don't actually iron our carpets do you?'

'Nope. But one day when I'm rich and famous – Are you mad at your parents? About that piano audition or else you're on your own?'

'How'd you know about that?'

'Mamma. She's diabetic, not deaf.'

'What else has she told you about my family?'

'Not much. I didn't mean she gossips. Plus she works six days a week and leaves early and gets home late. We get to talk more now I'm helping her. Quality son and mamma time over the feather duster.' He flicks his wrist like he's dusting the branch then inspects my swollen hand. 'Bit hard to play the piano now.'

A series of silent expletives roar in my head. 'I gotta get some ice. Maybe it's not broken, just bruised.' Dex looks doubtful. 'You're welcome to come by the studio anytime,' I add. 'It's soundproof. You can sing what you want.'

He lights up like I offered him a million bucks. I swing my leg over the branch, hang from my belly till my feet hit the bough below. Dex follows, instructing me to hang by my elbow – like he'd know.

'I'm gonna stay here a bit,' Dex says, when we're back on the ground. 'Good luck with the broken bones. And thanks for the offer – the studio and all. I owe you.'

♫

Dad visits the studio the morning after he hears about my hand. He adjusts his scarf. It's not cold outside, but ever since Mum said scarves add colour to his pale complexion, he wears them practically year-round. He glares down at me. I spent the night on the Lego sofa – as Harper nicknamed it. I guess it *is* a sofa made of foam Lego pieces. I pull on a blanket, stay curled up.

'I hear your hand is broken in two places.' Dad keeps his volume at normal, which is a good start. 'Correct?'

I draw my sigh out. The muted TV on the wall shows a green python hanging from a branch, waiting to ambush a lizard. The TV runs 24/7; it drowns out thoughts I don't want to have.

'Then you will have to sing at the audition. If you renege on our deal, you leave this house and make your own way in the world but this time there won't be any coming home again. I'll pull down this studio if I have to.' His forehead vein throbs and his skin is blotchy. He's like an albino gorilla trying to get the juice from a coconut without breaking it.

I glare back at him from my nest in the sofa.

He raises his virtually non-existent strawberry blond eyebrows, jerks his shirt cuff down. 'And no more bands or tours.' He's tightening his grip. 'We've almost lost you twice this year.'

Lost. Like a briefcase. Or a scarf.

'I understand how you're feeling, Jacob. Remember when my brother died?'

'Yeah. The same day Coda died.' I wrote a song to remember them both – everyone was so messed up. Tears prick, and I pinch them gone. Dad scoffed at the idea of a dog being missed as much as a brother. Sure, he was probably right, but I was a seven-year-old kid trying to reach him.

Dad taps his foot, sighs his next words. 'Maybe take a shower. Get dressed. Have you gone surfing lately?' I can hear the effort it's taking to soften his voice, to keep hold of his temper. When I shrug he adds, 'If you won't attend the grief counsellor's sessions I booked, at least talk to a friend.'

'*They're. All. Dead.*' Each word sends a punch to my gut.

'Clearly I don't mean them.' The fact that he has halitosis doesn't stop him looming close.

I draw my knees up. 'My school friends have gone to uni or backpacking.'

'Precisely my point. Noah down the road has gone to

Melbourne and if you remember my colleague Brian, his son has a scholarship to Yale.'

I snort. 'It's clear why you're so disappointed in me.'

'This is non-negotiable.' Dad pulls open the studio door.

Once he's gone I snatch my boardies from where they're drying over the tap and bag the surf wax, craving oblivion, craving the fate the ocean waves could deliver.

6

Astrid

I should be rehearsing or wandering around the majestic Berlin Academy of Music star-spotting famous composers or singers. Instead, I'm stuck in a cubicle with my head down a toilet.

This is the new norm.

Local performances and contests in Australia were one thing – but this is the professional scene; the world where my mum sparkled with stardom, where everyone knew Veronika Bell, and where they will now compare us. I can't help feeling I'll let everyone down.

This is why rehearsing *La Bohème* for endless hours is pointless. And all those alphabetised operas on Maestro's shelf –

Earlier this year, when I up-chucked in Seoul, we blamed it on food poisoning – the sushi from lunch the day of the competition. And when the nausea began two days before the contest in Sweden, at first I thought I was dead unlucky to get stomach flu.

'You're aware that winning the money isn't important,' Maestro said. 'We're here for the opportunity, not the bank balance. Don't let the nerves win. The international scene is merely the next step in your singing career.' The look he gave me confirmed this illness was far worse than food poisoning or gastro, because it's harder to cure a sickness of the mind.

Reaching for the toilet again, I gag. My gullet is raw, my teeth coarse. Random squares of toilet paper and empty toilet rolls litter the pale green floor. Both knees are wet. I don't want to think about what I'm kneeling in. My brain fuzzy, my pulse has changed from a restful adagio to a racing allegro. If this is what life is going to consist of from now on, I'm not sure I want to do it anymore. I will never be 'the most outstanding vocalist of my generation'.

When I next dry-retch my eyeballs nearly pop out and into the toilet. I shiver and retch again. *I can't do this anymore.* I try to distract myself with happy thoughts and think about the latest song I'm writing.

'I have something for you.' The clipped female voice comes from nowhere. For a moment I think I imagined it. But then I hear scuffling behind me. Someone is waving a strip of pills under the cubicle door.

'For the nerves.' She waggles the pills harder. Her accent is German, but I don't recognise her. 'They block the nerves. Take it. I must go now.'

I reach for them, just to get rid of her. 'Thanks.' The fingers disappear and I listen to the retreating footsteps on the tiles. The outer door squeals open and clunks shut. I gawp at the pills. Competitors pop beta-blockers like candy in this industry.

Perhaps I need them because I must keep performing. I owe Maestro. I owe Mum. In the past, Savannah and I would imagine the various reasons for our mother dying – she wanted a boy not a girl and died of despair, or according to Savannah, I was an ugly baby and Mum couldn't bear it. Or her singing sounded angelic and the angels insisted on taking her. But she died soon after my birth and Savannah probably hit the nail on the head when she said my birth caused her death. So I've always felt like I owe Savannah too; if I hadn't been born, Mum would be alive.

I grasp that it's not exactly my fault, but it's easy to see how Maestro, in his grief, could've blamed me. Yet he never made me feel less loved than Savannah, and for that I'll love him more fiercely than I'll love anyone or anything my whole life. I owe him for being both my parents rolled into one. I owe him for not resenting the fact I could still celebrate a birthday, but thanks to me, Mum could not. I owe him for homeschooling me and for all the overseas trips he took me on, instead of his wife. I owe him for being my only friend.

The feeling of missing Kara, my friend from next door who I met in year one, spills over inside my stomach. It's possible to mourn people who are alive, yet are not in your life anymore. Kara moved to Singapore four years ago. When she left it felt similar to losing Savannah. I decided it was safer to never get close to anyone again. Even swapping letters hurt, and we stopped communicating.

From that point Maestro became my whole world and I, his.

I throw the pills into the toilet. There has to be another way. Maestro gave me beta-blockers after Sweden. But they made me nauseous and dizzy and then I couldn't sleep for two days.

Wobbling to my feet I tie my cardigan around my waist and bemoan the dark circles on the knees of my trousers.

Maestro's waiting in the hallway, his expression sullen as a dirge. 'You all right, Buttercup?'

I burst into tears.

He pulls me into him, hushes me. I'm small, so being engulfed by Maestro has always felt like being hugged by the hero at the end of a movie or when the music score from the final scene of *Lord of the Rings* blasts in your head and you're sure everything's going to end well.

Maybe I should tell him how I spent the last two nights writing pop songs to fill the long hours after midnight, hoping to avoid the tossing and turning as pages of music notes crashed through my dreams. In one nightmare, I opened my mouth but nothing came out. Another time, what came out sounded like train brakes.

My body droops with every sob. 'I don't have what it takes, Maestro.'

'You'll feel better now you've got it all up.'

'No. I don't.' I pull away, clutch my arms around myself. 'I didn't eat today. Yet I need to vomit. I'm exhausted. I don't sleep. I'm dazed going on stage. I can't do this . . .'

'Yes, you can.' Maestro scours the passageway. Someone's approaching and he ushers me into our practise room. Three rows of chairs front a grand piano, and the secured blinds make the otherwise white room appear shadowy. He opens the lid of the piano. My tears have created a dark patch on his sky-blue tie. 'Part of learning to be a great performer is learning to handle the nerves. This is purely another lesson you need to absorb, like learning to sing an E6.'

I think how much easier it is to hit one of the highest notes a soprano can master when I'm back home in the music room, compared to going on stage and merely singing a basic middle C.

'This is what we've worked toward,' he continues. His features have moved on from disapproving to hopeful. 'Think of the engagement offers you could win – festivals all over Europe. You have the best voice here.'

I drag my fingers down my cheeks. 'Without the nerves maybe, but the nerves aren't going away.'

Maestro's lips press together. 'You have to believe in yourself, Buttercup. Be certain that you are the best and you can do this. Then let your mind and voice take over. Once you start, the muscle memory in your throat will know what to do. And the more you sing in these big contests, the less the nerves will affect you. It's something you must go through. Lots of people suffer from performance anxiety, and like them, you'll get over it. It's not the reason to give up.'

I wonder if Mum suffered with the same problem, but

I don't want to know the answer and don't ask the question; if she didn't, then that's further evidence I'll never be as good as her.

Swallowing bile, I say, 'Maybe hypnotism would work. And more practise. But until then – I can't do this. Not today.'

Maestro's lips twitch. He strokes his neck, then rests his palms on my shoulders. Their warmth comforts, but he has the air of a stern teacher – the person he becomes if I'm having a bad rehearsal.

I inspect the floor and his hands fall and grasp my elbows a little too hard. 'All singers must learn to trust their voices. After the hours of practise, let it free, without overthinking, without self-consciousness. Trust that everything you've done has led to this point and you're here because your voice is good enough.'

'I get what I'm *meant* to do. But I nearly fainted on stage in Sweden. My breath stopped working. It felt as if my neck was in a vice. I couldn't sing my best –'

'But you *didn't* faint.' Maestro drops his hands from my elbows and whirls away from me. 'And I have some pills that will help.'

'They make me feel sick and they're addictive – I've read about them.'

'It's not forever. Merely until you get through this.'

'No! They don't help. You stopped performing when Mum died. No more *Don Giovanni* or *Rigoletto* –'

I've never talked back at Maestro, so when he twists to confront me, my heart squats.

His expression folds into disbelief, then fury. 'You are being childish, Astrid. That was different. You must sing on to fully discover your capabilities, including how brave you are. Fear is healthy. It stops you becoming complacent, but you cannot let it cripple you. Harness the fear.'

He arranges himself on the piano stool, giving a flamboyant flourish of his hands when he's ready. In the shadowy room his nose appears huge, his eyes deep pits, as though he's wearing an opera mask.

'You will not give up today. You will not surrender to this fear.' His voices wobbles. 'Time to rehearse. Then we must hurry back to the hotel for you to change into your dress.'

I picture Mum's royal blue dress hanging in my hotel room, the matching shoes placed neatly below. Maestro has her dresses taken up for me, but we share the same shoe size. Like always, I've dyed my hair auburn, to match hers, and straightened it, so everything's organised. I can do this.

Sensing nausea, I trundle toward the piano.

Maestro flicks on a light that banishes his phantom mask. 'Good girl.' His transformation is dramatic; like stage curtains swooping open, his smile sweeps open his face. And with that, I know how much this means to him even though I want to snatch the smile from his face and snap it in two. 'I wish I could rip those nerves from you,' he adds, 'but you'll learn to deal with them. I promise.'

I take in deep breaths and try to open my constricted throat by bending at the waist and flopping forward while letting a groan escape. I curl back upright, one vertebra at a time, pulling in another huge breath.

Maestro begins with arpeggios, rippling up and down the keyboard. I stand tall. He counts me in, his index finger manically striking each beat in the air.

My life for hers.

♫

The walk-in cupboard of the guest room back at home is filled with Mum's performance dresses, her jewellery, shoes, capes, coats and hats. Savannah and I spent many hours dressing up in them. The dresses retain a faint scent of flowers, but that's probably wishful thinking because Maestro dry-cleaned them.

Now, after our lesson, my fingers run along the row of silk, chiffon, velvet – in every colour of the rainbow. I remember when she wore each one, thanks to Maestro building my memory bank. She wore the pink silk gown when she won the Richard Tucker Foundation competition. She should've left the red one with the spaghetti straps with the Paris Opera costume department, but she couldn't bring herself to part with it and left behind her own clothes as compensation. While most of her dresses are her own, each time a soprano wears a dress from the costume department her name and the date worn are sewn into it on a tag. This one contains the names Renee Fleming, Yolanda Gustav, and of course, my mum.

Maestro didn't keep anything personal – no brushes or perfume or diaries. Except for a while he kept a bundle of unopened letters addressed to her and tied together with string. When I was seven, I found them in what had been mum's bedside drawer. It was weird that no one had opened them. The return address was a mysterious John Miller of 7 Broccoli Street, Camden in London. I figured they were from an over-enthusiastic fan. But they too disappeared.

At least we still have the CDs Mum recorded. Maestro had set up a player in here for Savannah and me to sing along with her. We spent hours mimicking her trills and how she hit an E6. We must've sounded like caterwauling cats back then. Some days I still don't hit that note right. Like in Berlin. I didn't even place. Instead of discussing what happened, Maestro stepped up my training. Now I'm terrified that if I can't follow in Mum's footsteps, Maestro will disappear into himself again.

I twist the dial on the player to my favourite classical station. Mozart's *Don Giovanni* filters through the air. I wander across the hall into Savannah's room even though I should be doing schoolwork. Maestro never packed away anything that belonged to her, yet what remains of Mum's belongings barely fills the spare room cupboard. Maybe it's harder to lose a child than a wife. Every toy Savannah ever played with, every pair of unmatched socks, every hair band, every drawing, remains in its place. Even her collection of Disney character perfumes is displayed in a neat triangle.

Sitting at her desk I open one of her singing books.

I sometimes think if she hadn't died we may have competed with each other. But when I was four, I became her puppy dog, following her around, waiting for her to throw morsels of information about Mum my way. She harboured dozens of stories that Maestro had repeated in the years after Mum's death, and I couldn't get enough. After I turned thirteen and Maestro allowed me to use computers, an internet search displayed loads of official function photos but they were never real enough for me. Mum often had a cigarette in her hand, and a glass of wine or she'd be standing in a posh building wearing a party dress. This version of her didn't fit the stories Maestro told of baking cupcakes, pyjama movie days, and building forts out of blankets in the lounge.

When Savannah was old enough, I'd bribe her with jelly beans to read out articles about Mum. I'd paint a picture of her out of the words. My favourite story was the one where a violin player reported how Mum would often come home with the entire orchestra after a performance and she'd sing and dance with them until the sun came up the next morning. I had memorised his words: 'She never made it to a rehearsal before midday. Once I had to fetch her because she was two hours late. She was sitting on the front step popping olives and still in her pyjamas – well, more like a glamorous silk and lace nightie.'

I wish Maestro had kept that nightie.

Then there was Savannah's story about the times she was too sick for kindy and Mum would take her to the beach.

Mum always swam too far out though, which scared my sister, but then she'd eventually return and spin Savannah around and around until they fell over, dizzy, lying in a heap of arms and legs, giggling and covered in sand. And the time Mum came home with a puppy and when she accidentally let it escape out the house, she bought Savannah a human-sized teddy bear instead. To us, Mum was an enchanting movie star, a legend. Even her name sounded glamorous: Veronika. She was dazzling, and I wanted to be dazzling, too.

At the foot of Savannah's desk is the box of photos and newspaper clippings of Mum that Maestro saved. It's been years since I went through them. I lay each one on the carpet and a patchwork quilt of Mum – her red hair, her pale skin, her grey eyes, her delicate frame – forms around me. A square of paper slips from between two clippings. I pick it up, unfold it. The paper is old-fashioned with roses at the corners and the creases have torn in places. The cursive handwriting is small and neat.

Dear Sean,
People shouldn't try to be what they are not. It only leads to unhappiness. I'm sorry.
All my love forever,
Veronika

My pulse beats fast, a sharp, repetitive staccato note on my temple. I trace my fingers over the words, confused about why this precious note, addressed to my father, exists among the clippings. Did Savannah hide it from me? My whole body clasps with jealousy as I make for the stairs.

Maestro is reading a book. An old recording of Pavarotti singing '*Nessun Dorma*' plays on his prized gramophone.

'I found something,' I say, passing the notepaper to him. 'Is that what she called you – Sean? No silly nickname?'

His jaw slackens as he inspects me. 'Where did you get this?' he growls.

'It was in Savannah's room. In the box of clippings. Are you angry with me?'

Maestro swallows hard and takes a deep breath, staring right through the note and into another dimension.

'Her handwriting resembles mine,' I add, when Maestro keeps staring. His torso heaves as Pavarotti's voice crescendos. I nab a glass of pineapple juice left over from a session. Gulp at it, wondering if it's the right time to ask him for the truth about Mum.

I keep drinking.

I'm suddenly afraid of the truth.

Maestro rises to his feet as if his knees hurt. His glance flickers toward the photo of Savannah wearing the yellow taffeta dress she always wore to singing auditions. Even when I grew into it, Maestro never let me wear it.

The orchestra strikes up their finale and something inside me snaps. I have to shout to be heard. 'I'll be eighteen in March. What difference will another six months and five days make?'

'I said eighteen, and I meant eighteen.' It's his stern voice-coach tone. Behind his eyes live all the secrets.

'I'll find out another way then. I'll find her parents.'

'I've told you before, the Millers were estranged from your mum. John and Esmeralda didn't approve of her choice of career. They don't know anything.'

Miller. John Miller from the letters in the bundle. He's Mum's dad. My grandfather.

'They abandoned her when she was a teenager,' he adds. 'It was unforgivable and hurt your mother immensely. I don't believe she ever got over it.'

The room plunges into silence as the record finishes; the stylus blips with static, the arm lifts to return to its home. Maestro unfastens the top button on his shirt. Then, walking stiffly, he leaves the room. He's never walked out on me when I've asked about Mum.

Before he leaves, I blurt, 'What does she mean in the note?'

He snatches at the door handle, leans on it. 'I've no idea.'

'Didn't you ask her?' I say, sharper than I intend. His face pales and puckers, as if he's been left out in the rain and sun for several days.

His eyes rumble with memories. 'I – I never got the chance.'

Because of me.

His socked feet whisper on the stairs, and I hear two small sniffs.

There've been many times I've felt glad I didn't succeed at joining Mum and Savannah in heaven. Right now, the certainty that Maestro would not have survived my loss jolts me, like when the orchestra starts up at the beginning of a performance; sudden and dramatic and full of trepidation.

I vow to never leave him.

Except I do sometimes worry there's some kind of inverse law of the universe that says once you decide you *don't* want to die, then that's exactly what happens.

7

Jacob

Four days after breaking my hand, I bite the bullet and am standing outside the doc's house listening to Astrid sing. I like her sound even more than I like Yolanda Gustav. How can someone so small pack that much power? I sit on the stone wall until she stops. Then I go home, knowing I won't be able to sing. I thought I could, because I must, but my voice died with the band. And it should stay buried with the band.

When I get home, I tie my surfboard to the roof of my Jeep and head to the studio to pick up my board shorts and wax. But Dex is there. The studio's in the back garden, so I never lock the door. He's singing a Bruno Mars song – his back to me. His voice soothes. It doesn't make me sad, like I figured it might. I slip inside to listen, observing the TV I never switch off. The ticker tape states that two teens were swept out to sea. More dead people, their families numb.

'You're not clipping the notes off properly,' I say, stepping further into the studio.

Dex stops singing and spins round. 'What d'ya mean?' His buttoned shirt is half yellow, half gold and black stripes. Interesting.

'The notes at the end of the 4th and 8th bars are semibreves. You're holding for too long.'

Skittles used to do the same thing – he was always a better drummer than singer.

Dex cocks his head, bites his lip, then sings a couple of phrases.

'Better,' I say. 'But you're making your S's hiss.' I head for the fridge, desperate for a beer. The world needs anaesthetising. As I reach for the beer I reassess the situation and grab a Coke instead. 'Juice or Coke?'

Dex chooses Coke and tries the lyrics again.

'Good. Your phrasing's wrong in the last line though.'

Dex's shoulders sink. 'Buh. Show me, dude.'

'Nah. Give it another shot.'

He pokes his tongue into his cheek, peers at me from under his coif. Then he sings it again.

'Now you sound mad.' I smirk, crack open a Coke and gulp it down.

'You look like crap,' he says. 'How's the piano practise going?' He scans my cast and I swallow a chuckle.

'Don't even go there, kid. Why aren't you at school?'

'School development day for teachers.'

'So how long till you gotta go?'

'An hour. Your house wasn't dirty today.' His smirk mocks me.

I give him a shove. 'Maybe yo Mamma did it for her little boy before he got here.' He snorts and tries to shove me back, but I sidestep him on my way to the iPad that's connected to the studio's speakers. I select some tunes and when I turn around Dex is emptying the tea leaves from several tea bags into the sink.

'Check this out,' he says, unravelling the filter paper of the tea bags and standing them on their ends. Quick as a flash he pulls out a lighter and three little fires lift off the bench top, floating upwards like tiny fiery angels. They swiftly burn themselves out and debris drifts into the sink.

'You know playing with fire's dangerous, right?' I say.

'I'm careful. It's a buzz though. Don't you reckon?'

'You need a check-up from the neck up.' I press play on the iPad. 'I usually go surfing in the afternoons. But seeing as it's you, and I have a broken hand – how about you give "Pillowtalk" a crack?'

'Zayn. Love it.' The music and Dex's singing fills the cave of my music studio. The tension in me slips from ten to nine.

'You sound similar to him,' I say. 'Now, how are you breathing?'

'In and out. Just regular, dude.'

Coke spews from my mouth. I think about Callum in the hotel – before.

Dex launches into the next lyric. He's good. I cut him off to correct his breathing. He gets me straight away. This feels okay. I'm helping this kid and it's got nothing to do with the band. We work on his breathing technique and he sounds even better. He can sing anything. Then he starts dancing while he sings – turning big circles with his arms flung out sideways-type dancing, his face raised to the ceiling like the music breathes life into his body and he's surrendering to it. I edge up the volume and he hooks my elbow, makes me spin with him. I go with it.

The track's on repeat and starts again. Dex sings to me, as if I'm his girl or something. He gets on one knee and serenades me, and I'm laughing at him – this kid's nuts. And then we're spinning again, oblivious, and it feels so good to let go and I sing the lyrics at the top of my lungs. It's more of a scream. And we're both shout-singing in each other's faces, caught in a space where nothing else matters but that moment, knowing no-one can hear, and there's no pain, no numbing required. And the music frees us.

At three-thirty Dex's watch alarm beeps. 'Gotta go.' He shoves his feet into his sneakers.

'Need a lift home?' Dex considers the option.

'Nah. Don't wanna lie to Mamma even more.' He takes off, untied laces dancing around his feet. 'Your voice is smokin',' he yells before he leaves. 'Might let you sing with me again.'

I chuckle. 'Don't let the door slap your arse on the way out.'

But I don't mean it. I wish he could stay because I don't want to stop singing.

8

Astrid

The day I catch sight of Jacob sitting on the wall of our garden listening to me sing, excitement swims through me. The song finishes and I request another; I can't explain why I want him to keep listening. When Maestro says it's time to finish I spy on Jacob from the dining room, ready to beat Maestro to answer Jacob's knock.

During the last couple of days, Mum's note has hung between me and Maestro as we wander around the house like two lost melodies hoping to find someone to harmonise with. It reminds me of the years after Savannah died, before Maestro began to teach again – he ate what I thought were pale yellow M&M's and wore a mask that mimicked him but, being a mask, was lifeless. He told me much later the tablets helped his depression.

On top of tiptoeing through his current moods, I can't stop thinking about Jacob, hoping he'll come back for a lesson. And finally, today he has.

Except Jacob never even comes down the drive.

'I saw Jacob. But he came and then he left,' I tell Maestro, who's in the music room staring into the fire.

'Damn it. I wanted to help that boy. Kids with his talent don't come along often.' He takes a poker and stabs at the fire, a little too violently. My body tenses as I gauge his mood. Although he's no longer as sad, he's gotten more erratic since he started homeschooling me for high school. The dad I remember as encouraging and understanding is around, but there's something acrid smouldering within him, similar to a house fire no-one's detected; the contained flames seethe and fume and singe the edges of him when he's feeling low. Then some days he's so exuberant he seems manic – the batty professor side of him. During yesterday's lesson he ran his fingers through his hair so much he resembled a victim of electric shock treatment. On those days I'm on my best behaviour, but then he'll suddenly stop the lesson and waltz me around the room to Strauss.

'I'll go for dinner with Mikhail, instead,' adds Maestro. 'I've even told Mikhail about Jacob. He's on the audition panel at the Con. I'm a fool for mentioning him, but with my help – I got overexcited.' Maestro acts so glum and disappointed, I'm angry with Jacob.

Maestro stows the poker. 'While I'm gone, finish your English assignment and study the recording of Yolanda Gustov. See how she supports her breath, how she shapes her mouth for the high notes.'

A case of ants-in-pants starts up. 'How long's the recording?' I fail to keep a hint of whininess out of my voice.

'Two hours. And there's leftovers in the fridge you can reheat.'

I plod up the stairs to get the recording, the ants now crawling beneath my skin. It can't be normal to have this urge to run and run to stop the sensation of being trapped, not specifically in the house, but inside my skin. It's as if I've been told something big might happen, and though I have no idea what that 'big' is, I'm anticipating it with every pore.

I think of visiting Savannah's grave. The problem with graves is they can't answer questions. Maybe I'll go for a drive. Although I hardly ever drive anywhere other than the cemetery or the library, I love the sense of freedom driving gives me. But I have homework – and Yolanda.

In my bedroom I switch on a lamp. Dark clouds gather over the city, and I wonder if we're in for another storm. I imagine what people are doing there. Lately, I wish I went to a normal high school and knew friends my own age. I'm Rapunzel stuck in her tower. Never to be rescued. In another forty years I'll still be here, staring out this window. And if I'm Rapunzel, what does that make Maestro?

He's given me so much, shown me the world, taught me everything I know, yet the older I get the more I realise everything I've learnt and seen was selected by Maestro. What if there's more? How can I love him so much, yet sometimes want to push him away?

My fingers trace over the photo frame of me and Savannah in our swimmers, then the row of picture books that belonged to Savannah and were passed down to me. I wish she'd written in them – little thoughts, secret messages, a drawing. But she didn't even fold down a corner to mark her place. Kara left her mark on Pinocchio though, believing his nose should be longer and drawing an extension on every page. *Sleeping Beauty, Cinderella, Snow White, Alice in Wonderland.* Perhaps what I'm feeling is how Alice felt before she stepped through the mirror into the unknown. Except unlike me, Alice was born brave.

'Bye, Buttercup,' Maestro shouts up the stairs. His despondent tone tells me Jacob's fed the flames of his inner demons. I grip my hands into fists. Even if Jacob is grieving, he shouldn't make commitments and then walk out on them.

I bet Jacob doesn't think about me as much as I do about him. I find myself speculating on if he cries himself to sleep and if he struggles to focus on the present, or if he's lonely. Maestro said Jacob's a surfer. Does he escape from his grief by surfing, as I did with singing?

An idea blossoms: what if I can persuade Jacob to come back for his lessons which, in the end, will benefit him anyway? Excitement fizzes through my veins at the thought of Jacob and I sharing our grief and given he was in a band, he's bound to love chart music too. And there's a sense of heaviness lifting from me because if Jacob returns it'll put out the dangerous fire he's relit inside Maestro – and help Maestro forget about Mum's note.

Before I change my mind, I check Maestro's files for Jacob's address and even though I've never done anything like this before, never even been alone with a boy, I jump into my car and roar up the driveway.

The radio loud, I sing along with Ariana Grande and Drake while drumming my hands on the steering wheel. The sensation of crawling insects, of being trapped in my own skin, vanishes. But when I get to Jacob's house, I realise my unusual bravery was more likely boredom or wishful thinking. *He won't even remember me.* I pan across the sparkling structure that is his home. It's like a piece of cube art in a modern-art museum. I cut off the music and grip the steering wheel as if it's a life preserver. But this is for Maestro. And maybe it's a bit for me. I need –

'Something more.'

Forcing myself from the car, I walk past a yellow Jeep with a surfboard strapped to the roof rack. But when I'm standing in front of a double-wide, double-high glass front door, my reflection staring back at me, I can't make myself knock; I was stupid not to change out of my misshapen sweater. It's baggy and reaches the hem of my wool skirt.

I'm almost back at my car when a large woman comes out the house and ambles up the path toward me, followed by a teenage boy in a loud shirt.

'Can I help, dear? You want Jacob?' she shouts, her Italian accent strong. Her hair is braided into a thick plait, shorter hair at the front hanging loosely around her cheeks.

I take in a deep breath. 'Yes. I wasn't sure if he lives here.'

She points a pudgy finger toward a gate to the side of the house. 'His studio. Through the gate. You cannot miss it.'

'Thank you,' I say, but make no move to go. Neither does she.

'He won't bite. Well, not very hard,' says the boy. He links arms with the woman. '*Dai*, Mamma. The bus.' The boy tugs at his mother's arm. I lock my car and cross the road. When I open the gate, she's still watching me.

It's easy to spot the circular building in the back garden. I can't hear anything coming from it though, and decide Jacob's gone into the main house and I should go home. I retrace my steps, but then spy the woman and boy searching for something in her handbag through the crack between the gate and the gatepost. I retreat, dragging myself back to the studio, and after staring at the door awhile, I knock. A minute ticks by. I push at the door. It makes a noise like suction cups coming apart and the sound of someone singing streams out. The room has to be soundproofed.

The voice is rich and low and powerful; one that could sound soft and soothing or loud and commanding. I bet it could sing anything, even opera. The words to 'You Raise Me Up' wash over me. The low notes produce goosebumps on my arms and legs. As the voice rises an octave, then two, its clarity, its purity, startles me. I can't help but step inside to identify the singer, because it can't be Jacob.

But it *is* him. He's standing next to a grand piano as he accompanies a recording. His eyes are closed. Somehow, I expected boy-band music, given he was in an indie-pop band, although the open beer bottle on the piano isn't a surprise. The blue cast on his hand is though.

Unaware of me, he keeps singing. Perhaps he's remembering

the person he lost recently, letting the grief course through him with the music.

I'm intruding on a private moment. If he discovers me, he'll be embarrassed, and it'll get awkward. Chickening out, I tiptoe backwards and leave.

But I don't want to return to my empty house with its grandfather clock marking off sameness one minute at a time, with its piles of scores waiting to be learnt, and with Mum's dresses hanging like colourful ghosts.

I drive around aimlessly and end up at the beach. After last night's storm the surf's big. It's a windy winter's day, and only a few walkers brave the weather. A coffee shop entices me out of the car and, cradling the takeaway cup, I sit on the sand under a sky crammed with grey woolpack clouds. With each sip, I hold the coffee on my tongue, savouring its bitterness. When it's finished, I loosen my ponytail and let the wind flog my hair. I grin into the chilly breeze.

To my left a surfer in a wetsuit arrives. He drops a red towel on the sand. His blond hair whips around as he bends to attach his leash using one hand; a light blue fibreglass cast encases the other.

Jacob.

My whole body gasps. I sit upright. But he doesn't notice me and trots into the surf, pushing his way through the whitewater to the bigger waves. His fluid motion as he mounts his board, surfs the wave, then goes off the back of it, becomes another piece of the Jacob puzzle.

It begins to drizzle and then the sky splits open. Rain pelts down like bullets, leaving dints in the sand and the smell of wet wood. I run to my car, stripping off my heavy jumper. I ramp up the heat, but the windscreen has fogged and I have to watch Jacob through the small patch of clear glass that grows as the car warms up. I rub my hands together in the stream of hot air and spot the yellow Jeep I'd seen earlier in Jacob's driveway two parking spots over. Perhaps he'll come out soon and I can say hello – pretend it's a chance meeting.

But Jacob appears to relish the building waves; the sound as they crash on the beach is now thunderous. He takes on a wave that slams him into the whirling ocean. I lose sight of him and need to flick on the windscreen wipers. His head pops up in the whitewater. He fights to get back out to the bigger green waves. Everyone else has gone home.

Something feels off. I lean into the windscreen to keep sight of him.

Jacob surfs a couple more waves before getting pounded into the ocean by another breaker. His orange and blue striped board swerves through the waves until his body emerges and he paddles out again. A thought comes, but slips away. I grab at it again. I recall the wild look on Jacob's face after his lesson with Maestro, the grief he's dealing with, and then I remember how in the early days of my own grief I wanted to join Mum and Savannah in heaven.

I throw open the car door and race across the beach,

waving my arms to catch his attention. If I can make him understand that what he's feeling is natural, then one day he'll be glad he can still surf and sing. One day he'll be glad he didn't die today.

9

Jacob

The ocean's giving me a battering today. Being pounded by something so powerful and certain as these waves somehow fills the hollow inside – for a while. It gives me something to hold onto, instead of forever groping at emptiness.

I size up another wave, but with only one good hand, I'm too slow. I'm thrown forward into the washing machine. Saltwater floods my nostrils, stings the back of my throat. My ankle jerks. The leash snaps from my board and it's as if my tether to the beach has vanished. Letting myself hang under the waves, I release the air out of my lungs and drift down, arms out sideways, the leash drifting like an umbilical cord. I stare up at the muffled crashing of the waves above me. When my toes skim the sand, in a reflex action I push off and whizz toward the sky.

Rain pounds my cheeks before I dive into the foam of the next wave. The cold bites my face. In the break between waves, I cast around for my board. It's almost back on shore, but between it and me swims a girl who's being clouted by the surf. I duck through the next wave only to surface and watch her get tumbled by it. Her head bobs up eventually. She gulps at the air. She's not wearing a wetsuit, just a white T-shirt, and I'm suddenly certain she's got herself in trouble. *Stupid.* Swimming on a day like today.

Grumbling to myself, I bodysurf toward the girl. There's a sandbank practically *next* to her. She suddenly makes a determined effort to swim toward the sandbank, though she resembles a demented turtle. When I reach her, she's just struggled to her feet in thigh-high water. She's panting and coughing.

I move in beside her, pulling my stare away from her clinging T-shirt.

'You okay?' I ask. She wraps her arms around herself. I nudge her to warn of another approaching wave. We jump it in unison. 'What are you doing? *Trying* to drown?'

'Me?' she shouts. 'I thought – your leash snapped – your cast and the waves.' Her words rev, fast and clipped. 'Only a suicidal idiot would surf in this.'

I shrug and check out to sea. 'Sounds about right.'

Another wave crashes toward us and I bodysurf to the beach. The girl wades and jumps toward me in the shallows, ringing out her long hair. Her T-shirt is see-through and she uses her arms to shield her breasts. The only other item she's wearing is pink undies.

I pluck my attention away from her, scan up and down the beach. My board's been washed up a few metres away. 'Where are your –' *Jeez, she's insane.* '– clothes?'

She searches around, baffled. 'Probably halfway to New Zealand by now.'

'So you came to the beach on this awesome day.' I lift my face to the grey sky, which has stopped raining. 'And the ocean was so inviting you stripped off and jumped in.'

'And you came to the beach with a broken wrist on this awesome day and thought you could handle the surf.'

'Easy if you do one-hand pop-ups to get up. But yeah, I'm usually a lot better at it.' I pretend to check my cast, maybe slightly embarrassed, then inspect the girl, trying to figure out her story. There's a graze on her forehead. Grey eyes. Full lips. I check her feet. Dainty. 'Aren't you that opera chick, I mean, um – Astrid. What're you doing here?' Didn't peg her for the adrenaline-junkie type.

'Maybe I'm after a little adventure.' She sounds a bit flirty, but then she rubs out those words by blurting, 'And you didn't come to your lesson.'

Snorting, I turn away. 'Did your dad send out a search party?' I unzip my wetsuit, edge it down over my hips. I should be mad she came after me.

When I turn back to her she's wrapped her arms around herself more tightly. 'I smell beer on your breath,' she says. 'Please tell me you weren't surfing after you'd been drinking.'

'Drunk in charge of a surfboard. Guilty.' I'm only joking, but the words come out hard, like I'm throwing stones at her. She's pressed a button now, and I wish she'd scram. I lose my gaze in the horizon, hoping she gets the message.

She doesn't. 'Alcohol strains your vocal folds. Beer's the worst. It dehydrates you.'

I swing to her with a retort, but she's shivering uncontrollably. She's like a drowned kitten. I fetch my towel, pass it to her. 'Lucky I don't sing anymore then.'

She accepts the towel and wraps it around herself. 'Sounded like you were singing okay to me. You're a skilled vocalist.'

'That goes against your argument that beer's bad for the voice.'

'Touché.'

'Touché? Who says touché?' She's like a girl from a seventies movie. But wait. What the f– 'Hang on. What did you say?'

'Alcohol strains –'

'When did you hear me sing?'

Her cheeks burn a dark shade of red. She makes circles in the wet sand with her big toe.

Something's off. 'When did you. Hear me. Sing?' I repeat.

'I have a confession,' she says. She bites her bottom lip, then sighs. 'I saw you leave my house before your lesson and I came to your studio before I came here.'

'You what? Why?' This girl's unreal. I cross my arms over my chest, which is now covered in goosebumps. Before she can reply, I stalk off to retrieve my board. When I near her again, I say, 'Don't worry. Doc'll get paid for the lesson.'

'That's not why I came. I – um. I –' She pulls the towel tighter around herself. 'But back to the point – you sing beautifully.'

I kick once at the sand, as though it's a football. It fans in the air. She needs to let this go. 'I told your dad I won't sing anymore. He should give up on me. No-one can force me to sing. Go tell him that.'

'If you don't want to sing, I don't think anyone should make you.'

What? Her words stop my next tirade. I check back, but she appears to mean what she said. 'Right.'

'But –'

I'm not sure if I should laugh or yell at her. 'Yeah?'

'You *were* singing. You have an amazing tone.' She's shivering again, despite the towel.

'Coming from you, I'll take that as a compliment.'

Her cheeks flush again. 'If you won't sing at my house – why is it all right at yours?'

I rub the back of my neck, trying to understand it myself. How did Dex get me singing again? And how come it felt so damn good? I track a drop of water that trickles down Astrid's forehead, over her nose, and to her mouth. She licks her lips, which jolts my attention back to the horizon.

'I was helping this kid with some voice lessons earlier – guess the singing overflowed from there.' This is getting awkward. 'So Astrid's an unusual name.'

'After Astrid Varnay, a famous opera singer. Both her parents were opera singers – the family business. And she grew up backstage at –'

I hold up a hand. 'Whoa. No need for a frigging history lesson.' Why am I still here talking to this girl?

She fidgets with her fingers. 'My sister, Savannah, was

named after the place she was conceived,' she adds.

Laughter rumbles from the pit of my stomach until it's a full belly laugh. It's like she's never talked to a boy before. She seems confused so I add, 'Not sure we're on friendly enough terms for you to bring up conception.'

Her face drops and she touches the graze on her forehead, then fails to control an all-over-body shiver from the cold.

'I'm freezing my arse off. We should go,' I say, putting down my board. I reach for the towel to get my car key, but she drops the towel, revealing her bare legs.

'You can keep the towel.' I hand it back to her. 'But my car key's attached to it with a safety pin.' She wraps it around herself again and then, awkward, we search for the key, the towel continually slipping.

But the key's not there. 'Shit.' I hunt in the sand around our feet. 'I pinned it to a corner.'

'Maybe you were too drunk to do it properly.'

She's wrong, but her words find their mark. Is she suggesting I was drink driving? I pick up my surfboard and stomp toward my Jeep, shove the board underneath it. When I turn back to her, she seems surprised. 'Seeing as you know the way now – drive me home, would you?'

10

Astrid

I hop into my car and tell myself this will be over in five minutes. When I suggested Jacob had been too drunk to pin his key onto the towel, he'd scowled and his annoyance had expanded across his face until it splashed into his eyes. I don't think he likes me – at all.

Giving a ride to a fuming Jacob is worse than sitting in the same anteroom as your competitor before a performance.

'I wasn't drunk.' Jacob's voice cracks. 'I would never drive while I was smashed.' His words are firecrackers discharged into the space between us. They ricochet inside the car, crackling dangerously. I keep saying the wrong thing, unable to figure out this guy. So I say nothing.

When I pull up outside his house he pivots to me. His chest is hairless and defined. I inspect a jacaranda tree through the driver's window.

'So. Opera,' he states, his voice suddenly silky. I glance at him, but his body language doesn't match his words – it hardly ever seems to. He's impossible to work out.

'So. The Con,' I mimic.

'This isn't a good conversation, you know. How about I ask

you a question and you answer without any history lessons, and then you ask me a question . . .'

'Ha-ha. *Très drôle.*'

'There you go again. You speak like someone out of another century.'

I whip around. 'I do not. It's French for *very funny.* But if you're going to insult me –'

'Keep your knickers on, Astrid Bell.' His smile takes over his face. Yep, definitely laughing at me now. 'So you're not auditioning for the Con?' he adds.

'Maestro has other ideas for me in the professional music world. Festivals and competitions.' I fiddle with the heat vents and shiver. I'm wet and wearing Jacob's towel as a skirt. 'Do you want your towel now, or will you be back for a lesson?' What will Maestro say when I come home bedraggled and half-clothed? He'll have a blue fit. I never lie to him, but I'll have to about the going to Jacob's studio part. I'm sure it'll seem as unacceptable to him as it was to Jacob.

'You've gone above and beyond the call of duty to get me back for lessons. But I'd rather get you a dress from my mum's collection. What would you prefer? Gucci, Armani, Chanel?'

I giggle at the idea of wearing designer clothes. 'I think I'm more of a Cotton On girl.'

He swings his long legs out of the car. 'Come in for a drink. As a thank you for the lift. I'll find you something to wear.'

'It's okay. I don't really drink. And I should go.'

He bends to peer into the car as I fiddle with the gear shift. 'You owe me.'

'I owe *you*? How's that?'

'For making me think you were drowning out there. Besides. That's my favourite towel. Signed by Kelly Slater.' He contemplates my lap, grins. My retort blows away like dandelion fluff out the window. 'And I need a lift back to the beach, once I find my spare key,' he calls as he walks toward the side gate, 'after we warm up.'

I have no choice but to follow him.

'Studio's open,' he says, pointing to it. 'I'll get that dress.' He takes the backyard steps up to the main house two at a time.

A dozen different instruments clutter Jacob's studio. It's as if the Sydney Symphony Orchestra dumped their kit here after rehearsals. Except judging by the number of dirty scattered plates, glasses and bottles, they stayed for lunch too. A pile of clothes is bundled next to the kitchenette's sink and I'm willing to bet that's why the place smells of cheesy socks and stale armpits. The sofas are both odd – one's in the shape of giant red lips and the other is a material replica of colourful Lego pieces. Behind them is a music system that's bookended with shelves of CDs, and two huge speakers.

I move to the grand piano in the centre of the room and play a few scales. It's a Steinway and has an excellent tone. Untidy stacks of sheet music are piled on either side of the piano's music rack. I shuffle through them and find a batch of photos – all of the same girl: big white smile, long chestnut hair, tanned a deep brown.

When Jacob joins me, he's changed into jeans and T-shirt. He passes me a plain beige long-sleeved cotton dress and as he does, stares at my clingy T-shirt. I hug the dress to me.

He makes a beeline for the fridge. 'You strike me as the white wine sort. I hate drinking alone.' He's pouring a glass before I can answer, then grabs a beer. Because of the cast, he holds the beer between his knees and pries off the cap. I notice a long scar on his calf.

'You were drinking alone before – when you were singing. Or do you have some hidden friends in here?' I mock-search the room.

He chuckles, and I'm stupidly proud I made a joke.

'Bathroom's that way, if you want to change.' He points behind me with his bottle.

It's not actually a bathroom, only a toilet, but there's enough space for me to wriggle out of my wet clothes and into the dress Jacob's lent me. It fits, though it reaches below my knees thanks to me being vertically challenged. Jacob sits on the red lips sofa and nods his approval, which makes me blush. I choose the Lego sofa. It's so soft and squishy that I sink backwards until I'm practically lying down. A small shriek pops from my mouth. I yank down the dress.

Jacob's low laugh gurgles softly. 'That thing's a blob. If you stay there, you might never get out again. I won't bite you know.'

It's what the boy in the driveway said. Seems to me Jacob might bite.

'I'm fine here.' I slide to the floor, lean against the sofa. He points with his chin at the glass of wine on the table between us. I have drunk a little wine before, at rehearsal dinners and celebrations, but I don't enjoy it. I can probably blame Kara for that after she stole her father's wine when we were twelve. Since I have to drive home, I press my lips together as I sip and only allow the tiniest amount of liquid into my mouth.

'You weren't giving me the cold shoulder when you said you didn't drink,' says Jacob. He's laughing at me again. I stare into the wine glass, but finding no comeback, search the room for inspiration.

A large framed photo of the same tanned girl rests on the table near the fridge. She's thigh deep in the surf at the beach eating an apple, her hair tousled and sexy. In the back of the room a glass door leads into an area that resembles a spaceship containing a console with hundreds of knobs and buttons. 'Is that a recording studio?'

'Yup. Want a tour?'

I follow him, stepping over a flute and two guitars. Through the glass screen over the controls, a third small room emerges. The walls are covered in floor-to-ceiling grey curtains, and a baby grand piano graces the middle of the room. *Zut.* Two pianos?

'Soundproof booth for recording stuff,' Jacob explains. Then he shows me what the knobs and sliders on the console do. We listen to some music he recorded and as it ends he pushes a slider to distort it until we flinch.

'Do you write music?' I ask. He looms over me. He's got to be six foot.

'Yup. But I suck. Better at playing it. But now I can't.' He waggles his cast. It's covered in handwritten words.

'What will you do about the Con? You can't play an instrument and you won't sing.'

'I thought you said no-one should make me sing.'

'And I meant it.' I recall Maestro in Berlin. 'I *really* mean it.'

'You sound as though you don't want to sing yourself.'

My breath catches. 'Why would you say that?'

He crosses his arms, the good hand in his armpit. His hair falls across one cheek, his smile skeptical. Or perhaps it's wary.

'I love all music and I love singing,' I say, cautious. 'But I'm not sure performing in public is – what I want to do for the rest of my life. I prefer writing lyrics and songs.'

He studies me, like he's listening to every word with his eyes.

After a gazillion minutes, he asks, 'Are you any good – at writing music?'

I band my arms over my stomach. 'I think so. I don't know.'

His features perk up. 'Got anything you can play now?'

'Only if you come back for your lesson tomorrow.'

'There you go again. Tricking me into singing. The doc *did* send you.'

He's teasing now. We study each other. My belly performs an instant hip-hop dance. If Jacob understood how Maestro would disapprove of me being here, alone with a boy . . . Soon Jacob's going to guess this is the first conversation I've held with a guy my own age, other than some stranger in a concert hall surrounded by hundreds of people. He adds, 'And what's with this *Maestro* shit? I mean, it's a bit corny.'

'His students started it.' When he continues to snigger, I scramble for a new topic. A photo of him cuddling that same tanned girl is tacked to the glass screen. Is that the girl who broke his heart?

He catches me staring at it. 'Girl from next door,' he says, impassive. 'Her mum's into photography.' He glances away.

'Is she why you won't sing anymore?'

Jacob's eyes flash, then go dark; a glint of sunlight on a lake that's swallowed by the deep water. He swivels to the console, turns something on. 'The band I was in. They're – all dead. Accident – recently.' I can see he's battling against his emotions in the way he flattens his expression. 'It's not right that I carry on singing – as though I've moved on and forgotten them.'

The pieces of the Jacob puzzle start to fit together and I can almost forgive him his grumpiness.

I remember from my own experience that someone saying they're sorry is unhelpful and offhand, so I refuse to say it now. But what else do I say? 'Today, were you surfing in those conditions with a broken wrist so you could join your friends?'

'Broken *hand*.' Jacob's jaw works from side to side. 'My friend, JW. He broke his wrist once. Didn't stop him surfing 'cept he wore a plaster cast instead of a waterproof fibreglass one. After three weeks the cast stank like the armpits of hell.'

'That's your answer?' I coax.

Jacob reaches for his beer. Eyes bruised with memories watch me as he swigs. 'It's all the answer I have.' I blink at our bare feet while he seems to tower over me. He adds, 'Does your dad support you – with your songwriting?'

I fiddle with a button on the dress and shrug. After Berlin, I learnt that Maestro might not *let* me give up singing. Until then, I thought it was my choice.

Jacob cocks his head. 'My dad told me who your mum was.'

Memories press in on me. I scratch my shin with the ball of my foot. 'She died after I was born.' I nearly mention Savannah, but it feels like too much information, too much tragedy, all at once. Instead I say, 'I figured out that when I sang it was as though I was filling her shoes and my dad kind of recovered from his grief.'

'So you keep singing as a stand-in for her. To honour the dead. That's insane.'

'It's no crazier than someone refusing to sing because it *dishonours* the dead.'

Jacob hangs his head and knocks his knuckles rhythmically against the wall he's leaning against. 'This might be where I say touché.' He's teasing me again.

Our gazes bump into each other. A hush circles us. Heat rises through my chest and neck like a puddle soaking through sheet music. I inspect the words on his cast.

They were chosen instead of me
And you ask why I don't feel lucky?
I was left behind to live
A forgettable life.

Jacob straightens, slides his cast behind him. 'Play some songs? The ones you wrote.' He indicates to the baby grand through the glass screen.

Relieved to put some distance between us, I sit on the stool in the soundproof booth. Jacob lets me warm up, hovering at the console. When he joins me, I play an intro and breathe deeply to make myself relax. At first, I can't remember the lyrics, although my hands play the notes as if they're on autopilot. After the first few bars, the words return to me and when the song ends, rather than deal with Jacob's reaction, I sing a couple more. The acoustics in here amaze me and my confidence skyrockets.

'I didn't know what to expect, but I wasn't expecting chart music,' he says, after I finish a third song. He's sitting behind me on the floor, elbows on bent knees. 'I mean, the songs are awesome. I guess I've only ever heard you sing opera. I'm totally jealous. You have that voice and you can write pop hits. None of your talent should go to waste.'

'Thanks. I wish Maestro saw it that way. I don't get to write much because I'm either voice training or doing schoolwork, or he's with his students and I can't use the piano.'

'He wants you to be a singer more than he wants you to write songs?'

I'm surprised by how much his question, spoken aloud, jolts me. I hadn't realised how much this was bothering me lately.

'Without sounding like a sleazebag, you're welcome to use the piano out there, or this recording studio, anytime. It's never locked – as you already discovered.' His expression mocks me. 'That talent needs to be nurtured.'

'And you're welcome back for your voice lessons. That talent needs to be nurtured.'

He blinks hard, twice. 'I have no choice but to come back. If I don't get into the Con, my parents won't support me anymore. I'll have to leave home and get a job. But I'm not cut out to do anything else. I'm someone who *has* to live the music – as if the sound of music flows in my veins and if you take away the music then the life drains from me.'

He's described why I love music perfectly. But more than that, I'm ludicrously happy he's going to return to his lessons with Maestro. 'You're very philosophical,' I say, then grimace; he opens up to me and I respond with something glib. But he doesn't appear to notice; his stare bores into the piano.

'Been doing a lot of thinking –' He contemplates me as though he's weighing up whether to tell me something or not.

'There's this dude I'm helping out. Dex. In one afternoon he made me see how much singing makes me feel alive.'

'And your friends from the band – they'd understand. You have to keep going, even if it means singing without them. They'd never ask you to stop.'

After a time he says, 'You might be right.' His eyes tremble with jagged memories.

He considers me, the room, his fingers, for about a million minutes. Then the memories slide away and a playful grin slips onto his lips. 'I'll sing *if* you tell your father you don't want to.'

I giggle. '*Et puis zut.* That's not going to happen anytime soon. Maybe when I'm older.'

'I'll ignore the weird "zut" stuff, but how's it going to be easier then – when he's invested more in your future as a singer?'

The setting sun tinges the room with a wispy pink light. Somehow the muted glow is calming; it cocoons us. I haven't told anyone about my deal with Maestro. It's private and so – disturbing. But the way Jacob's opened up to me . . .

'Maestro's promised to explain how my mother died, on my eighteenth birthday. I'm speculating it was in childbirth. *My* birth. Maybe it was post-natal depression and she – you know. Which is pretty awful too. But I doubt it. After he's told me everything though, it'll be the right time to talk about my future.'

I wait for his shocked reaction. Instead he says, 'Sounds to me like you're just chicken and avoiding the conversation.

And in the meantime you're not doing what you need to do.' The way he's combing my face, as if he cares about my dilemma, as if he understands me on a deep level, makes me feel like I'm glowing from the inside out. He's not offering a bland opinion, or saying what he should say, unthinking. 'It won't be any better then, than now.'

The room is absolutely still. As are we.

Something deep inside me stirs and stretches, an animal coming out of hibernation.

A lamp in the main studio switches itself on and we startle, then chuckle to cover our embarrassment.

'It's on a timer,' says Jacob.

Jamming a chord across the piano keys, I say, 'Enough talking,' and escape into the intro to Post Malone's 'Better Now'. Jacob stands and picks up the song in the fourth bar. He stares beyond me, as if watching a movie on the wall. Even though we're disconnected physically, the music, flowing between and around us, somehow connects us, like we're two separate musical notes, but in the same melody.

Afterwards, he says he needs a beer and we move into the main studio. We sing 'You'll Never Walk Alone' and 'What I Did For Love' in the dimming light. When I sing the songs in a more operatic style, he easily copies me. I'm shocked at how beautiful his voice is: smooth and low, powerful. Listening to him feels like sinking into a silky bed of pillows. His voice wraps around me, lifts me, so it's as if I'm floating in sound.

'Gone,' he sings, then subtly flattens the note for the next phrase. The note tugs at my heartstrings. Tears cram into my eyes. The vulnerability in Jacob's face, in his voice, makes me want to cry for Savannah, who often sang this song, for Mum, for me and my dad, for the beauty of the music. And then for Jacob, for his lost friends and the scar on his leg, whatever caused it, and the wounds in both of our hearts.

The studio door suddenly opens. The outside security light blares into the dimness like headlights in the early evening darkness. Jacob stops singing.

I squint, holding in a sob.

With the dazzling light behind him, I decide the silhouette belongs to Jacob's dad. But as he steps into the studio I realise it's the boy I saw earlier when I first came to find Jacob. The door closes, turning the room shadowy again; I swipe at my teary cheeks.

'Wassup?' The boy grins as he pans from Jacob to me. 'Did I interrupt something? All I could hear was you, man. La-la-laaaaah.' He raises his arms and drifts across the room, impersonating an opera singer. Then he cracks up, folding himself in half.

'Well, *scusami*. Nothing wrong with popera.' I get to my feet. 'Jacob was great.'

'Dex De Brun.' The boy holds out a hand. 'Pleased to meet you, Miss Scusami.' As I reach for it, he pulls away and ducks into an elaborate low bow instead. I giggle. This must be the kid who got Jacob singing again.

'You speak Italian,' he adds.

'Um. Not properly. But I've visited Italy a few times. And I sing in Italian sometimes – mostly by rote.'

'Holy coif. Can you sing in any other rote languages?'

'French. Spanish. German. Some Czech. Rote means by memory or repetition. Although I do get the translation, and I study pronunciation and inflection.'

'What you doing back here, kid?' Jacob moves right beside me.

'Missed the bus. Mamma's gone to Aunt Ramona's for dinner – blood sugar – and I said I needed to go to the library. So popera?' He snickers.

'Hey,' I interrupt. 'I want Jacob to like operatic pop. It's just pop songs performed in an operatic style.'

'It's not that I don't like it.' Jacob peers down at me. 'I'm just not sure – it's me.'

'Have you ever noticed how when a huge international event takes place it's the classically trained singer the world calls on?' I say. 'Think "Amazing Grace" or Pavarotti at football finals, or the ceremony at Ground Zero in New York. Opera may have a smaller following –'

'Time to step off the soap box, Maria Callas.' Jacob jostles me with his elbow.

I need to fight for some personal space so I pick up an old plate heaped with leftover pizza crusts and march to the sink.

'And you.' Jacob wags a finger at Dex. 'Don't think I didn't notice the beer you swiped before I got here. It happens again, you're out.'

'But you drink it.'

'I'm eighteen, and I'm not having your mamma smell it on you. Got it?'

'I bet your papa would be straight round here to tick off Jacob if he found out you were drinking,' I add.

Dex shrugs and rubs the back of his neck. 'Not sure he'd care. He blew the joint before I turned one. Moron went to all the trouble of running away with Mamma to Australia, and then it dawns on him he doesn't want to be married after all.' For a moment, Dex's bravado drops away, similar to a superhero's cape unexpectedly slipping off and revealing the true person beneath – a vulnerable boy fighting to survive. But in the moment that follows he swirls on another cape. By the time Jacob flicks on a second lamp, mumbling something about people not being fit to be parents, Dex swings back to being Mr Attitude again. I suspect Dex is wearing all sorts of masks to hide a lot of hurt. Like Maestro did.

Jacob adds, 'I mean it, Dex. No drinking.'

'All right, dude. Take a pill. You sing, lady?'

'Her name's Astrid. You wanna sing for us, Dex?' Jacob slaps him on the back. 'Despite his manners, this kid's got talent.'

Dex bounds over to the music centre, jabs at the iPad. Jacob gestures for me to take a seat. I choose the red lips sofa this time.

When Dex sings 'Pillowtalk', he's spellbinding. His voice and his Italian-origin looks make a good package. Jacob paces behind Dex, sipping from an orange-juice carton and offering Dex occasional tips.

'Want to give something new a shot?' asks Jacob, once Dex proves to be a quick learner. 'Astrid's a songwriter.'

'Holy coif. It's my lucky day.' Dex pulls out one edge of the piano stool with a flourish. I get up and move toward the piano. '*That's* why the room stinks.' Dex points at my bare feet and pegs his nose. The boys chuckle.

For the next hour I write down parts of my songs, and Dex sings them. Jacob makes suggestions, correcting Dex's breathing technique or sight reading or phrasing. Jacob's mood is brighter, and I sense it's a little lighter in here, as if the air has been emptied of ghosts. This is the real Jacob. This Jacob isn't broken or defensive or confused. This Jacob draws me to him.

When Jacob's phone rings he whips it from his pocket. The caller ID image is of the tanned girl in the photos. He beams and swipes to take the call. 'Harper.'

The girl has a name.

'An actual phone call,' he continues, his face lights up as brightly as if Harper just surprised him in person. 'How's America?' He's smiling but as she replies shadows move across his face. He stares straight through me. He's not in the studio with us anymore. 'Sounds great.' His words are wistful. 'But I hope you miss home a little. It's not the same without you. The Purple Woods need you, too.' That smile again.

I swivel back to the keyboard and continue playing, extra loud to avoid overhearing their conversation. Dex takes his cue and sings until his watch alarm beeps, at which point

Jacob ends his call saying, 'Still love ya', like he's trying to be all casual, but by the way gloom straps itself to him as he hangs up, it's clear he does still love Harper.

To reach his bag, Dex vaults the Lego sofa. 'Gotta go, dudes. Can we do this again, Miss Scusami? Bring your music next time.'

'*Please*,' says Jacob.

'What's the rush, Dex?' I ask. He tornadoes around the studio searching for his shoes and mumbling about being a *bugiardo*. 'I could drive you home.'

Jacob chucks some empties into a big bin. 'We gotta keep this a secret. His mamma doesn't know about the singing.'

'It's not easy being the nephew of a bishop who threw out his sister – my poor mamma – when she got knocked up.' Dex pounces on his shoes. 'He used to slap her to knock out the evil in her. Mamma would never hit me, so she says sinning will come easy to me.' Holding his shoes by their laces, he makes for the door yelling, 'Pop songs are sinful. Byeeee.' And with that he struts out the studio impersonating Lady Gaga singing about going where others can't hurt us.

Jacob pinches the bridge of his nose. 'Jeez. Kid's got to brush up on his manners. But *I'll* say it for him – thanks for spending all your time on him.' Jacob's collating sheets of music but the inches between us are not enough to stop my blush. 'What's *bugiardo* mean?' he asks.

'A liar. Poor Dex.' I get up from the stool, patting my pockets for car keys. 'I better go.' Silence swings heavily between us like a pendulum. When I glance up, Jacob's studying me. I examine my toes.

'You were crying before Dex came in,' Jacob says, soft. 'I saw you wipe your tears.' It's such a contrast to his earlier wariness at the beach that the moment seems intimate. I suppose we did spend the rest of the afternoon sharing our biggest worries and secrets.

I jangle the keys and blurt, 'That song. My sister sang it a lot. Savannah. She died when I was five.'

Jacob brings the heel of his hand to his forehead. 'And here's me going on about *my* shit. And you – jeez, I'm sorry. Sucks.'

I let the stillness swing between us a little longer rather than respond.

He adds, 'But *four* singers in one family. That's – totally out there. My parents wouldn't know a D flat from a G sharp.'

'It's not always a good thing.' I check my phone. Maestro's texted me twice. I'll have to say I lost all sense of time in Mo's Music Shop. He won't be impressed that I haven't finished the homework he set. 'There's a lot to live up to,' I say. 'By the way. Dex is amazing.'

'Even if he is completely egocentric.'

'He's a fifteen-year-old boy with a father who walked out on him and an uncle who hit his mother for getting pregnant. I assume it's an act. You know, to cover up how he feels.'

'And his voice fits your songs like sand goes with surf.' Jacob ambles nearer. He waggles my ballet flats at me. 'You should team up with him – record something.'

A whole future of the three of us working on my songs lays itself before me like a picnic blanket inviting me over. But I doubt my songwriting is good enough. And Maestro would never allow it.

'I mean, if you want to,' Jacob adds, when I don't respond. He tugs at his earlobe and opens the studio door for me.

Stepping backwards I wave, and then turn and head for the gate.

'Hey, would you give me a lift back to the beach?' he yells after me. 'Just hang on while I find my spare car keys.' Without waiting for my answer, he takes the back stairs into his house, two at a time.

11

Jacob

Doc Bell's music room's high on a hill, so it's as though the room's filled with sky. Unlike my cave of a music studio, light and fresh air fill every corner; the three French windows are thrown open and, in the distance, there's even a glimpse of the tips of the sails of the Opera House.

I study the painting above the fireplace, where someone's lit a fire in the grate. The woman resembles Astrid apart from the dead straight auburn hair that makes her face seem long and pale. Veronika Bell, I presume. I'm not sure I could sing at all with my legend of a mother staring down at me.

Doc Bell welcomes me back without referring to me running off halfway through my first lesson or playing hooky yesterday. He leaves the room saying he needs to fetch juice.

My phone dings with a text in the silence. Dad. *This is your last chance.* He called the doc to explain about my broken hand.

'Jacob, you met Astrid during your last session here,' says the doc when he returns. He's carrying a tray of pineapple juice. 'I've asked her to join us.'

I check the door, but there's no sign of Astrid. He pours three glasses of juice.

‘I thought the two of you could amuse yourselves with some songs. How’s “You’ll Never Walk Alone”?’ He straightens and glances toward the door. ‘Astrid?’

Astrid’s small hand appears before she does. Her fingers brace the edge of the half-closed door for a few seconds before she pushes it open.

‘Right here.’ She flashes him a smile, then acknowledges me with a bob of her head. Her cheeks are fiery. I’m guessing she hasn’t told the doc about coming to my studio and how we sang together, and that means this duet idea’s all his. Except the song has to be her choice – we sang it before she ran from my studio like Cinderella at midnight, except what she left behind was more valuable than a glass slipper: I felt happy.

Smirking, I track her, but she won’t turn my way. She’s wearing a grey knitted dress that wraps around her tiny shape and ties in the middle. By comparison, Harper’s tall – almost my height – and strong, with powerful shoulders, and she never wore anything but jean shorts with singlets, or tennis clothes. Astrid dresses more like a mum than a teenager, yet I have the urge to watch out for her. Perhaps it’s the way she looks at me as though she’s afraid I might hurt her. When she does that I can see the person I’ve become, and I wonder if I want to be that person anymore. Problem is I don’t know who the hell I’m meant to be.

‘The Gerry and the Pacemakers version or some opera one?’ I ask the doc. Astrid’s on the verge of giggling.

'You can do both?' The doc arranges himself on the piano stool, rips through a couple of scales, and goes straight into an intro for the original version. 'Take it easy. Use it as a warm-up. Come, come.' He beckons us closer, then dips his chin at Astrid as her cue.

Her attention on her father, she sings the first line, soft, a whispering melody. Yesterday, Astrid asked if I went surfing as some sort of attempted suicide. I guess I was leaving it to fate. Or luck. Right now, singing this song, I feel the same and decide to go with it – see where fate leads me.

'Have fun with it, Jacob,' says Doc. 'Enjoy the music.'

My mouth goes dry as I shove aside thoughts of the boys – they worshipped this song. But I remember how good it felt to sing, first with Dex, and then with Astrid, and I make myself breathe through the emotion of it and open my mouth. And sing about the end of the storm, about sweet silver songs and about walking on.

The doc's lips purse – in approval – I think. We launch into the chorus and finally Astrid pans across to me, smiling through the words. But she splutters and giggles.

Her father frowns at her in a *not kidding* way. 'Again,' he barks.

We begin again, soft and cautious, building to the chorus. We sing it another three times.

'Good. I want to attempt something. You have some rich classical tones in your voice, Jacob. A good range. Can we change it up a bit, a little vibrato, more full-bodied. Astrid, the *Carousel* version. Listen first, Jacob, then join in. We'll do a few scales first though.'

After the scales, which involve lots of agility exercises including complicated octave jumps, Astrid begins the song again. This time her soprano voice cuts through the sky in the room like a rainbow.

'Join in when you can, Jacob.'

I shift my weight, fingering the micro memory card in my pocket. Yesterday, I recorded Astrid while she sang in the soundproof booth. I need to find a moment to slip it to her. Doc Bell doesn't pay me any attention and instructs Astrid to 'give more support' or have 'higher resonance'. At the end they go straight into the start again. Astrid focuses on a point out the window, perhaps to avoid giggling. I remember singing with her last night and want to repeat the moment; my chest busted with that much exhilaration it could've split wide open.

I make a tentative start, adjusting my throat for a fuller sound as Dr Sofia taught me. I feel stupid in front of Astrid, but my voice sounds okay so I keep going. When the corner of Astrid's mouth lifts for a moment, I commit to the song, wanting to impress her.

The room swells with our melody, and I'm astonished at how my skin pricks with goosebumps. It's like rushing headlong through the Purple Woods in the old days, a kind of explosive joy bursting from my pores.

The classical style of singing seems more intense and empowering – perhaps it's the tradition behind it, of hundreds of years of music, that gives it more soul and more muscle. Or the fact you sing it using your entire body, from the head right through to the gut. Whatever it is, somehow singing the classical greats allows me to release every emotion I've ever wrapped up and buried, as if they were lifeless birds; now each one flies free of their grave and swarms the air.

When the song ends it feels like I've been dropped back to earth.

'You should've sung opera not jazz at your audition last year,' says the doc. 'You've got quite an instrument there. It's unique. And you're first-rate at placing your voice in the mask – in the nose and cheekbones where the sound resonates.'

I snort at him blowing smoke up my arse. 'If I can sing Astrid's opera garbage, she can sing what I normally sing.'

'You think I can't?' she fires back, the first words she's directed at me all morning.

'Maybe. Prove it. Olly Murs. "Troublemaker". Can you play it, Doc? I'd offer, but –' I lift my cast in the air.

'It's Dr Bell, not Doc. And no I can't, but I can find it on the iPad. Wait a moment.'

When he gets up Astrid peeks at me from under long lashes, her freckles lost in a mild blush. 'Is "Troublemaker" your middle name?' she asks.

'*Très drôle*,' I reply, slipping the micro memory card into her palm.

The music starts and I launch into the lyrics, pointing

and gesticulating like a rapper until she joins me. She knows the words – guess this is the kind of stuff she writes. When we hit the chorus I have the urge to dance, but Doc wouldn't approve. He straightaway clicks off the music when the song finishes. But Astrid carries on, turning the chorus into a rap at the speed of light. I swear her lips move so fast it's as if she's pre-programmed. She adds hand gestures, as though she's Cardi B in some rap battle.

My laugh comes out full-bellied. It loosens something inside me. 'You win. You win. That was awesome.' I fist-bump her.

'Where did that come from, Buttercup?' Doc appears kind of shocked, and not in a good way. 'I didn't know you liked the genre. Impressive.'

'I like everything.' She transforms back into dutiful daughter and passes round glasses of juice. 'Music is music.'

'True. Similar to sport, all music unites.' The doc turns to me. 'Jacob, your voice is an immeasurable gift. If it could be sold, it would fetch a high price – you could exchange it for a Stradivarius. It lies smack bang in the middle of two worlds of music – pop and opera.'

'Popera.' I snort, recalling how strongly Dr Sofia urged me to sing opera and popera.

'Your voice is big while at the same time having accessible pop tones. You need to nurture it. This will become your inimitable brand. Your style and voice cuts across cultures and ages. It speaks to all music lovers. It's what'll get you record deals.'

'I don't know about that,' I say. Astrid gives me a 'told you so'.

'You play the flute and the drums? Classical and modern. Popera is merely modern music sung classically.'

Astrid crosses her eyes. Harper used to do that. Laughter gurgles and pinballs a bunch of memories into my brain: the times when I rehearsed in the Hunters' kitchen with Aria last year – Harper listening in and tossing popcorn at us if we made a mistake. To prepare for the Con audition we competed for Harper's applause on each instrument. She'd award scores and Aria and I would squabble. I miss those times. I miss being part of their family. I miss my Purple Daze family. A lump forms in my throat and I'm struggling to hold onto my shit.

Spinning away from the piano, I stride over to the fireplace. The ashes in the grate take me back to the funerals. The band would have a giraffe if they could hear me sing popera. *Geek. That crap's scarring my ear drums. Evil, man.* I turn toward the windows. 'But I don't want to sing that stuff. I'm into chart music.'

'No reason you can't do both – sing modern music with a big voice, with more vibrato. It's how it was in the fifties and sixties anyhow. Those artists did all right. Otherwise you're no more than a copy of the next guy, trying to make your mark in a sea of sameness. Let me show you.'

With more cajoling from them both, we spend the morning converting my favourite pop music into 'full-voiced' songs that aren't quite opera but are big, open-throated affairs. Astrid helps me adapt them, hearing harmonies that compliment, and I have to admit the sound is good enough to forget everything in my life but the music.

♫

For ten days straight I have a lesson with the doc. And Astrid and her father step into the gaping hole in my life. Twice, I even stay for dinner. Doc Bell usually teaches at the Con most afternoons and privately in the music room the rest of the time, but some young talent he's been nurturing, Heinrich someone, has laryngitis, leaving an opening for me. I have a reason to get out of bed every day, even if my bed is the Lego sofa. Even if I don't get up till midday.

The doc pushes me; he's strict and doesn't let up. But neither do I. It's similar to when I'm surfing dangerously large waves – the complex lessons, the discipline, the repetitive vocal exercises are something to grab hold of, instead of emptiness. They need my absolute focus and take me away from – everything. And I finally make the doc smile. His smiles are so rare I count them, but stop after reaching eighteen. I'm less proud that I made him cry once. He'd asked about Purple Daze. I became defensive, angry even, and turned the question back on him.

'Astrid told me about losing your daughter too,' I said.

Doc stopped collecting sheet music. He faked a smile, tears brimming.

'It seems neither of us are ready to talk about our loss.' He gave me a complicated look though, one that said *sorry and I understand and we're in this together* all in one short, brilliant moment.

Is this what it feels like to have a proper father?

'He's really happy with you,' says Astrid one night as I fetch the salt and pepper and she places three bowls of spaghetti and meatballs on the kitchen table. The sound of the doc humming in the music room is an excited, high-pitched purr. 'You made his week.'

'Don't know about that.' I remember one set of vocal gymnastics we repeated fifty times.

'He's not usually this cheerful all the time. He can get horribly moody. And last night, he said despite your attitude to opera, you're his best student ever and he's never met anyone –'

We turn at the sound of footsteps. Doc, his hair bushy from running his hands through it, seems to float into the kitchen, his smile wider than a keyboard. He slaps me on the back. 'This young man,' he says, 'is destined for greatness.'

'Greatness at what though?' I ask. Maybe fishing for compliments. 'Eating the most meatballs?' I pinch one from my bowl and lob it into my mouth.

Doc pulls out a chair. 'Your parents don't mind that you're staying for dinner?'

I haven't asked them. They won't be home for hours and would expect Maria to feed me.

Dinner turns into a couple hours of talking about music genres and their strengths and weaknesses, and Doc reveals a secret passion for cricket. By the way Astrid stays silent, I'm pretty sure they don't usually do sport talk over dinner. Afterwards, he wants us to listen to a new talent from Italy. We return to the music room, Astrid and I in an armchair each, while he paces the room and describes the technical strengths of the voice we're studying.

'Before you go,' says the doc as he packs up. 'Astrid's competing in a contest for young singers in Vienna at the end of the week. Heinrich Vogel-Jung was meant to be entering too, poor soul, but his laryngitis has resulted in vocal-cord paralysis and he cannot attend. I think you, Jacob, should take his place. I can pull some strings. I've worked with the organisers.'

It's like he locked me into a box and I can't breathe.

'No.' I gulp in air that's thick as cold soup. 'Not yet.'

The last time I was on stage was the last time we – my blood brothers – were together.

'That's terrible for Heinrich,' says Astrid. 'Will he be okay?'

'It could be permanent, I'm afraid. His career could be prematurely over.' He turns back to me. 'We've got three days to rehearse. I'll discuss the expenses with your father. What else have you got to do? I can adjust my schedule to give you some extra hours.' The doc's whole body seems to sparkle with excitement, as if he's impressed with me. It's a big contrast to Dad's air of disappointment.

I toe the piano leg. My blood brothers and Harper have

gone. I'm lonely. And singing is all I have left. As Astrid said in my studio, they'd be okay with me singing again. 'Would Astrid and I sing together in the competition?' I glance at Astrid. She's nibbling on a thumbnail.

'No. Astrid has her own repertoire. But you don't need to sing together. What you have on your own is enough. It could get you some interest – live festivals, scholarships, vocal agents, something to add to the Con application.'

From lead singer of an indie band to popera soloist? It's all fine behind closed doors . . . No. I don't think so. It's not who I am. 'No. It's in three days.'

'Son. If you want this enough, you'll find a way. If you fear it, you'll put obstacles in your way. Blithely declaring it's too soon is an obstacle. Never let fear dictate your decisions. Do you want a career in music?'

'I do. But I wasn't expecting this. And the style of song –' Inside my mind, the boys are busting a gut laughing.

Doc drops the lid on the piano, now copying my dad's disappointed expression. 'You're going to reject an enormous opportunity because you weren't *expecting* it?'

I shrug and go to crack my knuckles, but can't because of the cast. It *has* been kinda cool converting pop songs into popera this week. I mumble, 'I can be pretty dumb.'

Astrid passes me some sheet music, adding, 'You said it,' without looking at me. It's maddening how she does that. 'Jacob's more of a bar singer, Maestro. He likes to stay within certain *limits*.'

'Think it over,' Doc adds. 'But sometimes a disparity exists between the music you're mad about and the music your voice was meant to sing. I need your answer by tomorrow morning.'

Could that be right? I peer at the sheet music Astrid gave me. It's a pop song she's written. It's called 'Touché'. The word releases snippets of memories from that day in my studio and with them, a ripple of happiness. Instinctively, I know I need to grab hold of that happiness before I get lost down a path I might never return from.

Astrid's pouring juice. She rolls both lips and bites down on them, smirking. Alone in my studio with a beer for company or performing in Vienna with these two nut-jobs? No-one will know where I am or what I'm singing. Except my parents. And Dad will totally approve.

For all those reasons, and to prove Astrid wrong, I say, 'I'll do it.'

12

Astrid

It's after midnight and I should go to sleep because we leave for Vienna in the morning, but I have to finish this song; melodies are pouring out of my head and onto the page as though my brain is an overflowing jug of notes.

I've played the USB Jacob slipped me every night. If I hadn't remembered which songs I sang, I swear I wouldn't have known it was me singing. It's the acoustics in his recording studio. I want to go back and sing opera and see how that sounds. And this new song.

Maestro busts into my room, hair sticking up like a mad professor. Black storm clouds appear to follow him in. 'Astrid. Tonight of all nights.'

'Two minutes.' I hold up two fingers, clinging to the last phrases of the song. My pen jerks across the page as Maestro snatches away my book.

'Now you've made me forget the end.' My throat bloats with unshed tears as I climb off the bed.

I brace myself for his reaction, but it's not like I'm breaking the law. It's just chart music. Maybe it's better he finds out this way. He scans my work, a puffy sourness mauling his features.

This is the erratic version of Maestro, when the smouldering fire inside him burns most fiercely. I remember going to see the musical *Dr Jekyll & Mr Hyde* and sometimes Maestro can be scary like that – Dr Dad and Mr Maestro. I recall how the actor fought with himself, as if a demon lived inside him, one moment showing the open, concerned face of the doctor, the next turning to reveal the pinched, angry expression of Mr Hyde. It's only me that ever gets to see Mr Maestro.

'What is this?' he demands.

'Music!' I rummage for a clean PJ top, having spilled hot chocolate earlier.

'I can see it's music. But you're writing pop songs?' He paces, studying the book, then spins back to me. 'And tonight? We leave for Vienna in the morning. You should be sleeping or you'll sing worse than a cawing raven.'

I stiffen. He's never talked to me this way before.

'I should never have invited Jacob. You are not focused. Vienna is a huge event –' His fingers spear his hair.

'And this helps my nerves how? What happened to having fun and not worrying about the win?'

The cords in his neck twang. 'This is not the time for *that* discussion. It's after midnight and you're writing *pop music*. Is this because Jacob prefers this sort of music?'

Exasperation balloons inside me. I've never felt so breathless with it before; I want to slam doors, punch walls and jump out the window. 'I won't sleep anyway.' My voice is a high-pitched bark. 'I'm too nervous.'

Maestro's face pinches. 'Do *not* shout at me, Astrid.' He points a stern finger.

'Maybe I have to because you're not *hearing* me. I prefer *writing* songs to singing them.'

There. I've told him. With no way of taking it back. Except I want to when Maestro pulls himself tall and the storm clouds he brought in with him thunder across his features.

'*Enough*. This is Jacob talking. Get yourself to bed, Astrid Bell. Vienna's calling.' The music book in his grasp, he stalks from my room.

I stare at the door as if it slapped me. I expected him to listen and then we'd hug and say sorry – like the time I hid in the cupboard because he wouldn't let me miss a voice lesson to go to the cinema with Kara. Or when I refused to wear an orange dress until he discovered it was because Savannah hated the colour; he's not worn orange since.

Something has changed. *He's* changed. It's as if the older I get, the more the unpredictable side of him is taking over. Mr Maestro's winning. It's like living inside my own opera and the demon has gained ground.

And I'm to sing, whether I want to or not.

13

Jacob

Astrid's brown boots march alongside my black ones on the cobbled street. She has to walk fast to keep up. I slow down. Even though it's September and the leaves are only just starting to turn in Vienna, the evening temperatures drop to ten degrees. It means thongs and shorts are out and I'm as uncomfortable in woolly gear and boots as I was the time I lost a bet to JW and wore a bikini to the Aquadrome.

'Your dad told me that Savannah is the place he loves visiting the most.' I tug at the neck of my jumper. 'Guess that's why she was conceived there,' I tease. 'Where's the place you love most?'

'Paris. Maestro says he scattered Mum's ashes there. It was her favourite city.'

'Paris is a good name for a girl. Don't go conceiving a kid in Zimbabwe or Lahore though.'

Astrid punches my arm. '*Zut*. Don't mock.'

The doc had arranged to meet an old friend and I argued we needed a break while he swanned off. He swirled on his cloak while inspecting us as though I'd asked if we could get drunk and go skinny dipping. What's got his knickers in a twist? He borrowed that critical expression from my dad. 'Don't be a bad influence, Jacob. Two hours free time. Competition's tomorrow.'

Like we needed reminding.

To humour Astrid I agree to watch a performance of the Spanish Riding School. It is pretty cool: one of the horses springs off the floor, four hooves at once. And it's pure white, similar to the walls of the Hofburg palace we walk past afterwards.

'Vienna's stupidly clean,' I say. 'Every building's spotless. Even the apartment blocks. Isn't this city about a gazillion years old? Reckon the pavements are scrubbed with toothbrushes. No gum or litter, cigarette butts.'

'It's like an historical movie set. I keep hearing a movie score in my head.'

'Which one?'

'Something dramatic. *Empty Chairs and Empty Tables* or *Phantom of the Opera*.'

Astrid has dyed her hair auburn and straightened it. She resembles her mother in that portrait above the fire even more now. I tweak her hair. 'You realise you don't need to look identical to Veronika Bell to sing like a star.'

'I happen to love the colour.' She ups the pace. 'That's all.'

We walk past a news billboard on the pavement. The headline declares 'Day of terror in Thailand' and I remember we have to fly back to Australia via Bangkok. No matter where you live in the world, we must deal with death.

'Yeah, it's a nice colour,' I say. 'But reckon you're kidding yourself. You have crazy amazing talent of your own, and great hair.'

She wraps her arms around herself, peers at me sideways, eyes filled with shadows. I'm surprised by the urge to hug her, but she's about as rigid as a music stand right now. I ram my hands into my armpits.

'My dad gave me this leaflet about the stages of grief,' I say. 'I can't remember them all, but one of them was the guilt stage. And we're meant to pass through all these stages – shock and denial and anger and stuff – until it doesn't hurt so much. I reckon you got stuck at guilt – if you keep living your mum's and your sister's dreams for them, you can feel better about being the one who didn't die. And until you get past that guilt, you'll never move forward with your own life.'

Astrid's steps quicken. I can see I'm right: blame and grief leak out of her – they're even in the way she clutches at herself. And I know how the guilt's tearing at her organs, leaving her bruised and aching – because I've felt it.

'And what stage are you stuck on, Jacob?' Her jaw set firm, she's suddenly fired up.

I scan for a distraction because the air has become too chunky to breathe.

A man wearing a felt grey hat with a green feather poking from it blocks our way. '*Kutschfahrt*?' he asks, then points to an open white carriage drawn by two white horses. It reminds me of something out of a fairytale.

Astrid studies the horses. 'No thanks, it's okay,' she says. But by the way she glances at the horses again, I can see she wants to.

'Why not?' I say. 'We're tourists today.'

Astrid pinches her bottom lip but then goes ahead and negotiates a price.

'I owe you,' I tell her, as we climb into the carriage.

The buildings are draped in a twilight that adds to the movie-like atmosphere of this city. While we clip-clop down cobbled streets, I wish Harper was here. I commit each sight to memory so I can tell her every detail. First, we pass St Stephen's gothic cathedral with its intricate spires and coloured roof tiles that resemble pieces of a kid's puzzle. Then Demels, the famous royal confectioner; their wood and brass doors open to let loose the aroma of sugary Bundt cakes. Outside Mozarthaus a trio of violinists play for coins and we lean over the edge of the carriage to toss our spare change into their open violin cases. We pass Mozart's statue and Astrid stands and gives a dramatic bow. We're chuckling and joking until the sight of the Vienna State Opera House muzzles us, our words sealed behind face-aching smiles.

The lights are coming on, highlighting the pale-green domed roof. The building sparkles like a palace and each dramatic arch promises entry into a grand world of musical dreams. The history of this building, the people who have walked up those stairs – Pavarotti and Maria Callas, Mozart, Strauss and Wagner – even a non-classical ignoramus like me can appreciate the enormity of what we're about to do. But to walk in the shoes of her stupidly famous mother, here in Vienna, must be *more* than overwhelming for Astrid.

Sitting opposite each other, I watch her, both lit up and pensive.

'My parents met here. On the stairs to the left.' Astrid points to one end of the building. 'Whenever we visit, I feel closer to my mum. She sang here often – *Evelyn Bolena, Il Trovatore.* She won the Belvedere Singing competition here, when she was my age. It launched her career.'

'And you have *her* blood in your veins. Wow.'

Astrid's face crumples. She folds herself over, clutching her trousered legs. I jump across the carriage and put my arm around her. *Way to go, dickhead.*

'What if I can't do it?' She clings to her legs, talking into them.

I lean in closer. Her hair smells of flowers. Different ones to Harper. 'Do what?'

'I get performance anxiety,' she says, muffled. 'And this is bigger – way bigger than anything I've ever done. In Berlin, only recently, my gullet constricted and my voice didn't flow. I struggled to reach the upper register or keep my breath. The higher I went, the worse the strangling panic. My skin was soaked with sweat and the theatre walls wobbled and throbbed around me. I'm amazed I sang at all.'

'You're kidding.' I fall back in the seat. She's such a pro – what hope is there for the rest of us? I add, 'You'll be fine. I mean, you're an expert and you've practised loads.'

I recall glimpsing her landing card at Vienna airport, and noticing how she wrote 'student' in the occupation box, while I wrote 'musician'.

She straightens, dry-washes her face with her hands. I hop to the opposite seat, grasp her wrists. 'It'll work out okay, yeah?'

She reads what I've written on my cast in big black pen: *Why wasn't I enough, Harper?* Pulling away, she gives me a weak smile. '*Bien*. Course it will.'

The carriage stops and I recognise the Hofburg palace, the ride now finished.

'I could eat both my legs,' I say. 'Let's go get some food. I owe you.'

Astrid wraps her arms around herself. 'I feel sick. Sorry.'

'The sight of me makes you sick?' I joke. But Astrid doesn't laugh. She walks in the direction of our hotel and I almost put an arm around her, but stuff my hands into my pockets instead. She's not Harper, after all.

♫

The air con in the hotel room whispers like a ghost.

I can't sleep. It's 3.14 am.

I haven't stayed in a hotel since that night.

All hotel rooms smell the same – carpet cleaner and stale, dead air. Memories pace inside my skull. My legs jig. The lost remote control, the freezing air con, the weighty voice of the policeman. I pulled on the socks of a dead man.

I'll never hear their voices again.

Blood rushes until the need to get out of the room makes me roll out of bed. But there's no balcony. I slam my arm against the window. The memories thicken. They take hold. I re-live that night; grief and guilt burn through me until I'm feverish. I pull off my T-shirt. When my breaths come faster, and I'm sucking back sobs, I yank open the minibar fridge.

'Here's to you, boys.' I raise the small bottle of Jack Daniels and take a swig. 'Jesus effing Christ.' I slap my thigh, kick the bed. 'I miss you idiots.' They promised to have a designated driver. A-holes. My body trembles and I sink to the floor, prop myself against the bed. 'Why? Why did you have to die? I should've been with you.'

Instead, I get to sing in Vienna.

Their faces parade around a dozen merged-into-one hotel rooms; Skittles going through the running order for the next gig. No-one's listening and he's calling us all neanderthals. He chucks a Skittle into his mouth, swigs at his beer – he swore the Skittles stopped hangovers. JW's on the phone to his mum – such a mummy's boy.

His mum's totally alone now.

Emery's combing his flick to one side, then backwards, then to the other side, smiling idiotically into the mirror. 'Doesn't matter what you do, you'll always be a dumb arschloch,' yells Mad Dog, snapping open another can. Emery's baby daughter has no father now, dumb or not.

Mad Dog's climbing onto the balcony railings twenty

storeys up, chasing the adrenaline rush from jumping to the balcony next door. I always figured that would be what killed him.

And Callum. Sitting in the corner on the tiny round table, scribbling in a pad. His novels will never be read. His songs will never be heard.

They're probably stalking me from heaven. Opera. I snort. *Heaven will shake with their laughter.* Or hell. I grapple two bottles of beer from the fridge and slug them back.

I have to stay in another hotel in England. As we're already in Europe, the doc talked my parents into another audition at a music school in London. It was last minute, but Doc reckons it's a better school for me. More than anything, it's a ticket out of home. Reckon the doc knows I need to get out of Dodge. To do that for me – give up on his teaching time – Doc's quite a guy. And imagine what my parents' friends will say if I'm accepted.

Hiding inside a beer-brain fog, my thoughts slide to Astrid; how her expression of awe slipped into fear when she saw the Opera House. That's what happens when you walk in the footsteps of a famous mother. I wanted to comfort her so badly, but the right words wouldn't come.

I punch her mum's name into Google on my mobile and read an article about how Veronika-with-a-K Bell disappeared from the music scene. They don't say how she died. Next I check Callum's Instagram account. It's gone now, same as Emery's. Mad Dog's remains, his jaw as square as ever, but the number of followers has dropped to 911. Did people unfriend him because he's dead?

A text comes through from Harper: *In Paris for training.* So close, yet so far.

I throw back a couple of shots of vodka and wash them down with Coke, then download some music and hum to myself until I fall asleep on the floor.

14

Astrid

We're backstage, minutes from my performance, and I'm darting downstairs to the bathroom to throw up. Again. I barely have time to rinse my mouth before running back into the wings. My hair, looped into a fancy bun, lies flat and damp against my skull. The freckles I'd covered with make-up peep through and the tight strapless bodice of Mum's red ballgown seems to constrict around my chest.

'Better?' Jacob asks. When I shake my head, he puts an arm around my clammy shoulders. I droop into him. 'If *you* can't do this, how can I?' he adds. He's sweating in his penguin suit and bow tie. When he first put it on he laughed at his reflection, thinking he looked dumb, then argued with Maestro about tying back his hair. Now, his hair hangs loosely around his face, strands of it sticking to his sweaty neck and jawline.

Ripples of music filter through the thrumming in my head. I peer between the leg curtains onto the stage where a baritone is performing. A slim, grey-haired man accompanies him, striking out a series of chords on the piano. I hold my breath and push back at the nausea. 'That accompanist,' I say, eventually, 'has played for loads of big-name singers around the world. Including my mum.'

'And now he'll be playing for the great Astrid Bell.' Jacob points to the contestant currently on stage. '*He's* sending everyone to sleep.'

I glance at the judges sitting near the front in one of the rows of red seats. As it's a contest, it's much brighter than during an evening performance, and there are no spotlights on the performer. The circular theatre yawns behind them. It's smaller than I imagined, compared to the Sydney Opera House, but also filled with hundreds of people I hadn't expected to witness my probable humiliation. I reach out to hold onto something and Jacob grabs my elbow.

'Should I fetch your dad?' he whispers.

And then they call my name.

I draw myself up, like shoving a rod through my entire body. 'Vienna's calling. The show must go on.'

Jacob squeezes my arm. 'You can do it.'

I make myself put one foot in front of the other. Fear slips and slides through me, but I keep moving forward and pass my music to the pianist. I've been clenching it so tightly, it's creased in one corner. I wonder if he knows I'm Veronika Bell's daughter, or if he remembers her. He smiles at me, but I can't make my face smile back.

My body sways as I turn to face the audience. Fear becomes a bird trapped inside my ribcage, frantically beating its wings and trying to escape through my throat.

The accompanist coughs. When he does it again I turn my head to him. He's waiting for my nod. But my mouth is dry, my ears throb with my heartbeat, making me dizzy. My gaze swerves back to the audience and over all their heads to the very back of the auditorium. Mum floods into my brain and suddenly I'm her, gazing out at the very scene she once did, wearing this same dress and shoes. What if the judges compare us and are disappointed? I check my feet, half expecting to see her ghostly footprints on the stage from years ago.

The theatre fills with the intro to 'Summertime'. I count the beats, my body shivering yet hot. On cue, I open my mouth. Nothing comes out. The music continues. Then stops. There's a prickly hush that snaps me out of the haze I'm swaying in. I twirl to the pianist.

'Sorry. Would you mind starting again?' I ask.

The music begins again, but when I look up my oesophagus tightens. I swallow hard and take in a deep breath, but it's too late. I've missed my cue again. I try to catch up to the music yet it's flying ahead of me. Then someone else is singing. I turn my head and watch Jacob slowly tread onto the stage. The lighting silhouettes him and alters his blond hair into a bright halo. He's an apparition in a tux.

I feel my mouth stretching into a smile so big my cheeks cramp. I focus on Jacob's mouth, shaping the notes. He moves nearer, his rich tone sending goosebumps up my arms and spreading a balm over my nerves. I snag Jacob's hand, in case he's thinking of leaving me here – he has to be more familiar with the Ella Fitzgerald version. My throat loosens. He times his breath perfectly and I join in. The audience applauds and we turn to them.

My voice does what it's trained to do, climbing to the heights I ask it to, and Jacob expertly accompanies me in the lower keys. Then our voices soar toward a dramatic finale, and even before we've finished holding the final note the opera house boils over with applause and cheers.

Jacob waves his cast and bows while I curtsey. A bubble of happiness bursts inside me.

We retreat offstage and I grab Jacob in a hug around the waist. 'That was the worst and best moment of my life,' I shout over the continuing applause which only stops when they announce the next contestant. We clutch each other's elbows. 'You were incredible.'

'*You* were awesome.'

'I've never enjoyed singing on stage so much. But, oh my god, I'll be disqualified.' I pull away, spin in a small circle, and almost trip over a curtain. I turn to Jacob. 'Maestro's going to have a kitten.'

'After that applause? Never.' Jacob's smile is unguarded and it's as if I'm seeing him truly happy for the first time. 'And I get to do it all over again.' He slaps a palm over his forehead. 'Holy coif, as Dex would say.' He peers through the leg curtains.

We listen to the next contestant, and when they call Jacob's name he glides onto the stage as though the floor is ice and he's a professional skater.

Jacob commands every ear to listen; his vibrato rings out poignantly and I brush away the tears as I wait in the wings. I glance around me. Others have tear tracks too. His voice is a tray with his heart laid out on it. His tone sounds so vulnerable you can't help but let it touch your own heart, maybe even unlock it after it's been sealed and buried.

He finishes a faultless performance. The audience rise to their feet and continue applauding even after he's rushed offstage, arms spread wide for a hug. I throw myself into them. He lifts me off my feet and I lean forward and kiss him on the lips. I don't know why I do it; with the air in the opera house jammed full with an intense zing, it feels right.

But it's as though a needle has been yanked from a record.

Everything stops.

Jacob drops me to my feet, his expression spiked with anguish. With a final pained stare, he whirlwinds away.

15

Jacob

Being a competition, the lights in the auditorium are dimmed only a little. As the pianist begins to play, I can see the expectation on everyone's faces. It's distracting, so I place my focus beyond them, at the back of the auditorium, and lose myself in the song. I get back to that place where I was with Astrid moments before, singing together in a way that had made me feel elated for the first time in months – longer.

After a while, I sense people are smiling and nodding. Some have tears that make their cheeks glisten, and some gawp at the person beside them, their faces filled with wonder. They look at *me* with wonder.

It comes to me, shadowy at first, but then like the dawn sun splashing around the gaps in a curtain, brightening the air so everything in the room gains definition: I know this is the purpose of me in this life. I know the purpose of my voice because it can affect people in an awesome way. It's like my voice is a cure for the way life can numb you.

I wonder why I resisted Dr Sofia when she steered me toward popera. And that answer comes to me now too, making me smile into the audience: it was what my *dad* wanted. Plus who ever heard of a surfing tenor? I suddenly don't care about that. Watching the audience and how they respond to me is so powerful my body fills with emotion like I'm an expanding accordion.

For the first time since the funerals I'm honouring Purple Daze – singing for them, never forgetting them, dedicating my voice to them.

And then the applause comes and the audience is on their feet, cheering. Some clap their hands above their heads. But at the same time that an intense happiness streaks through me, I'm struck by the sense that I'm saying goodbye to the boys, that our paths are forking, and I am leaving them behind.

I smile through bittersweet tears and rush backstage to Astrid. She's jumping up and down on the spot with excitement. I sweep her into my arms.

And then she kisses me.

My body pulses and responds. Except kissing Astrid means saying goodbye to Harper.

I can't do it. That's one too many goodbyes today.

16

Astrid

The next morning when I walk into the hotel dining room for breakfast, Maestro catches up to me, and leans in close. 'You've been disqualified.'

'I'm not surprised. I'm not cut out for this.' I choose the nearest table and drop into a chair.

He seems not to hear me. 'When you did finally sing though, you sounded incredible. I'm not sure whether to be mad or ecstatic, Buttercup.' Somehow, even after his disappointed lecture last night, he's in a good mood. He pulls out a chair and sits opposite me, casting around for a waiter.

I'm about to reply when Jacob appears behind Maestro. He perches on the seat between us, rapping his fingers on the table.

Maestro pats his hand. 'There you are. We couldn't find you last night, but you were extraordinary. It wasn't just your voice, but the expressiveness of your face, your ability to project your personality –'

'Got it, Doc.' Jacob searches over our heads, then gets to his feet and crosses toward the coffee machine. Maestro doesn't take the hint and follows him, still wearing his cloak like some sort of villain in a comic book. I watch Jacob go through the motions of making a coffee from the jug on the hot plate while Maestro's arms gesticulate wildly. He's still talking when they return to the table.

'You never let anything hold you back, Jacob.' Maestro's glare plunders mine. I need Alice's 'drink me' potion so I can shrink down to the size of a pea, but I needn't have worried because Jacob doesn't appear to be listening. He glugs down his coffee, surely burning his mouth.

'I'm not hungry.' He stands again, stares at the exit like he's a trapped animal. 'I'll see you at the rehearsal room, Doctor Bell.'

Only then does Maestro stop talking. He frowns at Jacob's vanishing shape then at me. 'What's happened?' I turn my empty juice glass in circles. He crosses his arms. 'Astrid?'

I've never discussed anything like kissing a boy with Maestro. He thinks I'll stay a virgin until I'm fifty-five. He probably thinks I have a virginal mind, and the thought of kissing Jacob wouldn't cross it. And I'm still so confused. Jacob seems angry with me. Why would kissing him have that effect?

'I really don't know.' The words are congealed lumps stuck in my throat.

Maestro stands and with a flurry, takes his cloak off, laying it over the back of the chair Jacob just vacated. 'Perhaps it's his band again. It would be hard not to miss them after a night like last night.'

♫

Jacob progresses to the next round and continues to be civil but distant, his smile pinned in place, his gaze never meeting mine. In response, I get a little angry. If he's not interested in me in that way, he should move on. He's being childish. Why can't we go back to how it was?

He and Maestro rehearse for the final, but mostly Jacob eats quickly and leaves and seems to sleep a lot. I stay out of his way, all the while wishing he'd look in my direction.

The night before the final he plays with his food at dinner, cutting the pasta with his fork. He chops it into smaller and smaller pieces and eats nothing. Beside his dinner plate his phone buzzes. It's a text from his mum asking if he's won the competition yet. A second text comes in. I can't help but glance at it and see Harper's name. He texts straight back but this time puts the phone in his pocket. His elbows on the table, I glimpse the new words he's written on the cast.

If I become the person they want me to be
Will you let them free?
If I do all the things expected of me
Let them be free

Jacob's third place is controversial, given there are better singers in the contest, technically speaking. It's seen as a popularity win – and his actions to 'save' me from my onstage faux pas also earned him points, even if they weren't the kind of points on the score sheet.

When I hug Jacob to say congratulations, he's stiff and I bang my forehead on his cheek. He excuses himself and goes back into hibernation in his hotel room. No doubt he's converted it into a replica of his pigsty studio. And he's surely spending hours talking to Harper on the phone.

A wedge of melancholy slides itself into my heart.

Later, when we're packing suitcases, Maestro asks if something's happened between us.

'Nothing. He's a bit blue.' I slip my dirty socks into a bag and take a sip of juice. 'I suppose it's Purple Daze.' My words are muffled as I talk into the glass.

Maestro stops rolling his bright silk ties. My cheeks flame and I keep my head down. I can hear his breath passing in and out of his nose. 'He is *not* to be a distraction, or he'll have to go. He may be a remarkably talented young man, and he may have the X-factor, and the music world would lose something precious if he didn't continue, but your singing, your goals, are more important to me.'

When he moves away to pack his suit into its carrier, I study him. He's taut; a clockwork form of him, his face stern with concentration. Where did the softer version of my dad go, the one who sympathised and supported? The one who made up the secret sign for *I love you* so we could convey it to each other when we couldn't say the words out loud – mainly at auditions. Nowadays, I can't imagine Maestro sticking his finger in his ear while pressing his nose like it's a button. I know how Luke Skywalker felt when he learnt his father went over to the dark side.

There's no time to celebrate before we fly to England for Jacob's audition. Maestro sits between us on the plane, for which I'm grateful. The one time my gaze glances off Jacob's, we're in the customs line and I'm mumbling the words of a Spanish aria to myself.

'It's what I do in queues,' I explain. 'Helps me remember different languages.' But he's texting and not listening.

Getting too close to Jacob feels like I'm opening myself up to a world of misery. He's too unpredictable. Moody.

In the new hotel at Hyde Park, I steel myself at the prospect of spending hours alone in this room while Maestro and Jacob practise. I've feigned a cough to dodge rehearsals. Once we're home it'll be easier to avoid Jacob. The question is, how do I avoid Maestro? If Jacob passes his audition, he'll move to London. Life will go back to how it was before. Just me and Maestro.

The sensation of being trapped in my own body returns. Ants crawl under my skin.

After a sleepless first night in London, I eat room-service breakfast alone. The sun cracks open the skyline and with the early wave of drizzly light, I come to a decision: when we get back to Sydney I'll tell Maestro I don't want to perform anymore. I can't go through that again. I want to be a songwriter. Just as Jacob is moving forward and not letting his guilt and grief hold him back, so must I.

Someone knocks on my hotel room door. It's probably Maestro, come to talk me into practising. When I complained of sickness last night he completed a thorough check of my temperature and glands, and declared me healthy. Perhaps I should tell him about my decision now.

My pulse shifts up a gear.

I suspect he'll refuse to let me give up, like he did in Berlin. But maybe if we have this out, he'll let me continue song-writing too. He'll see how important it is to me.

Except when I answer the knock, it's not Maestro.

♫

Jacob bounces on his toes, hands dangling at his sides as if he's baffled about where to put them. 'Can I come in?' he asks. He smells freshly showered, or else he's growing lime trees in his room.

I pull the door closer, ensuring I'm sandwiched between it and the frame. 'I don't think that's a good idea.'

His face pleats with dejection. I almost want to snatch back my words. He bites his bottom lip. 'I've been a dick. I want to explain.'

The steel inside me melts like snow in the sun. After a moment, I step aside to let him in.

And then remember I'm wearing flannel pyjamas patterned with musical notes.

He traipses into the room, says, 'It's complicated.'

I shut the door. 'It was a kiss. It's not complicated.' The words are hot coals on my tongue; I need to spit them out.

'I get the message. It's fine. I don't see why we can't *move on.*'

Jacob takes two steps toward me and his hand suddenly warms my cheek. His mouth meets mine. My fingers splay stiff at my sides. His tongue slips between my lips and his palms slide to my hips to tug me against him. My fingers go limp. My bones soften and knit together. Only to steady myself, I hold onto him. The muscles on his back tense under my touch. His chest expands against mine. He runs his fingertips down the side of my jaw and across my collarbone. Every thought gets severed from my mind. Feelings loosen themselves from where I'd pinned them down. My body sings an aria and a movie score plays just for me: 'Love Me Like You Do'.

Warm fingers thread under my pyjama top and my body careens. Wait.

Stop. Too fast.

When I pull myself away from him it's like yanking open that damned suctioned studio door. I lurch toward the bank of windows, my palms flat on the cool glass. The view of Hyde Park blurs behind gullies of rain that tendril down the window panes. I can feel the downpour spluttering against my palms on the other side of the glass.

'Sorry, Astrid. I didn't mean to do that.' Behind me, Jacob's breaths come in puffs. 'I meant to explain – *then* kiss you.' I hear the smile linked in with the last few words.

Swallowing hard, I cross my arms, turn around.

He half-smiles. 'I was in love with someone and it didn't work out. Guess it still hurts like f– hell.'

'When?' I shuffle backwards and knock into the window.

'Nine months ago. Ten. That's a good sign – I'm not counting the days anymore.'

I want to seize his grin and fling it out the window to the road below where it'll be run over by every passing car.

Instead I tell myself to breathe. 'Harper? She broke your heart?'

'She broke more than my heart. I think she broke *me*.'

'She doesn't sound very nice.'

'It's not that. She wasn't a bitch or anything. She didn't love me back – enough. And I was a dick. It's how I got this.' He points to the scar on his calf. 'I kinda lost it, got drunk, then took off on a Harley and didn't care if I died on it.'

I picture my five-year-old self pedalling my bike with its wobbling training wheels, hoping to go fast enough that I'd have an accident and join Mum and Savannah in heaven.

'I thought I was getting over her. And I am.' Jacob takes a step nearer. I push myself against the window. 'It doesn't hurt as much to think about her. But when you kissed me, it felt –' He crosses his arms, then scuffs his foot against the bed. '– like I might lose her all over again. It confirmed she's gone and I'm moving on, and it was like losing one more person in my life – you know, after the band.'

Jacob peers at me from under long eyelashes. 'But this is the good bit.' His worried expression morphs into a grin. 'It's taken me a while to sort through this stuff, but when I understood why I reacted that way, after you kissed me, I knew I was ready to let Harper go. Because I couldn't stop thinking about *you*. I feel – good – when I'm around you. And that's not something I've felt a lot of lately.'

The room seems to expand like an inflatable toy being blown up. I half cringe, anticipating the disappointing pop.

'You helped me shut the door on that part of my life and open a new one. Sorry if you got a bit – messed around – in the process.'

'You're over her?' The words, tinged with hope, tumble out of my mouth.

He studies the pattern on the beige carpet. 'That sounds too – final.'

Pop.

I'm not looking for love, so I can't explain why I'm disappointed. In fact, I spend my life pushing everyone away to remove any risk of losing them. I've whittled my life down to one person: Maestro. But now he's going loopy or he's fighting demons or something, and I'm so, so alone. And a little afraid. And here's Jacob: I want him like Cinderella wanted her prince, but I can't gamble on the fact he might want me back in the same way and if he does, he might not stay. He might move to London. As Kara moved to Singapore.

Jacob licks his lips, stares out the window at the steady drizzle. The sky is dead and white and flat and feels as though it's pressing in on me. He adds, 'Let's say I'm loosening the grip Harper has on me.'

'I'm glad I could help,' I say. 'It sounds as though you're on the road to recovery.'

Jacob's grin smudges. 'I'm saying sorry, but you're still mad.'

'What happened? Between you and Harper?' I shift to brood out the window, not wanting to see his face in case it confirms what I already know.

'It's complicated. I mean – it kinda involved her whole family because it was like they adopted me. I practically lived with them. And before Harper, I was with her sister Aria. And Harper and me – we were in love but we had to keep it a secret – I messed everything up.'

'Don't ever kiss me like that again.' I can't let him finish because every word is twisting me tighter like I'm being wrung out. My breath fogs up the window.

'Ever? Was it that bad?'

Loosening the grip Harper has on me.

I draw a heart on the fogged-up glass and write J4H inside. 'You can't kiss me when you're not over your ex.'

Jacob moves in behind me. He reaches to rub out the heart. 'That's what I'm trying to tell you.' The warmth of his breath on my ear sends a tickling heat swarming through me. I can smell the toothpaste I recently tasted in his mouth. 'For the first time I believe I *am* getting over her.'

It's not enough.

'Jacob, we can only be friends. You said yourself, you're getting over Harper, but you're not entirely over her. And you might be moving to London.'

A stagnant moment passes before Jacob moves away from me. When he doesn't speak or leave I turn around. He's staring through the floor, shaky, as though something eroded away his edges.

He looks over at me. 'Friends then?' His smile is the closed-lipped one, needing his teeth to prop it up.

I reply, 'Always.'

'Bon Jovi version or Atlantic Starr?'

I swipe a cushion from the chair beside me and throw it at him. Although I paste a happy expression over my frown, it's as if I got busted apart and put back together again, except the pieces of me don't fit as well as they used to.

17

Jacob

My audition's the last one of the day at 5.45 pm, then tonight we're going to listen to Yolanda Gustav and Renee Fleming at the Royal Opera House. This morning Doc has meetings with industry dudes. He's the kind of man who has buddies – associates – in every corner of the world from the old days when he performed. He suggested I distract myself with sightseeing. He doesn't realise that Astrid is the distraction.

For once, the sun's shining in London. Astrid and I wander across Tower Bridge. She gets all poetic about how the River Thames sparkles beneath puffy clouds that chase each other across an endless sky. For me, it's the kind of day for holding hands, for eating outside, and for taking idiotic selfies in front of famous buildings. I doubt she'd hold hands though.

'I've always thought Tower Bridge was made up,' I say. 'With the blue paint and the castle turrets. It's as if it's been extracted from a fairytale.' She laughs and shoves me, teasing. Her touch creates a zing through my veins.

'You do know the Eiffel Tower is part of this world, right? The Statue of Liberty. The Leaning Tower of Pisa?'

'Reel it in, smart arse. How do we get to Covent Garden from here?'

She pulls a folded map from her back pocket, smug. She's wearing something she bought yesterday: a jean skirt and a flowery blouse that slips off one shoulder. She looks her age instead of like a teacher and I keep wanting to pull the blouse up – or more accurately, touch her bare shoulder. Kiss the skin there.

My phone rings. I check the screen. It's Harper, but I don't want to talk right now and reject the call. Astrid glances away, pretending not to have seen. She ups her pace but keeps her finger on the map as we walk. Each time she looks up she seems to be studying people, searching for something in their expressions.

'Why are you inspecting everyone we pass? Or are you trying to read their minds?'

Astrid stops abruptly. The person behind walks into her. He growls something, and she apologises then steps aside to stand next to an old red post box. Her face is crinkled with thought.

'What's going on?' I ask.

'My mum's parents live in London. Whenever I'm here, I can't help people-watching. I search for grandparent-aged people that resemble her. Stupid, because if we ever met, I'd be furious at them because they didn't support my mum.'

'It's pretty unlikely you'll be on the same street at the same time –'

'That's why I've made a decision. We're not going to Covent Garden. Well, you can. But I'm going to Camden.'

'Okay.' I stretch the vowels out. 'Why?'

Astrid stares into space, the map hanging limply from her fingers. 'When I was seven, I found this bundle of letters in Maestro's bedroom, tied together with string. They were unopened. They were from a John Miller and the address on the back was 7 Broccoli Street, Camden. I remember because we'd just been to the Camden markets after a summer break in London, and – well a street called broccoli is hard to forget. Anyway, I recently figured out John Miller must be my mum's dad but there are too many John Millers to find him online, and none listed in Camden –'

'And you want to go visit him now?'

'Yes and no. This is kind of spur of the moment. I've been angry with my grandparents for years. They thought singing wasn't a respectable profession and threw my mother out of the house. Maestro never even met them. Mum told him that they were ignorant and should never have borne a child. That's why I haven't written to them – it feels a little like I'm betraying my mum. But there's a part of me that wants to know them because except for Maestro, I have no family in the world. And I'm curious about my mum. They could tell me more about her when she was my age. Maybe they could tell me how she died. If I know her better, maybe I'll understand myself better – you know, like who I am?'

'Okay. So, let's go.'

'You'll come with me?' That smile is back.

'Of course. Impulsive is my middle name.' I gesture to the map and she searches for a street sign. As we set off, she hooks her arm with mine. It's all I can do not to bend and kiss the top of her head.

'But what if they don't want to know me? They banished my mother from her home!' She slows her pace. 'What if I get angry at them and we argue?'

'Why wouldn't they want to know you? It's not like you want anything from them. And you won't get angry. You'll just ask about your mum and stuff. Who knows when you'll next be in London.' Astrid studies my face. I nod like a bobblehead until her expression moves from uncertain to decisive and she ups the pace again.

'Here we are.' Astrid points at an underground station sign for Leicester Square. We clamour down the concrete stairs, racing each other to reach the turnstiles. Being the morning rush hour, it's packed, and we're forced to slowly weave with the crowd along a bright underground passageway toward the train platform.

'By the way, did your dad bring up your stage fright in Vienna?' I ask.

'We talked forever about what my inner voice says and how to feed myself more positive instructions, repeating *I can do this.* And other secret weapons like visualisation and a new breathing technique. He's suggested a hypnotist when we get back to Sydney. Except there's one problem with all those solutions . . .'

I put out an arm to stop some guy hitting Astrid with the huge sport bag he's flung over a shoulder. 'What problem?'

'I'm going to tell Maestro I want to stop performing and write songs instead. And this time I'm going to make sure he hears me. It's still music after all.'

'Yes! Put it there.' We bump fists, but there's no sparkle in her, only doubt.

A train zooms out of the tunnel bringing a warm gust of wind that whips my hair around. I tuck it behind my ears. The crowd propels us onto the train and my face encounters the armpit of a man in five-inch heels. Astrid and I hang onto the same central pole as the train lurches out of the station.

'Did you think about letting Dex sing your songs – recording them?' I ask.

'Did you think about singing popera instead of indie pop? Vienna was awesome, right?'

I have to fight to stop tracking her curvy lips as she talks. 'Why do you always answer my questions with a question?'

She folds her map and pockets it. 'Well, did you?'

'I dunno,' I lie. It was awesome, but I'm not sure if I'm ready to say it out loud.

'You need to sing what you were born to sing, not what others tell you is cool. You're being disappointing.'

'What the hell?'

'There's a reason why anything good has the word "classic" in front of it – classic car, classic rock, classic clothing. Anyhow, you can't choose your future based on how *cool* it is.'

'That's where you're wrong. Have you heard of the cool-career-ometer?' But Astrid has a point. Somehow the applause Purple Daze used to get never lifted me in the same way the applause in Vienna did – maybe because I was sober. Or maybe because of the grand setting and huge audience. All I know is in Vienna, I was thinking something along the lines of, *so this is what it feels like to be alive.* 'Anyway, back to recording songs with Dex?'

She studies me for a moment. 'I wouldn't want to hold back Dex.'

'What? You don't think your songs are good enough? Are you crazy?'

'They're okay. But they're for me. I'm not a songwriter yet. I have a lot of learning to do.'

'Not based on what I've heard. You're a natural.'

She snort laughs. 'You're biased. I'm not ready for the world to hear my songs.'

'You're afraid. That's what you mean.' Just like I'm afraid to leave behind the world of indie pop. 'But you are good enough and unless you take that risk and put your songs out there into the world, they don't exist. You have to be brave.'

'I guess I'll have more time now, without the singing rehearsals. And it'd be a good way to practise my songwriting. If you're sure.'

'I'm sure. We could submit something to some music labels. Get some feedback.'

She jiggles her head, not to say no but like she can't believe what she's hearing. 'I'm not sure about *that.* And I don't understand that side of the business, do you?'

'Sure. I submitted demos for Purple Daze. With Dex's voice and your songs, who wouldn't sign you?'

A shadow crosses her features. 'What if you move to London?'

'I doubt I'll even pass this audition.'

We travel in silence for a while. Compared to Harper, Astrid's not a huge talker and I kind of like that. It feels as if there's space for me. I'm not used to it. Harper could dominate a conversation. I realise also that when Astrid and I look at each other there's an honesty in each glance – it's like what I see there is what she's feeling and thinking. Harper had too many secrets, and parts of her tennis world I couldn't understand just as she didn't understand my music.

A couple of stops later the crowd thins and we find a seat. I read the graffiti on the opposite wall about fifty times; *don't die wondering,* being my favourite, and *bombing is a religion* my least. I check my phone when it vibrates; a text from Dad asking how the audition went. He's a bright guy, and can work out the time zones well enough to know my audition is later today. Clearly, he couldn't be bothered.

When we reach Camden, Astrid doesn't get up when the train stops. I grab her hand. 'Come on. You have a date with your grandparents.' But her face has paled, and fear barges all the hope out of her.

18

Astrid

Broccoli Street doesn't contain a single tree or flower or blade of grass. Maybe that's why someone's added colourful graffiti to the metal garage doors that line the blackening pavement. Occasionally, there's a shop instead of a metal door – a drycleaners, a greasy café, a pawnshop that's closed. Gloomy brown-bricked flats perch on top of every garage or shop, each with two windows, like blank humourless eyes.

I had pictured someone as dazzling as Veronika growing up in a stylish London address. But perhaps she didn't grow up here.

Jacob points to a number seven on a green door that has a mailbox in the middle, a mouth threatening to bite. I stop and inspect the building. The windows are shut. Maybe no one's home.

'Are you ready?' asks Jacob.

It's like someone's trampling in my head and I'm suddenly confused about why I'm here and what I'm going to say. They probably don't even know they have a granddaughter, given they were estranged from my mum.

'Come on. I'll be right here with you. Why wouldn't they want to know about their grandchild?'

'I'm a singer like my mum. They didn't approve of her profession.' I study the grubby streets and wonder how something like singing would be disapproved of. What profession were her parents in that singing was so bad? I had pictured them as snobs living in a big mansion and demanding my mum become a doctor.

And then the green door swings open.

An elderly man whose clothes appear too big for his scrawny frame fiddles with the lock. He takes us both in. His glare sharpens. 'You lost?' His accent sounds the opposite of the Queen's.

Words become butterflies in my headspace.

Jacob answers for me. 'We're looking for John Miller?'

'Who wants to know?'

An umbrella pops open inside my chest.

This man is my blood, yet he doesn't resemble me or Savannah. We can't take after Maestro's side of the family, because everyone says we both look like our mum.

'It's hard to explain,' answers Jacob. 'This is his grandchild – Astrid. Her mum was Veronika Miller. But we live in Australia . . .'

The man's inspection pierces me now. He begins to smile. 'Veronika's child? I haven't seen Veronika in maybe thirty years. We used to live on the street behind 'ere, back then. She went to school with my Debbie. You're the spit of Veronika.'

'So you're not John?' continues Jacob, because I still can't speak. I'm not sure why, but I'm relieved he's not John. I glance around, now knowing Mum was here, perhaps playing on this square of pavement that I'm standing on. I squint at the windows again and imagine her singing and passers-by listening to her voice. Nothing about her childhood was glamorous.

'John and Esmeralda moved not six months ago. To Cambridge. John's brother died and left 'im some money. I'm Tom.' He offers his hand.

Air that I hadn't known I was holding in rushes out of my mouth. And he's reminded me that my grandma's name is Esmeralda – very exotic. I shake his hand.

'I have an address for them. We forwarded their mail. I can't believe 'ow much you resemble Veronika.' All his previous wariness has been replaced by nostalgia. 'I was just off to get some milk, so I can't invite you in for tea, but I'll get tha' address.'

When he goes back inside Jacob gives me a thumbs-up. I can't decide if I'm happy with the lead or not. Being here, where Mum grew up, is confronting enough.

Jacob pulls out his phone, jabs at the screen with his finger. 'Shit. It's nearly two hours by train to get to Cambridge because there's a bus replacing part of the route – repair work. And that's if we make smooth connections.'

'Your audition,' I say.

'It's not till five-forty-five. We can still make it.'

'But what if we can't get a train back when we need to, or there are delays? Or the bus is full? Why don't we go tomorrow?'

'We fly home tomorrow.'

'Not till the evening. Or I could write to them.'

'You're stalling. You'll just change your mind. Your dad had us up at frigging early-o-clock. It's only like nine-thirty now. We've come this far. Let's just do this.'

Neither of us have noticed Tom standing in the doorway again. He holds out a ripped triangle of newspaper, the address written in thick black pen. Jacob pockets it with a thanks.

'You can drive in just over an hour. There's a car hire garage five minutes that way.' Tom points south along Broccoli Street.

Jacob glances at me. 'Then we'd definitely have time.'

I scuff at the pavement.

'You must visit 'em,' says Tom. 'It'd make 'em so happy. After Veronika left, their life became very empty.'

'I was told they threw her out.' My voice sounds weak and rumpled.

'You were? I didn't know them that well, but I knew 'em well enough to know they would never do that. They were very proud of 'er.'

'So maybe there's more to the story,' says Jacob. 'Let's go find out the truth.'

♫

Green fields roll past as we speed up the M11 toward Cambridge. If my grandparents didn't throw Mum out, why were they estranged? Why didn't Mum open their letters? Why have I never met them?

We hired an automatic car so Jacob could drive with his cast; I'm too tense to drive. He's put the radio onto a classical station, probably for me. It's only 10.30 am, so we have plenty of time.

'Do you want to talk, or do you want to think?' asks Jacob.

'I don't know. A bit of both?'

Jacob remains silent for a few seconds, then glances sideways at me. 'I've been wondering. I hope it's okay to ask. But how did your sister die?'

'Meningitis.'

'That's rough. I mean. Wow. So it's unlikely that's how your mum died. Funny how the articles on Google say she withdrew from public life, rather than saying how she died.'

'You googled my mum?'

He shrugs. 'I was bored.'

'I asked Maestro about that once. He said he announced her death as a withdrawal from public life because he wanted to spare Savannah the media attention. Back then, the press dogged him and Mum a fair bit.'

'Odd her death didn't get leaked to the press, but I guess it happens.'

The longer the journey takes, the more this feels like an audition – to be a granddaughter. My blood buzzes in my veins. My skin turns clammy. Like a vine, a thorny fear grows from the pit of my stomach and up around my neck.

'No. Stop. I can't do it.' The words clatter out of my mouth.

'It's okay. I'll be with you.'

'I'll write to them when I get home'.

'You're just scared of being rejected.'

But this is worse than stage fright. I clamp my hands to the dashboard. 'No. Please stop. Please turn around. I've changed my mind. They don't even know I exist. They don't approve of singing as a profession. They threw Mum out. I'm being disloyal to my mum. They're not nice people. And what if they don't know their daughter's dead? Maestro will be furious. And your audition.' Words catapult over and through each other as they fall out of my mouth and I'm suddenly sobbing.

The car swerves, skids as Jacob tries to take an off-ramp too late. His arms straighten on the wheel. He pumps the breaks. The hand with the cast slips off the wheel and we swerve again. We're going to collide with a huge service station sign. The tyres screech. The car slides askew. I slam my own feet on where the brake pedal would be, were I driving.

There's the squeal of breaks behind us. I whip around. A truck is bearing down on us.

'Shit,' yells Jacob.

The smell of burning rubber clogs the air. My head whips back and forward when the truck hits the corner of our car on the driver's side. We spin sideways and slide toward the sign.

19

Jacob

I brace myself on the steering wheel for the impact. My broken hand twinges. The truck hits the back of the car on the driver's side so the car skews. I pump the breaks but we're sliding sideways and breaks can't stop us. We're going to hit the sign. No avoiding it. My stomach somersaults. I think about the boys in the van, and wonder if it felt like this for them too. Suddenly, I'm grabbing at ways to get out of here, sure I'm not ready to die. Sure I must protect Astrid.

Panic is like a fishhook being pulled through me, snagging on every organ in its path.

The noise of the collision is as loud as a gunshot only it's a bigger, dead-sounding thud, then a crunch of metal. And the clap of the side of my head hitting the driver's door window is dull and hard. Pain spikes through my skull as the window becomes a spiderweb of cracks.

Skittles's face. Mad Dog. JW. Callum. Emery. They line up.

I don't want to swap places with them anymore. I want to live. I want to sing. I want my voice to affect people like it did in Vienna. The thoughts come so fast they knock each other over. I want to surf the ocean just as the light of a new morning peels back the night. I want Astrid. When she smiles at me it feels like I'm tripping over and falling into her eyes. I want that every day. Before I look over at her, I glimpse a blurry image of the truck narrowly missing the railings ahead.

Astrid's watching the truck too. The urge to hold her – but my limbs are too spongy to move. I want to tell her something – that she's important to me. That I want to be a better version of myself when I'm around her. But my brain won't link to my mouth. My heart pounds at my ribs and I think I hear Astrid's heart thudding too, and maybe she can hear mine so our hearts are like drums sending signals to each other.

The air smells snappy: metallic and smoky. It layers my throat. Something warm and wet trickles onto my cheek and I push my hand against the throbbing where I hit my head, pull away a palm covered in blood.

'Are you okay?' Astrid's mouth seems wide, like she's shouting, but I can barely hear her. Her face twists and she's screaming. Is there another truck? Another collision coming? Are we going to die?

♫

Hushed words. Whispering footsteps. The smell of bleach and carpet cleaner and half-dead flowers combine in my nostrils. My mind scrambles for a solid memory, but it can't get any traction, like shoes on ice.

A hotel room. No, a hospital.

The ghosts of Purple Daze rush at me. My eyes zip open. But there's no Mad Dog or Emery in the room. It's not even Astrid staring down at me. It's Harper.

My quick intake of air hurts my skull.

'Jacob. You're awake. How do you feel?' She places her hand on my forehead. It's cool, but callused as usual, thanks to hours of tennis practise.

I split my dry lips to speak, but my tongue sticks to the roof of my mouth.

'Are you in pain? Nod once for yes.'

I grin. 'Dumbass.'

Harper leans closer, her long hair tickling the inside of my arm. 'You're back with us then. As witty and entertaining as always. And your vocab has improved.'

But her hair isn't auburn.

'Where are we?' I ask.

'London, dummy. Maybe you *do* have brain damage.'

And maybe I do. Because I can't stay awake. And I dream of Astrid.

♫

I'm aware of conversations happening around me, the smell of instant coffee, beeping machines, nurses lifting my arm, but I can't pull myself out of sleep for long. They must've sedated me. Or maybe I don't want to wake up – because *where's Astrid?* I remember the car crash. She was fine. But did we get hit by another vehicle? All I know is I want to be with her. She has to be okay. The thought of her being gone makes it feel like the ceiling just dropped on me. Maybe I love her.

Later, I hear Doc Bell's voice. I fight to wake up.

'Thank God,' Doc says in a low, dawdling kind of way. The room's dark. I can't even make out his shape. But then I grasp that my eyelids are as heavy as bags of sand and are actually closed. He sniffs twice. 'I nearly had another empty bed in my house.'

Nearly. Astrid's alive.

The doc suppresses a sob. I hear him slump into a squeaky chair next to me. He mumbles something I don't hear the start of: '– would serve me right for trying to separate you.'

♫

The next morning I sit next to Astrid's hospital bed, holding her hand while we wait to be discharged. It feels like we've been here for days, but it's only been overnight. I touch the three bumpy stitches on my head. I have a concussion and Astrid has severe whiplash, and mild concussion. Before I'd passed out in the car, Astrid had been screaming because my face and hand were covered in blood, not because another vehicle was about to hit us.

Astrid's face shifts to grave. 'You missed your audition. Maestro says my first words when I woke were, "Did Jacob miss his audition?"'

I'm not upset about the audition even though I wanted to move to London. Things have changed; Astrid doesn't live in London. 'That's not important. It's Lilliputian, as Callum would say.' I'm surprised to find that a random band memory doesn't have me sinking into a gloomy mood.

Her face creases even more. 'I'm so sorry. It was all my fault.'

'No, it wasn't. I probably shouldn't have been driving with a cast.'

'But I made you panic. You were only trying to get us off the motorway because I lost it.'

I squeeze her hand. 'Let's hear you sing wearing a neck collar.' I flick the soft collar, then let my fingers trace down her arm.

Her chest rises in two short beats.

She covers her face with splayed fingers. 'How is it possible that music and magical ballgowns and opera houses and the Tower of London can exist right next to car accidents and dying during childbirth? Sometimes the world scares me.'

I peel her hand away from her face, kiss her fingertips, certain that I want to be with her. But her expression changes to stony.

She pulls away, nibbling on a cuticle. 'I met Harper,' she says, flat.

'Oh.' My gaze fumbles in hers.

'Maestro introduced us. You were asleep. She's very pretty. And confident.'

I crack my neck. 'I guess.'

'She must love you – to fly out from America.'

'That's not true. I mean – not like that. And she wasn't in America. She was only across the channel in France for a tennis thing. She planned to surprise me by dropping in overnight. It's the kind of thing she can do. Money isn't an issue. And she had a gap in her schedule.'

'But still.'

'But still nothing. We met when we were five. We'll always be friends because her family are basically my adopted family. Besides, she's in love with someone else.' I lean forward and kiss Astrid on the nose. She pulls away, lays her arm over her face.

Sunshine leaks through the edges of the blinds. Shafts of light sever each other.

My words collide in my mouth. I dig through them, for the right ones. 'When I woke in the hospital and Harper was there, I straightaway thought, *Where's Astrid?*'

'Because you didn't know what happened to me.' She speaks into the crook of her arm.

'It was more than that.'

She lifts her arm. 'You're only not together because she loves someone else.'

We survey each other, ready for combat. I open my mouth to retaliate, but this is the last place – and moment – I want to argue.

And what if she's right?

'Nothing can happen between us, Jacob. You're not over her, and . . . and –' Tears pool in her closed eyelids.

'And what?' I ask, frustrated.

'I nearly died yesterday. So did you. Death is around every corner. I won't survive losing anyone else that I love. I won't.'

Her expression challenges me to contradict her, but I can't. Death does seem to stalk us. But she dropped the L-bomb. Is that what she feels for me?

'If you were granted one wish from the Genie of the Lamp,' I say, unwilling to give up yet, 'what would it be?'

She turns her face away.

When it's clear she's not going to answer, I say, 'Mine would be this: when you kissed me in Vienna, I wish I'd kissed you back.'

♫

After the hospital discharges us, Astrid and Maestro return to the hotel to pack for our flights this evening. I have lunch with Harper – how can I not when she came all this way? In a pub in Leicester Square, she asks for a reenactment of the whole accident and I oblige.

'If there's anything between you and Astrid, I hope my coming here hasn't caused a problem.' She picks out the tomatoes from her steak salad. She's hated raw tomatoes since I dared her into a cherry tomato-eating contest maybe ten years ago. It ended in her vomiting. 'I can reassure her I'm nothing to worry about. I'll tell her you're basically my adopted brother –'

Our eyes touch, then ping away to view the street out the window.

She adds, 'Have you spoken to your parents?'

'Astrid's dad phoned them last night. He gave them all the update they needed in between court cases.'

'Should you be flying with a concussion?'

'Probably not. We'd have to stay another week or more to be sure the symptoms won't worsen on the flight, and Doc can't do that. It'll be fine. I have strong pain pills. Astrid's concussion is really mild. It's whiplash that's bothering her.'

'I called Aria. She was on a flight from New York to Rome. By the time she landed we knew you were fine. She has a performance tonight. Principal second violin. She sends hugs.'

As Harper talks, her million-dollar smile doesn't set my body alight, and when she loops a twist of chestnut hair and sucks on the end, it doesn't send me into a tailspin as it used to. I don't even mind her calling me her brother. But when she massages her neck, I stop myself from reaching out to do it for her. Old habits die hard. She tells me stories about the circuit but I drift into a daydream about being in my studio, working on songs with Dex and Astrid. I'd rather be there with them, than here with Harper. Perhaps I *am* over her.

But if Harper leant over to kiss me, would I turn away?

I focus on my shepherd's pie.

'So I have news,' says Harper, interrupting my thoughts. 'I'm buying a house in Florida. I spend half my life there anyway, and the long flights back to Sydney are exhausting.'

I drop my fork, my appetite gone. If I'm so over Harper why do I feel like she just dropped a bomb on me?

'I'll probably only come back once a year for Christmas and the Australian Open from now on.'

I gulp down my beer in one go. A part of me wants to cry. Astrid's right – we have to keep it friends only, because I'm pretty likely to hurt her. Break her. Ruin everything. Like I always do.

20

Astrid

'I nearly died without knowing what happened to my own mum. You *have* to tell me.' I curl my hands into fists and pace the length of the grand piano and back again. Maestro removes his suit jacket and continues to build the fire in the grate of the music room. Mum's portrait watches us. She preferred the cold weather and loved a fire; the sound and smell would transport her to chalets in the Alps. Very different, I guess, from Broccoli Street. Now Maestro makes fires when he's particularly missing her, or upset about something. He must be really upset if he's lighting fires in September. My resolve to get the truth from him weakens, but not enough to let him off the hook.

I wait for an answer, but he continues to build his pyramid of logs. 'Maestro.' The word comes out between clenched teeth. 'Ever since Mum's note, you're snappy and distant. It's as if something's bothering you and it's eating away at you. I don't know who you are anymore.'

'I said when you're eighteen and I meant it.' He positions another log in place. 'Now stop behaving like a spoilt child.'

The unfairness of those last two words unlocks something

inside me. I slap an open palm onto the piano. 'It's insane. It's a matter of months. I have a right to know.'

'We discussed this a fortnight ago when you found your mother's note. And right now, you need to focus on your recovery and your singing.' He stands and wipes his hands on the cloth he was kneeling on. 'And you're recently out of hospital. You've been through an enormous ordeal. That's *enough* to deal with.'

I rest my chin on my sternum as if locking the anger inside before I say something I'll regret. 'Why would Tom have said that Mum left home, that she wasn't thrown out? And if they were estranged, why did John keep writing to her?' After Maestro had demanded I explain why we were driving to Cambridge, I confessed about finding the unopened letters, and the visit to Broccoli Street.

'For the last time, I don't know.' He opens the French doors and a cool breeze enters the room. 'I've never met your grandparents. Maybe Tom didn't know the whole story. Why would your mum tell me that if it wasn't true?'

'Do her parents even know she's dead? Is that why her father kept sending letters?'

'I said *enough*,' shouts Maestro. His face turns red. 'It was your mother's choice not to open them. Now I have a lot to do, and we're going around in circles.'

I storm past the piano, knocking over a music stand.

'Where are you going, Astrid? We need to test your range.'

'My voice is fine.' I give a few impatient trills to prove

it. I'd decided to start the 'tell me about Mum' conversation first, but maybe I should've begun with the fight about wanting to write songs rather than sing. But now's not the right time. Now I need to lash out, to vent. 'You're crazy.' I grab the cloak hanging on the hat stand and twirl it around myself. 'For example, what's with the cape? Who are you? Elvis Presley? The Phantom of the frigging Opera? Pava-fricking-rotti?'

I'm amazed at myself. I've never spoken to Maestro like this.

'That Jacob is a bad influence.' Maestro sits down heavily at the piano stool and bangs out a scale. 'C Major. I want to check your range. Whiplash can affect it if the laryngeal nerves were especially strained.'

A gust of wind makes the fire waver and crackle. It seems to cross the room and blast through me. It snatches away my breath. The cloak slides to the ground. 'Why didn't you tell me that was possible?' The words wobble from my tongue.

Maestro blinks over his shoulder as I pull my expression back from freaked out. But I'm too late. His own Maestro mask slips and in the twist of his lips and the flicker of alarm across his face, I catch a glimpse of the softer dad from my past. He closes in on me and draws me against him. 'Because I didn't want to worry you.' His voice is warm, comforting.

It's good to be held together. Maybe he is my cloak. And he has no-one to hold *him* together.

'Now come, Buttercup.' He leads me to the piano.

When he begins the scale, I'm shocked at the possibility the accident has affected my voice. Instead of singing I chomp the air in my mouth.

Maestro stops, places his hands on his knees. 'See. I shouldn't have told you and you'd have sung the scales without worrying. Can you let me be the parent?'

Shaking, I pour myself a pineapple juice, sip it. Then we complete some breathing and warm-up exercises before I accompany him on a scale. It feels good. We climb up the octaves until I reach my head voice. I keep going.

My voice falters. It fractures and cuts out. It's as broken as a split flute.

One of my hands swoops to cup my neck. So there *is* an inverse law of the universe: once you decide you *don't* want to die, then that's exactly what happens. Once you decide you *don't* want to sing, then that's exactly what happens.

I was meant to die on that road to Cambridge.

And now my soprano voice has been taken from me.

Maestro stops playing the scale and appears to shrink into a hunched old man. He inspects his patent leather shoes on the pedals of the piano for a long time, as if he's forgotten I'm here.

I whirl away from him toward the fire. Above it, Mum stares down at me and I want to climb inside the portrait for a hug. 'I can't believe it.'

Maestro's suddenly there; he rotates me to him. 'Don't panic. The laryngoscopy revealed no damage. It's likely to be a weakness in the laryngeal nerves. It's not permanent.'

What if he's keeping the truth from me – like with Mum's death? A silent sob crowds my throat. I pull away and pace around the piano. 'How long will it take to heal?'

'With so little data, it's difficult to say. Maybe a couple months.'

'Months?' I should be happy. This is my excuse not to sing in public anymore, but suddenly, now that the choice has been taken away from me, I'm not so sure. I recall the years of voice training, how I never did quite hit a perfect E6, how hard I've worked for the San Francisco performance next month.

'You're alive. And it's not permanent. It could be worse.'

I step out onto the balcony. Behind me, Maestro keeps talking. Firm. Certain. Overly loud. 'We'll make an appointment with a laryngologist. We'll work out a voice-treatment plan. All signs are your voice will be fine. I promise you, I will find a way.' When I glance at him uncertain, he adds, 'This is not the end of our goals.' Then he slumps into the armchair as though he's spent every ounce of energy and can no longer stand.

I turn away from the desperation pouring out of him, from the alarm that's making his complexion grey. He *needs* me to become a soprano. How could I think of taking that from him? And now the choice has been stolen.

Mum and Savannah died and with them, their singing gift. Yet I was going to throw away my gift. I deserve to endure my punishment for the rest of my life.

My fingers touch my neck, my mouth twisting. I whirl back to Maestro. 'Will I ever reach those notes again?'

He inches his gaze toward mine. I can see he's holding himself together by how tense his jaw is. 'We will *never* give up on your dream.'

And now that my dream might be gone, I realise how much I stand to lose.

♫

After the blinding glare of the sunshine outside, the studio is pitch-dark. The blackout curtains are still drawn. We landed from England earlier this morning. Perhaps Jacob's up at the house sleeping off his jetlag. About to leave, I pause to wonder why Kendrick Lamar's ELEMENT is blaring from the huge speakers. The explicit version. I walk further into the studio, giving my vision longer to adjust. I identify the smell of old bananas. Then I spot Jacob lying on the floor in front of the Lego sofa. At the foot of the sofa are two banana peels and four empty bottles: three beers and a vodka. A pair of sopping wet boardies lie discarded next to him. He said he was going for a surf when he got home.

I collect the bottles, letting them clink loudly. Jacob jerks, working to focus on me. He's not wearing a shirt, only jeans.

'Astrid! You gave me a friggin' heart attack.' He pushes up onto his side. His abs ripple and their v-shape disappears into his jeans. A sharp tingle dives from my belly to the top of my legs.

'I could say the same thing.' I chuck the bottles in the bin while he struggles to perch on the sofa, drops his face into his good hand. He rubs at the stubble that's grown since London, making him seem older. 'Drink?' He pushes to his feet, but rocks there for a moment before stumbling toward the fridge.

'You're wasted,' I say. 'And it's not even lunch time.'

'But in what time zone? That's the question.' Jacob twists off the top of an orange juice, slugs it back in long gulps.

'Are you okay?' I probe. 'Has something happened?'

'Why would you care after giving me the cold shoulder the whole flight home?'

I suppose I deserve that. I pull my cardigan around myself and glance at the TV that's always on. Today it's paused on a newsreader mid-sentence, his mouth frozen around a word and the news ticker stuck on, *Shopkeeper feeds thief in supreme act of forgiveness.*

Jacob finishes the juice and tosses the carton aside, then reaches into the fridge for a beer. 'Just when I thought I had it all figured out. I could've died. Again. My parents wouldn't give a shit. Death keeps trying to take me, but they don't care. I placed at Vienna, but why should they be here to celebrate with me? They'll never change.'

He releases the words like they're arrows; they puncture me one by one and I'm suddenly sure I'm way out of my depth with someone as complicated as Jacob Skalicky.

'Of course they care,' I say.

'Death failed again.'

I lose hold of the words I was going to chastise him with, and soften my tone. 'I get it, Jacob. It was awful. But we survived. And getting wasted isn't going to help.'

'You sound like Harper. Did I tell you she's moving to Florida?'

At the mention of her name my organs clench. Is this why he's drunk? He can't cope after seeing her again. Anger pulses through me in a series of shocks. 'Listen to me. When you're drunk you make bad choices. The Harley accident, for instance. Surfing with a broken hand in that storm.'

Jacob ignores me and hollers along with Kendrick Lamar. He starts dancing, his beer spilling. He grabs me, pulling me against him, revolves his hips against mine. His face is inches away, his breath hot on my retreating cheek. He stinks of beer.

I shove at him. 'Stop it, Jacob.' He throws his hands in the air, drains the beer. I snatch the bottle away. 'Why are you doing this, when you have everything going for you?' He plunges into the Lego sofa, slipping sideways. I kneel in front of him. 'You're alive. *You* have a second chance.'

Jacob jams shut his eyes. 'Guess how I get through each day? I count the minutes. Then the hours. That adds up to another day. Rinse. Repeat. Beer helps numb things.'

'You have to focus on the good things. Remember Vienna? How your voice had people crying and cheering? Your voice. It's your reason for being on this earth.'

Jacob doesn't move or speak and I wonder if he's gone to sleep. Gritting my teeth, I spin onto my butt and lean against the sofa. On the table his phone buzzes with a message.

Harper: *Landed safe. Miss you.*

Harper is typing . . .

Harper is crushing my heart in her fist.

'Sorry.' Jacob's voice creaks. 'For acting like a jerk.'

I get up to lower the volume of the music, then flick on a lamp and fill a glass with water. 'Sit up and drink this.' Jacob drags himself upright. 'You didn't die. You have another chance. And you should be grabbing it. Shall I tell you why?'

Jacob burps. 'I'm sure you're going to.'

I refrain from shoving him, only because he's holding a glass. 'I kept thinking I didn't want to sing anymore. I was going to tell my dad, remember?'

'Yep.' Jacob rolls onto his side, hugging the empty glass. 'Is this part one of the opus?'

'You're such a jerk when you drink.' My irritation keeps me upright; it steels me enough that I can add, 'The whiplash has affected my upper range –'

The words pour out of me like water onto fire; my anger sizzles away, leaving me limp. I slump to the floor.

Jacob moves close, throws an arm around me. 'Jeez, Astrid. I'm such a dick.'

I don't have the energy to push him away. 'Now I don't have that choice, I'd give anything for a second chance. And here's you. You survived the Harley, you weren't travelling in the van you were meant to, and even the car accident. You still have a choice. Don't throw it away.'

'I can't – I don't understand.'

'Maestro says the muscles in my larynx got strained or stretched and now they're weak.' And then I can't talk anymore for crying. I let my head rest on him.

Jacob rubs my back and holds me. 'But you sound normal when you talk.' His words are no longer soggy with booze.

After a while I manage to say, 'If I wasn't a singer, it wouldn't matter. It's not a severe injury.' I swipe at my wet cheeks with my wrists. 'And I can sing. But I've lost my head voice. I might never follow in Mum's footsteps. I feel as if I'm betraying her because even though I planned to talk to Maestro about not singing, I think I knew he'd never let me stop. It's as though I needed to push back at him so he took my songwriting seriously. So I could do both.' My mouth twists and fresh tears arrive. Jacob pulls me to him again. His fingers trace through my hair and I relax into him.

'You've lived out your mum's dream for most of your life – maybe this is a sign –'

'*No*. This has shown me I'm not ready to give up on it. To emulate her is *my* dream. I wasn't sure before. Lately, Maestro's made me feel like it was more his dream than mine. But I think I was scared, with the stage fright. I was feeling trapped. And my dad. What if this means he loses his fight? When he suffered from depression, it was as if we lived in a black and white silent movie. He needs this goal. I might lose him again. He's already acting weird. Everything's so messed up. But do you hear me? About second chances.'

The sound of the studio door opening interrupts his answer. We blink at the bright sunlight that floods in.

'What the hell is going on?'

I jerk away from Jacob and jump to my feet. 'What are you doing here?'

Maestro stalks toward us. 'You drove away upset.' He inspects me, his jaw gripped so that his lips are a thin line. He glares at Jacob, who hasn't moved from the floor and is currently reading his cast. Maestro examines the studio. 'You've been drinking.'

'Jacob's having a bad day. It's been – tough for him. The car accident. He could've died and hoped his parents would be here. It's dredged up a lot of stuff about the band too.'

Maestro's finger wags at Jacob who remains slumped on the floor against the Lego sofa. 'Bad day or not, you don't get drunk with my daughter. And you sure as hell don't touch her.'

Jacob hauls himself to his feet. 'All right, Doc. Hold it right there. I didn't ask her to come here and she was upset –'

'I thought I told you the drinking needed to stop.'

'You told me not to come to your house if I'd had a drink. This is my home. Not my fault you guys gate-crashed my party.'

Maestro inspects me, then the room again. He gestures at the floor, littered with dirty plates, glasses, bottles, instruments, record covers, broken CD cases, sheet music. It's worse than I've ever seen it. 'This is no home,' he says. 'What do your parents say about this?'

'Hah. They don't care if I live in a tree so long as I keep out of their hair.'

Maestro's rigid stance softens; even under his cloak I can see his shoulders fall. As he studies Jacob, his anger slips away a little. He's going to want to help Jacob. He's never been able to resist fixing people's problems. When Kara ran away from home and hid in my room after her parents explained they planned to emigrate to Singapore, Maestro called her parents and let her stay the weekend and told her stories of Asia – places and people, traditions and history. She went home a little bit thrilled about the adventures she was about to have. For a while after she left Australia, she sent him photos: Tiger Sky Tower, the Sentosa Luge, her first experience of Buddhism, a bowl of chilli crab –

Jacob careers toward his desk, slaps shut the laptop like he's suddenly remembered he left something private open. I get a glimpse of a website listing death certificates. He stumbles to the sink and slugs another glass of water then throws the glass at the wall. I startle when it shatters, hand flying over my mouth. I expect to see rage biting at his features, but instead his face blots with sadness. He slumps against the wall and slips down so he's sitting on the floor among the broken glass.

'Could've died on that motorway,' he mumbles, 'but my parents weren't even here when I got home. At least they left a note. Being in court was more important.'

I move to go to him, but Maestro holds up a hand. He considers me, the room, then Jacob.

'I can't get involved where your parents are concerned, Jacob, but I can be someone you turn to if you need to. And I can be the one to tell you that *you*, and only you, can get yourself out of this quagmire you're stuck in. Drinking will have you sinking further. Feeling sorry for yourself will keep you down. The only way out is to make plans and to have goals. Get into the Con and you can leave home. Bargain with your parents to make getting your own place a part of the deal, but *you* have to get into the Con.'

Jacob thrusts his head back against the wall. Fingertips rush over his stubble.

'You have nothing to occupy you. That's half the problem. Do you have a job?' Maestro's concern for Jacob glows in his every feature. He's in full 'fixer' mode.

Jacob scowls. 'I was in a band. That was my job.' He throws his words at Maestro like they're knives. 'I've been kinda getting over five deaths, if that's okay with you.'

Maestro swallows and scrutinises the ceiling. When he regards Jacob again, he stands taller. 'Do you want this, Jacob?'

'Want what?'

'A life in the world of music. For me to coach you. To work at the career you've begun. Because you could become huge, son. *If* you want it.'

Jacob considers me, expression loaded with mayhem. 'I guess,' he says. He traces a finger down the scar on his calf.

'Seeing as I'm not dead. Yet. A second chance. Or third. Fourth.'

'Okay. We need some new rules though.' Maestro strides over to the music system and switches off the rap music. 'First. We're going to hold our lessons here, you and me, but it has to be tidy and clean or the lesson is cancelled. Second. No more drinking at all. Show me you have self-discipline. *Prove* you want this. This is your job. Turn up for it every day, ready to work. Third. Astrid is off limits. If I ever see what I saw when I came in here, our contract is terminated.'

'No way.' Jacob's straight arm strikes the wall beside him. 'Astrid's old enough to decide for herself. What's whether we get together got to do with anything?'

I blush. Maestro's never mentioned boyfriends, and now he's banning them? I fall back onto the arm of the sofa, shocked Jacob objects to that rule over the no-drinking rule, or having to tidy up.

'Because she doesn't need you as a distraction from her career.'

'What career?' I say, louder than I mean to. But Maestro ignores me.

'Already you've got her writing chart music,' he growls. 'And she argues with me – just like you do.' Maestro turns to me now. 'Astrid. You can go home now.' He deposits his glare on me, waits for me to move. Here's the version of him I dread.

I consider him, then Jacob, each of us a point in a triangle. The room fills with unspoken words.

'I heard you in the hospital, Dr Doc,' says Jacob from the floor, surrounded by broken glass. 'I've only now figured out what you meant when you said you'd been trying to keep us apart.'

My whole body clenches.

Maestro sputters over his words as though they're coming to him too fast, then says, 'What are you talking about? *I did not say that.*'

'You thought I was asleep. I'm starting to see through your mask,' says Jacob. 'On the outside you're the supportive father, the wise voice coach, but you control everything and everyone, even whether Astrid chooses to be an opera singer or not. She can sing *and* have a boyfriend.'

Maestro scrubs a hand over his reddening skin. 'This is the drink talking.'

'And I thought you were such a cool dude to convince my parents to let me audition for the music school in London. To take time out of your schedule. But you didn't care which school I went to, did you? If I stayed in England, then you could keep Astrid and me apart. Isn't that true?'

'Maestro?' I want to obliterate Jacob's words from the charged air. Except I'll still have heard them.

'I said to go home, Astrid. Do as you are told. I will discuss this with you at home.'

I step toward him, stall. 'But –'

'Now!' Maestro roars. His face distorts. I hardly recognise him. He's let whatever demon he's fighting take over, and my old father has vanished. I trip forward, casting around for my car keys and patting each of my pockets.

Behind me Jacob hoot-snorts. 'You're more frigging cuckoo than a clock.'

'Jacob. I'm on your side,' shouts Maestro. 'And those are my rules. If you choose to accept them, call me. I'll come over tomorrow. Ten am.' He pauses to take a deep breath. 'But I have my doubts about this. Can I trust you to keep to my rules? *All* of them.'

'What about *me* being able to trust *you*? What about your own daughter being able to trust you? When are you going to stop lying to her?'

For a moment the world stops with only the light of the music player winking on pause.

'What are you talking about?' demands Maestro.

'Start telling the truth.' Jacob hauls himself to his feet, crosses his arms. 'About Veronika Bell. How she didn't die after Astrid was born.'

I can't stop blinking. It's as though I'm watching Maestro's bulging eyes and dropped jaw as a series of flash cards. Palms up and backing away, my throat throbs. 'She's not dead? You lied?'

Maestro has put on a mask I've never seen. His skin is grey and slack, the creases in his face deeper. Mouth quivering, he says, 'I can explain.'

21

Jacob

'I can't even look at you.' Astrid turns away from her father and runs from the studio.

'Astrid. Stop!' The doc launches himself after her, but stumbles down the brick stairs outside. He's on the grass, clutching his knee. There's a rip in his trousers and a bit of blood. 'Please, Jacob. Stop her. Don't let her drive.' He points to Astrid, his face coming apart.

Memories stack on top of each other: the Harley, the van, the car accident. I chase Astrid up the lawn, out the gate, and snag her elbow before she climbs into her car. She's crying and keeps her head turned away. 'No way am I letting you drive when you're this upset.'

'He lied. *He lied.* She's not dead.'

Jeez, I've stuffed up. 'No, that's not right. She *is* dead. But there's more to it.'

She blinks, processing this, and then glares at me, furious. I've never seen Astrid truly angry.

'Spit it out,' says Astrid. 'Whatever you think you know.'

I crack my neck nervously, and then plunge in. 'So I was bored. And I was thinking about you this morning. And I got to thinking about how you want to find out about your mum. So I searched for her death certificate online – to find the cause of death.'

'You found it? I couldn't find it when I did a search.'

'It can be tricky. But I've done it for –' It sounds insane that I researched the death certificates of my friends. Cause of death: stupidity. 'Anyhow. I remember you said she died soon after you were born, and you thought it was childbirth, or maybe post-natal stuff. But the death certificate is dated twelve years *after* your birth.'

Her head snaps round. 'Are you sure? Maybe it's a different Veronika Bell?'

'I cross-referenced her birth certificate and marriage certificate. The death certificate was in the name of Veronika Miller – she must have changed it back. It was her.'

'Twelve years! Twelve. Years.' Fist clenched, Astrid bangs the car roof. 'Why would he lie?' Her tone could explode lightbulbs right now. 'How did she die?'

'It was lung cancer.'

The look Astrid gives me buries me ten feet deep – but it's not her anger that kills me, it's the headlong, breaking-apart loss that's muddling her features, as if her mum only just died today. She's going to have to mourn her all over again.

A sob jags her throat and she slumps against the car. I reach to touch her, but she jerks away. When I heard about Purple Daze I felt sure I would drown in a grief so deep I'd never climb out of it; I didn't want to eat, breathe, talk, kiss, love, laugh, sing again. And I believed I was completely alone. I want to hold Astrid, and comfort her, but I remember how I hadn't wanted to be touched – back then touching felt too real. Physical contact poked a hole in the box of emotions I was fighting to contain. Touching's the last thing she needs.

A mess of emotions clutters Astrid's face now. The doc planned to detonate this bomb when she turned eighteen, in a careful, well-thought-through way. And here's me blurting it out. I'm an a-hole.

She slices multiple straight lines in the dirt of the car roof with an index finger. Then her lips move into a wary smirk.

'What?' I ask.

'You. After everything. The accident. Your parents not being here today. You stood up to Maestro. You're amazing.'

It's a beautiful realisation – I *amaze* someone.

It's all I can do not to kiss her.

She leans her back against the car, the small smile suddenly blotted out.

Apart from not wanting to be touched, I remember wanting quiet – space in my head. I keep my lips sealed.

'Lung cancer,' she says. 'She was always smoking cigarettes in the press photos . . .'

Odd for an opera singer to smoke. I think it, but don't say it.

'Maestro will have to tell me everything now.' Astrid claps a palm to her mouth, talks through her fingers. '*Whoa.* Mum was *alive* when Savannah died. How could she not come to the funeral? Such a big part of my life is now *not* a part of me. My memories are all false.'

'Astrid.'

We turn to see a shrunken Maestro limping toward us. Up until now I've seen him as a kind of fictional hero – wise, focused, talented, self-assured. But today that image slips away and he's simply human.

'Come home.' His words are monotone; his body stooped. 'It's time.'

Astrid's fists clench and unclench. She pivots to me. The rage has drained from her features, and what's left behind is fear. I pull her keys free of my pocket. She yanks open the car door and closes it behind her. Before Maestro moves to follow her, he pans back to me and mouths, 'Thank you.'

22

Astrid

I was six years old before I learnt to tie my shoelaces because I wouldn't let my dad teach me before then. 'Mum will teach me,' I declared early in the process, stamping my foot on the floorboards in the entry hall.

'And how will she teach you?' Maestro asked, although I called him Dad back then. He remained calm as he knelt next to me on the floor. But I couldn't tell him that I planned to jump off the high wall in the playground and in a few hours I'd float up to heaven with Mum and Savannah. Instead, I replied, 'In my dreams.'

Maestro gave a considered nod, as if in approval, and reached for my shoes with the buckles. 'Why don't we wear these today then, so we're not late.' It was a reasonable request, but if I wore those to school, when I went to heaven at break time, I wouldn't be wearing the black patent lace-ups and Mum would never teach me how to tie them.

So I ran out to the car, the laces clacking on the wooden floorboards, and of course tripped down the front steps. I expected Maestro to get angry – I deserved it. But Maestro raced to my side and brushed me down. He dabbed a hanky at the blood trickling down my shins. I saw my shoes and began to howl not because my knees hurt but because my shiny shoes were scuffed and Mum wouldn't think them pretty anymore. I told Maestro this and his response stayed with me, guiding and comforting me throughout every day of my life.

'A mother's love is strong enough that even though she's in heaven she is everywhere around you, too. When you hear the wind rustle in the trees, it's her singing to you. When you feel the sun on your face, that's her hand stroking you. When you see the light glinting off the ocean, it's her waving. When it rains, those are her tears from heaven, because she's so sad not to be with you. Therefore, she already saw the shoes when they were new and shiny.'

'And when I fall down the stairs that's her saying, "Let your dad teach you to tie your laces"?' I replied, thinking I was getting this 'mum' stuff.

Maestro shrugged. 'Maybe. Mums move in mysterious ways.'

But every word had been a lie. Every time the sun warmed my cheek and I laid my hand on what I believed was hers, she wasn't there at all. She sang and waved and laughed and cried somewhere else in the world, living her life without me.

She didn't love us. She didn't want us. She never saw my new black patent shoes.

By the time I reach the third set of traffic lights Maestro's BMW pulls up behind me. I watch him through the rearview mirror. Sitting behind the wheel, he seems smaller.

When we pull into the driveway I don't wait and shoot indoors to place myself in the dining room. I don't want to do this in the music room. I need a table between us. I don't want to be touched, cajoled, comforted. I want the truth.

I study the candy-striped wallpaper – Mum's choice. As was every bit of furniture in this room, this house. And her choices helped me piece together what sort of person she was. She liked antique furniture, so she had sophisticated taste. Maestro always said we should keep the house neat and tidy because Mum would've approved, therefore she must've been an organised and calm person. She loved real fires and the ocean view across the treetops, so she loved nature. All these little details helped me imagine her, along with her dresses and Savannah's and Maestro's stories about her.

Now I wonder if *any* of it's true.

When Maestro walks in he resembles the ragged teddy bear on my bed, the one Mum gave to Savannah before Maestro passed it on to me. Everything about him sags, as if the stuffing's fallen out of him. He sits down opposite me.

'Is it true? Jacob says she died when I was twelve. *Five* years ago.'

'She left, Astrid. She left us.' His words come out in a breathless flurry. They echo and vibrate in the air like each word is a gong being bashed one at a time, their meaning cruel, certified, undeniable.

My face flinches, as though he cuffed me. 'She left right after I was born?'

His glare stabs the table top. 'That's why I couldn't tell you. I knew you'd blame yourself. I didn't want you growing up hating yourself. I didn't want Savannah to blame you either.' He gets to his feet, paces toward the music room and back.

'But I thought it was my fault anyway. I thought it was *my* birth – I thought *I* killed her.' Fury blooms in my chest. I jump to my feet. 'You should have told me. I have blamed myself for her death every day of my life. I spent my life amazed that *you* didn't blame me. And now I know why. How *could* you let me think that?'

He swings to me. 'I didn't know you thought that. Why would you think that?'

'Because if she'd been murdered or something awful like that, the media would've been all over it. Because why else did you make it such a big secret? Even Savannah believed that.'

He scrunches his face, drawing all his features inwards as though he wants to obliterate them. 'No. No. It had nothing to do with you. I'm so terribly sorry.'

'*Why* did she leave then?'

'It's complicated.'

'*The truth.*' I bang my fists on the table. The ornamental vase in the middle jumps and rattles.

He lugs in a huge breath, holds it in, then lets it go. 'Yes. The truth.' Maestro's lips distort. 'Veronika had been suffering from a hoarse voice after performances. I begged her to visit a specialist.' He gulps down a sob that becomes a low squeal. 'She didn't go. Instead she took a break.' He stares over my head into space, slowly forming the words like they hurt to speak. 'Savannah was almost four when she left us for six months. She had run off before: three or four times a year, she'd disappear. She never told me where she went. Sometimes her suitcase came back with labels from places like Morocco or Venice. But usually it was just for a week or two, not six months.' He lets his breath trickle out.

My legs as weak as wet paper, I sit down again.

'And when she got home we had two problems. One, she hadn't visited the voice specialist. And when I finally convinced her, it was too late. She had vocal nodules – calluses on the vocal folds. The damage was permanent.' His gaze searches my face. 'And it meant she had to stop performing. To someone like her, the doctor may as well have told her to stop breathing.'

Maestro plods from the table to the music room entrance and back again.

'What did that have to do with her leaving us?'

Maestro stops pacing, rubs the back of his hand across his forehead. 'It wasn't you girls. I promise. It was her. Some people aren't cut out to be parents. She struggled with the responsibility. I'm afraid she wasn't as perfect as I may have painted her to be. Savannah's puppy? Veronika didn't accidentally let it escape: she hated how it piddled on the rugs and yapped all night so she gave it to someone in the staff at the Opera House and bought Savannah a teddy instead. And there were more tears than cookie baking. The one time she did try baking, Savannah burnt her fingers on the cookie tray. It was the second visit to the hospital in a month because Savannah had slipped getting out of the bath and knocked herself out – your mother had been on the phone longer than she realised even though I'd lectured her many times about watching Savannah. And while she was away from home performing and travelling, she coped with the occasional responsibility. But the prospect of living in one place, being a mum every single day, and never performing – she couldn't do it. She said parenting made her feel trapped and inadequate. But the truth is, she was too self-absorbed, always seeking pleasure and fun and avoiding – well, real life.'

Her words on the flowery notepaper. *People shouldn't try to be what they are not.*

'But what about you?' I remember Maestro's story of how they met on the steps of the Viennese Opera House, how they fell in love by the next day.

'*I* wasn't enough to fill that hole in her life. In fact, I became a reminder of the life she could no longer have. As were her dresses. I stopped her cutting them up. She got into a terrible rage. She called her life a living death. She couldn't stay.'

'And that's why she left behind her opera dresses. She'd never need them again.'

'They haunted me day and night. The lingering smell of her . . .'

Therefore, he dry-cleaned them and stored each item in the guest room cupboard to give us memories to touch with our fingers.

'Where did she go?'

'I genuinely don't know.' He grips the back of the dining chair, peeks at me from under heavy lids. 'She packed, emptied our bank account, took all her real jewellery, and left when I was out at a performance, leaving you and Savannah alone at night. She couldn't even wait for me to come home. She left that note you found lying beside you.' He pauses, lips trembling. 'But when she did die, her lawyer told me it was lung cancer. Oh, Veronika.' For a moment he's lost in his memories, his knuckles white around the rail of the chair. 'She had an addictive personality. Wouldn't even stop smoking when she was pregnant. '

'What else?'

Maestro looks at his feet. An eyelid twitches. 'Five years ago some lawyers in New York City contacted me. They couldn't tell me much. She never remarried or bore more children. She had no money to speak of. I have no way of finding out what her life entailed. But it wasn't much because when she died the press never picked up on it. I suppose she hadn't sung in twelve years and she'd changed her name back to Miller. But she did bequeath her daughters two identical rings, taken from the diamonds in our wedding ring. Shall I fetch them?' He moves toward the door.

'No. Not yet. She didn't know about Savannah and that's why she didn't come to the funeral?'

Maestro reaches for the ornaments on the bookshelf, straightens them into a neat line. 'How could she have? I had stopped performing and wasn't in the public domain, so it wasn't in the press. And I had no way of reaching her.'

'Who bought the furniture in this house?'

'I did. She hated shopping.'

I study the straightened ornaments. 'And it's you who is tidy and organised. Not her.'

'She left enough mess in her wake she should've hired a person to walk behind her to clean up.'

I had imagined the tiny scratches in the table top were made by Mum while she ate or learnt lines from operas. But maybe not. Everything I constructed about her recedes, vanishes. And there's such a big blank that I have nothing to hold onto.

'Did she adore the view over the treetops from the music room?'

'It would've been her favourite room in the house. Had she lived here. After she left I gave up performing and moved to this side of Sydney for a fresh start with you girls.'

'What? You always said she lived here. Why? Why did you tell us she was dead rather than she left?'

'There were a lot of reasons.' Maestro can't seem to stop blinking. He wipes a flat palm over his mouth.

'Which were? You have to tell me everything now.'

'Mostly, it was Savannah.' His words come quickly. 'She panicked every time your mother left. The first words that she spoke each morning and the last each night were to ask when her mum would be home. Even when she was gone for six months she asked every day. She had nightmares, lost her appetite. It was awful to watch. There was nothing I could do. When Veronika came home, Savannah wouldn't let her out of her sight in case she left again. Of course, it made things worse for Veronika, who already felt trapped. If she'd been drinking and couldn't drive, she would lock herself in the car just to get away from Savannah's clinging. She said Savannah's constant talking made her want to drink until she couldn't hear her anymore.

'So for Savannah it was better that she dealt with the fact her mum wasn't coming back. Because this time I knew it was for good. And I know you might not agree, but having seen what being abandoned by her own parents did to Veronika – her low self-esteem, her anger and hatred that she'd express when she'd had a few drinks – I didn't want that to happen to you. For me, being abandoned by your mother was *worse* than her dying. When you die you don't get the choice. Leaving you was her decision. And that affects a child in too many irreparable ways.'

She lost her dream and then threw us away.

'What else?' I ask.

Maestro bites his bottom lip, then says, 'Nothing else.'

'Whose ashes did you sprinkle in Paris?'

Maestro strains to keep his face from puckering. 'No-one's of course. But she always said she'd want me to do that. Now I have no idea what happened when she died.'

'Her parents. Did they throw her out?'

'That's what she told me. They wrote to her. She said whatever they had to say was too late. She returned the letters unopened. After she left, they kept coming and I didn't think it was my right to open them, so I saved them for her – until I heard she'd died.'

I let those facts sink in a while.

'I set the idea of your eighteenth in motion because I thought you'd be mature enough to deal with the reality by then and to understand why I lied,' continues Maestro, 'because I knew you'd be angry and might not agree with my reasons for lying, but at the time it felt right. I decided if you wanted to go find her, which was your right to do, you could do it then, but not before. I wanted you to be all grown up, to know who you were and what you wanted in your life before you went to find her. She was irresponsible and selfish and she wasn't a stable person. She didn't like herself . . . and she drank and smoked too much. I was afraid of what you might find when you located her. I also wanted you to feel loved, so I told you those stories that made her seem like a doting mum because I can't think of anything worse than learning that your mum didn't want you.' Maestro's voice cracks. 'You can surely see why I couldn't say these words to you when you were younger. I knew they would hurt you.'

My mouth moves before I realise it's me speaking. 'And then she actually died.'

'I'm sorry, Astrid. I took away your chance to know your mum and I'll never, never forgive myself.' Maestro blinks away tears. 'The guilt has plagued me for five years now. Some days I believe I'm losing my mind with it, because I cannot fix it or solve it. And it's made telling you the truth that much harder. All this time, I've been dreading your eighteenth birthday. And dreading that I'll lose you –'

As he surveys me, moments of time spark and die around us, but I cannot give him the reassurance he needs.

He sits down again. 'I'd imagined the discussions on your birthday would be about whether you wanted to go find her and how we'd start to track her down –' His voice is feeble, spongy.

Even with the table between us, it's as though Maestro's pressed up against me. I back my chair out, twist and glare through the window. This isn't some dinnertime chat. This is the truth. The big secret revealed. And it sucks.

The truth is my dazzling mum never wanted to be my mum and I can stop grieving for a person who never existed.

I chose to become a soprano to honour her and help Maestro get through his grief. Do I continue to carry that burden? His grief looks different now.

'Every time I thought you were grieving for mum you were pretending?'

'Not at all. I grieved the loss of my wife, my old life. And I grieved *your* loss of your mother. But that grief turned into fear and worry after I learnt she had died.'

'So when you got upset when I mentioned Mum it was because you dreaded telling me you lied?'

'The thought of losing you – after losing her and Savannah –' He turns away. 'I would die inside.'

Mum was cut short in her prime. The day they told her she couldn't perform was probably the day she died inside. As would I, if I couldn't sing again. It's the *single* thing I will *ever* understand about my mother.

'What I have – it isn't the same as what she had wrong with her vocal cords?'

'No. It's completely different.' Maestro stands and starts pacing again. I'm grateful for the distance it puts between us.

'All this time she lived a different life, knowing we were here. She never wrote, never came back?'

'Never.' Maestro exhales. 'I'm sorry. But she didn't.' He pivots and trudges toward the stairs. 'I'll fetch the rings.'

I listen to him climb the stairs in his socked feet. I always imagined Mum loved bare feet, never socks. But that's probably wrong. I'm envious of Savannah because no-one ever tore apart her memories of Mum. Worse, I've been following in Mum's footsteps all my life. Now who am I meant to be?

Maestro returns, two rings on his flat palm. 'They're yours,' he says. I peer at them; their diamonds are alive with light. They were more a part of her life than I was. 'She left them for you in her will.'

I stare at the rings, unable to touch them. 'You said there were a lot of reasons why you told us she was dead. What were the others?'

Maestro balls the hand containing the rings, turns away

to look out the window. After a too-long silence, he says, 'No. There weren't other reasons. It was for Savannah.'

'I want all of the truth. Look at me and say that.'

He turns to face me, crossing his arms so that his suit jacket scrunches. 'It was for Savannah's sake. I was stalling when I said there were lots of reasons . . .' I hold his gaze until he breaks contact and shows me the rings again.

I coax myself to pick one up, but a dark swirl of another question waits to be asked. 'You said there were two problems when she came back. Her voice and – what was the other problem?'

Maestro lets the rings drop onto the table. We watch them roll and spin until they stop. Chaos rumbles in Maestro's eyes. Before I even comprehend the answer I start to cry.

'She was . . . pregnant.'

I lean back in my chair, picking through the debris of truth, failing to create a picture that makes sense. I'm about to ask what happened to the baby. But then I realise the baby was me.

I'm panting as I stand. My chair falls backwards. Something inside me shatters and the shrapnel slices at me. Somehow my shaking legs carry me forward.

Before I exit the room Maestro calls, 'I'm here for you, Astrid. If you need me.' He pauses. 'I love you. You will always be my daughter. And I'm sorry.'

But I can't look back at him. I can't say thank you. I can't say it's okay. Because it's not.

He stayed. He lied. My life is a lie.

The truth is Mum was a flawed, selfish soprano star who abandoned her family and died from cancer not childbirth. The truth is Maestro has lied to me for nearly eighteen years. The truth is Maestro is not my father.

But who am I?

♫

Later that night the anger hits me like a train. I storm into the guest room and tear each gown off its coat hanger. I toss the hats through the air, throw the shoes at the walls. And then I squat in the middle of the mess, huffing and crying and willing her ghostly form to appear. To explain. To redeem herself.

I leaf through the memories I've pinned to the walls of my life. I had cherished them as works of art; they were beautiful Monet landscapes or Degas portraits. But now they're cracked and altered, like a Picasso painting – nothing's quite in the right place, everything's out of alignment, misshapen. They convey shapes of light and colour rather than reality.

She baked cupcakes *once*. She didn't care about building forts. And waking at midday or dancing all night until the sun came up now seems selfish and irresponsible, rather than endearing or glamorous. And why did she swim far out to sea if it scared Savannah? I pick at the splintered works of art, plucking them apart and all the while feeling the cut of their sharp edges deep inside me.

After a while I scan the floor, her dresses and hats scattered around me. I recognise, without any doubt in my mind, that even if I had a pair of scissors I could *never* vandalise these dresses. And the more I realise I don't resemble Mum at all, the more I begin to see who *I* am.

Maestro's playing Prokofiev's dramatic 'Dance of the Knights' from *Romeo and Juliet* at top volume in the music room. He's set it to repeat and he's accompanying it on his violin. It's an appropriate soundtrack to end this day. I get to my feet and hang up each dress, placing the right shoes under the matching gown. There are eighteen hats, and I remember their exact order. When I leave the room you would never know I'd been there.

23

Jacob

The room bursts with the sound of silence.

It seems wrong that there's the scent of Astrid in the studio, yet she's not here. It's wrong that I'm not with her now, standing by her side as she learns the truth she's waited for all her life. It's like turning up for a concert and discovering I'm a day late.

I inspect the room from Doc's perspective. The person who lives here has lost his way, or doesn't care. The person who lives here needs to grow up.

Do I want what Doc's offering me? There's nothing else in this world I *do* want. I try to re-live that certainty I felt on the stage in Vienna – that singing is what I must do with my life. That my voice is more than a song. It's the one way I can lead a life that might be remembered. And with Astrid and Doc by my side, getting into the Con doesn't seem so hard.

Three rules to follow until the Con auditions at the end of November. Just over two months. Tidy up. No drinking. Keep it platonic with Astrid.

I remember waking in the hospital and being goofy happy that Astrid was okay; the same moment I knew she'd found a crawl space into my heart. I was ready to let her push Harper all the way out of my head. But Astrid's made it clear it's not what she wants. Besides, she needs me in more important ways now. As a friend I can act as her rock. As a boyfriend, I come with Harper-shaped baggage. I let Harper down. I won't let Astrid down.

So I have no choice but to stick to rule three. And then how hard can the other two be?

My hangover kicks in but I pull open the curtains and pick up dirty dishes. Instead of counting on beer as a cure, I sit on the sofa with a glass of water and painkillers. My feet squelch on an old banana peel. 'You filthy pig, Jacob,' I mumble. I survey the bombsite around me. Nothing's going to change unless I change it. I need to put down the baby rattle and man up. I'm going to get into the Con and move out of home.

After switching on some dance music, I find an empty box left over from the new piano stool and take the first step into my future. I start clearing up rubbish near the fridge and come across the photo of Harper, the one where she's eating an apple at the beach. Wistful, I pick up the frame and gather the other scattered photos and picture frames of her and place them in the bottom drawer of the cupboard.

'Yo! My man. What crawled up your butt?'

I laugh out loud. If anyone can keep me off the grog, Dex can.

'Tidying up, kid. You can help.'

'*You* tidy up? You wouldn't know one end of a feather duster from the other.'

'But I can learn. Know anything about fixing vacuum cleaners? Mine's busted.'

'I got this.' Dex gives me an elaborate salute, clicks his heels together and disappears out the door.

I finish throwing rubbish and food leftovers into the box and start dusting. Dex comes crashing back into the studio lugging a contraption that bears no resemblance to the vacuum I'm used to. He boogies with the vacuum, pretending it's a dance partner and twirls himself around the room.

'You should be a ballroom dancer,' I tease, but when I next turn around, he's juggling fire – literally.

'They're cotton balls soaked in alcohol,' he explains, closing his hands around the balls of fire to extinguish them. 'Your dad's booze cabinet's well-stocked.'

'Doesn't it burn you?'

'A bit. But a moment of pain never hurt anyone.'

'You should find a safer hobby, kid.'

Dex dries up while I wash dishes and we haul four bags of rubbish and the box up to the main bins at the side of the house, fist-bumping after it's done.

'Do we get to sing today?' Dex glows at the prospect, reminding me of how I used to feel about singing, and underlining how much I take for granted. Sure I don't have 'normal' parents, but I have a lot. Compared to him. Compared to Astrid.

''Course we can. Let's do this.' I ruffle his hair and he slaps away my arm before using his fingertips to re-shape his coif.

Later, when his alarm beeps he slumps against the piano.

I feel bad about wasting his singing time by having him clean up with me. 'See ya tomorrow, kid,' I say, closing the music book. I vow to help him clean the main house next time, so we've got more time to sing.

'Where's Miss Scusami? I liked her songs.'

'She has more for you. If you like them, maybe we can record something.' This is how I can help Astrid. She wants to be a songwriter but her dad's not going to help her with that and she knows nothing about the pop market or submitting demos. Writing and recording songs with Dex will keep her mind off her injured vocal cords, her mum, her dad – everything. And at the same time, I'll be helping Dex. The kid's had it tough; he irons my carpets and cooks for his sick mother but he's hiding a talent that needs to be discovered. He just needs a lucky break.

And I need to concentrate on the living.

Dex scours the soundproof booth as though it's an ice-cream stall and I told him to help himself to all he can eat. He whoops and punches the air. 'I'm gonna get signed up. Be famous.'

'That's what you want?'

'It's all I think about.' Dex's face flickers with the hard edges of ambition. I consider him, with his absurdly angled cheekbones and boyish charm, his boy-band body and dreamy dark looks. Teenage girls will go mental for him.

I pound him on the back. 'We'd better get you signed up with a label then.'

'You can do that?'

'I can help you record something. You'll have to do the hard work. We can give it a go.' I tried submitting demos to labels for Purple Daze earlier in the year – not that we got anywhere.

Dex whoops and breaks into a high-stepping victory lap around the studio. 'Holy coif, I'm gonna be a pop star. Promise I won't go biting heads off bats or any of that trippy shit you read online.'

'Where's "holy coif" come from?'

'I dunno. Can't say "holy shit" around Mamma. It's better than what she suggested. Holy Hail Mary?'

'You get on with your ma?'

He blows a kiss out the window in the direction of the house. 'She's the love of my life.'

I ruffle his hair, grimace. 'That's not weird.'

'Why? She washed my cuts and grazes. Cleaned my nose. She's worked here all my life to feed me and make a home.' His voice goes soft. 'She was the first person to love me. I'm gonna write a song for her one day.'

We fist-bump again and a little of his excitement and hope spreads through the cleaned-up studio; it lifts me. I feel lighter inside than I've felt in a long time.

♫

'How much longer do I have to do this?' Dex watches me from his position on the floor, flat on his back doing breathing exercises after his sit-ups. 'I hate these things.'

‘To a count of twenty-five. As usual.’

Dex sighs. ‘I’ve been breathing and singing at the same time for years. I don’t want to sing opera.’

‘As I’ve said about fifty times now, breathing right is for *every* singer. I’m not explaining it again, okay?’ Dex falls silent to finish his exercises.

I’m being a shithead right now. But I’ve stayed dry for twenty days, partly to follow Doc’s rules, partly because it makes Astrid happy and since she found out The Truth, I’ll do just about anything to make her feel better. But memories still remain raw and in need of numbing. Using distraction, like the doc said, helps.

It’s not working today.

At least the doc’s keeping to his side of the bargain. Maybe he blames himself for keeping secrets rather than me for letting them out.

My phone pings with a message from Harper, but I’m not in the mood for catching up. Instead I check for texts from Astrid. She’s late today.

‘Okay next exercise, Super Boy.’ I throw over a hardback book. Dex catches it then lines up with the mirror at the end of the room, and balances it on his head. He takes a few steps and the book slides off.

‘My soul repels books. Even ones balanced on my head.’

‘Shoulders are hunched,’ I say.

He tries again. It falls again.

‘I know, I know,’ he says. ‘Head level, knees loose, torso

relaxed. Just like surfing.'

Dex may have the voice of an angel, but he's no surfer. Two Sundays ago he turned up unannounced as I was about to hit the waves. He had the whole afternoon free, so I offered to teach him to surf before we sang. He looked like a monkey on speed trying to stand still. The boys would've had a good laugh. But he did some of his voice exercises on the board and sang pop songs. It was kinda stupid, but fun. So we did it again the next week.

When he makes it to the mirror now, I tell him to repeat the book balance walk four more times. Dex is working hard with me and Astrid in the afternoons. He might even be skiving off school so he can fit in cleaning and singing some days. Last week I convinced Astrid to let us record some of the stuff she's written. She reckons her songs only sound good because Dex has a star-quality voice. That set Dex off and he's started playing up to the image of what he thinks is a pop star; for instance, throwing away all the yellow M&M's.

'What's this you giving me, girl?' he shrieked one time. 'Surely it's not tap water because my throat won't take anything less than the magical flowing spring water of Mount Everest.' And with a flourish he threw open his hand revealing a pool of blue flames.

I check my phone. Nothing from Astrid.

She's told me the bare minimum about how her mother walked out on them, and that nodules stopped her singing and she couldn't hack it. Instead Astrid's crawled into herself and an invisible mist of gloom surrounds her. Funny how I miss her, even though she's here every day. I miss how she looks at me as if she can see through all my bullshit and still likes what's left.

For the millionth time I re-live our kiss in London. Which must mean I'm over Harper. I still miss Harper, and of course I still love her. Won't I always? But I don't visit our shared memory bank as much as I used to. When I do, the memory doesn't feel like another drumstick spiking my heart.

Doc teaches at the Con in the afternoons, leaving Astrid to complete her homeschooling. But maybe today he's busted Astrid for sneaking out. I text her a vague: *you ok?* My phone dings almost immediately, but it's just Mum: *Won't be home until ten. Eat with Maria.* She knows Maria leaves at seven. I've eaten dinner alone most weeknights since I was ten, except when I ate it with the Hunters next door.

Dex moves on to the lip roll, his hands either side of his mouth to hold up the weight of his cheeks. He blows out air through loose lips then walks around making *mmmm* and *brrrrr* sounds. I'm pleased with how much he's working to take this seriously. When we first started the exercise he couldn't do it for cracking up. But when I showed him how it opens up his upper range and makes his notes sound sweeter, he buckled down.

I straddle a dining chair, the only one in the room. Mad Dog extracted it from his garage. He brought it for Callum who liked to perch on it backwards, his legs spread either side of the backrest, notebook on the back slat. He'd rock on the legs, lost in his own world of music. It was how he found his muse.

Someone took down Skittles's Instagram page. His last post was a video of him singing. Somehow, he'd *gained* followers, unlike Mad Dog, who's down to 899.

While I rock back and forth on the chair, Dex sings 'Stand By Me' replacing the words with *mmmm* and *brrrrr*. The repetitive sound starts grating on my nerves. I make a beeline for the fridge but a man can only drink so much juice. I massage my brow and fall into the Lego sofa, sitting on my iPad. Pulling it free, the news feed tells me our tap water might be infected with E.Coli. Thousands could die. And a passenger aircraft crashed in Indonesia. 324 dead.

A beer would taste so good right now.

Last night the ghosts of Purple Daze haunted my dreams again. It would be easy to raid Dad's drink cabinet at 2 am, but I don't because of Astrid. And because of Dex, who looks up to me. And because I have a gut feeling that if I don't want to fail at life, I have to fight the demons without the grog.

The problem is, on some days like today, the demons are winning.

Dex finally finishes his warm-up exercises and stops beside the piano, expectant.

I rouse myself and sit on the piano stool. We begin with scales using *ooh, eeh, ah, aah* applied to each scale. Then *doh, ray, me*. My cast's off and I can play a little, but stick with my good hand for now. We need Astrid to take over. I make him practise his staccato and he sighs before singing short, tight notes. With each one he pulls at his white singlet.

'Okay. Enough already. Can I sing now?' he says, hands on hips.

'What do you think you've been doing? Jogging? One more round on your own. I'll be right back. Gotta do something.'

I head to the Jeep, not sure what I've got to do. I watch a taxi disappear and search the road for Astrid for several long minutes, like somehow this'll make her arrive faster. I phone her, but it rings out, reminding me of the night I'd called five numbers and all five rang out. As I hang up, the front door opens and Maria appears. I wave but she falls back against the door, hunches, then crumples to the ground.

'Maria.' I run toward her. Her face is white and sweaty. She's attempting to breathe in a controlled way; in through her nose, out through her mouth. I kneel beside her. She raises a hand to her chest.

'What's wrong? Do you need an ambulance?' I ask.

'I called them already.' She hacks a sharp cough. 'I cannot find Dexter.'

'I'll find him.' I stand. 'But I don't want to leave you.'

Maria winces. 'Find my boy. Please, Jacob.'

♫

When Dex reaches his mother he unzips her handbag and rummages inside it. 'Where are your pills?' he asks. 'It's the angina, yes?'

'I already took them.' Maria gasps for a breath. 'Not helping. The whole world is sitting on my chest.'

Dex helps her straighten her legs, which are curled awkwardly beside her. 'When did you take them?'

'Trenta.'

'Jacob,' he says, without taking his focus off his mother. 'Can you get come pillows? Come, Mamma. Let's lie you down.'

I dart inside to fetch some cushions from the lounge and when I come out, Dex has his mother's head on his lap.

'Put them under her knees. To raise them,' Dex tells me. I'm impressed at how calm he is. 'Keep trying to breathe slowly, Mamma. Why did you wait thirty minutes to call the ambulance?'

Maria doesn't answer but shuts her eyes. Her hand seeks out her son's and he grips it hard.

Tears brimming, he whispers, 'It'll be alright, Mamma. Relax. I got you.'

24

Astrid

When I arrive at Jacob's he's sitting on the front porch steps. He's at my open window before I turn off the engine.

'Everything okay?' he asks. His expression is creased with worry.

'Sorry I'm late. I was at an appointment with the laryngologist.' Every muscle in my face holds onto a smile. I look away.

'What did they say?' Jacob opens my door. I climb out, keeping the car door between us, always careful not to accidentally touch. Although I itch to break every rule Maestro ever uttered, it's simpler to keep things platonic with Jacob. Everything is too messed up and jumbled in my life to open up another can of worms. Besides, because of the Harper question mark, why would I expose myself to more agonising, more confusion?

'My head voice is still restricted,' I answer. I keep my talking voice soft, ensuring I use my middle voice and mask resonance when I speak like Maestro said to do – to protect my throat. 'And my pitch isn't consistent. Apparently, it'll take time for the inflammation to reduce, but there are no structural issues.' I don't want to talk about it though; it makes the fact my voice is lost too real, and fills my already full head with chimes of fear. 'I'm sorry if I worried you. I left my phone at home.'

'Dex had to go. His mum needed an ambulance. It might be a heart attack.'

'That's awful. Is she going to be okay?'

'Don't know yet. It was scary. I found her. But you should've seen Dex. He knew exactly what to do. Cool as a cucumber. They left like twenty minutes ago.' Jacob stabs at his phone to check for messages, then adds, 'So no singing practise today.'

'Let's go for a drive instead,' I say. 'I'll tell you about the new song I've written for Dex. It's the one we should record.' Jacob agrees and walks round the front of my car. 'The song's called "A Forgettable Life".' I started writing it after seeing the phrase on Jacob's cast.

Jacob stops at the passenger door. He says something with his eyes. *You saw what I wrote.* Only there's something more intimate there. The idea of being in a small space together suddenly doesn't seem like such a great idea. To delay, I add, 'It's good and catchy, and suits Dex. I've learnt where his sweet spots are.'

Dex is my lifeline these days – a way to make a songwriting career happen. He's also the buffer between me and Jacob when we're in the studio. In this instance, three is not a crowd.

'What are the lyrics about?' asks Jacob.

'About being broken.' I stare up into the surrounding jacaranda trees. 'And lost in a forgettable life. But then finding the strength through love to rise up stronger than ever.'

'Tell me all about it while we walk on the beach. Let's go.' Jacob's cheeriness sounds fake and I wonder if the lyrics have hit a raw nerve for him. He opens the door but doesn't get in. Instead he says, 'You've let your hair go curly.' It's a simple observation, but behind it I can see he still, like me, re-lives that kiss in London.

My phone dings with a text from Maestro, checking up on me from the Con. I ignore it. Jacob gets into the car. I settle in next to him, turn over the engine. It's like the car's too small to fit all of our unspoken thoughts and feelings. We sit in silence as I drive. The engine hums, the indicator clicks. Through the window, bruised clouds crowd the setting sun. The horizon frays.

'I haven't touched a drink in three weeks,' says Jacob. 'I know I scared you before. That it's important to you that I don't drink.'

'And the studio is always tidy. You're doing better than me.'

He looks at me like he wants to hug me. I want to hook his hair behind his ears, but resist the temptation.

'I was thinking about what the doc said about getting a job,' he says. 'Skittles saved a load of cash. Maybe I can. And maybe I can get a grant for the Con.'

'But you're busy with Maestro in the mornings and Dex in the afternoons now.' I'm surprised how the thought of not having our afternoons together stings. Or is it that this is my way into a songwriting career? A way of getting away from Maestro.

'S'pose. The Con isn't far away. I'll get a job afterwards. Dex is making me see I'm a lazy rich kid. I thought I wasn't, because I worked hard at my music. But the truth is it's easy to stay as I am. I need to leave home, but it's impossible to grasp what's out there – if I'll survive on my own.'

'Don't do anything rash. Maestro's not always right.' He made the wrong choice by lying to me for all these years. And something about the way he turned away to look out the window, the way he was silent for a little too long when I asked what the other reasons were for his lie about Mum dying, suggests I still can't trust him.

Minute by minute, the dim evening swallows the day. A giant drop of rain splats on the windscreen, followed by another, and another. I pull over and turn off the engine. It's going to pour so we won't be able to walk on the beach.

Jacob's staring at me. 'What's happening with your father?'

'I don't want to talk about him.' I forget to use my middle voice. I'm still not ready to tell Jacob that Maestro isn't my father.

Every day I tell myself I just have to be civil with Maestro for one more day, but I'm kidding myself – it's not like I have any other family to live with. I'm trapped more than ever.

'I've been considering writing to my grandparents. They're the only blood relatives I have. But I guess it's not like I can go live with them.'

'No. S'pose not.'

Pellets of rain drum on the windscreen. Thick rivulets of water run down my window. I feel numb and sad, a lifeless doll version of myself. I remember the times Maestro bandaged me up after I tried to join Mum in heaven. But she wasn't even in heaven back then. All the hours of his own life he wasted playing at being my dad: the nappies, the fight to make me eat my vegetables, the times I was sick, the homework, the clothes shopping, the haircuts. What sort of man brings up another man's child? Probably a good one. But I resent him. He's made me live a lie.

I think of Dex and his single mum. Except Dex is Maria's blood.

Jacob pulls out his phone, jabs at the screen. A piano intro gusts into the car before Adele's words sweep up the silence. I cross my arms and listen, needing the music to soothe me. To ground me. But not even Adele can unearth an emotion from me. It's like I'm no longer me anymore. Instead I'm watching myself, the doll version left behind in my place, sitting in a car next to Jacob.

Adele's lyrics are bittersweet. I wonder if Jacob chose them on purpose because they're about being unable to make someone love back. Except I do love Jacob. I think. Maybe I'm confusing love with need. I have no one but Jacob. Maestro was everything. And now he's – I don't know what he is to me now.

The rain eases and Jacob lowers the volume, brushes his fingertips over my arm. I feel myself slip into my body again.

'Are you angry with your mum?' he asks, soft. I flinch as though he shouted the words. 'It's okay if you are. Reckon I would be.'

My lips wobble. 'I don't even know if her parents threw her out, after what Tom said. Who's lying? Maestro or Mum?' Maybe that's what Maestro is still keeping from me.

We listen to Adele's closing phrases. The windows have steamed up so it's like we're inside a white tent.

'I'm not feeling sorry for myself,' I finally say, talking to my fingers in my lap. 'Sure, it hurts that she left me. And the truth about who she was hurts. Maestro's filled in the gaps. She was selfish and egotistical, one-tracked. She chased pleasure and fun and hated responsibility and commitments. But I'm more confused than anything. That was *her*. It's not me. I suppose that's it – I don't know who *I* am because I've been trying to be *her* all my life. I know I wanted to become a singer too, but I partly did it because it seemed to help Maestro get over his grief – except she wasn't even dead. I'm angry because of that and because thanks to her and Maestro, my past is not what I thought. And to top it all, my future is – uncertain. I want to leave home, but I have no money. I don't know how.

'And there are no words to describe how it feels to have my past blanked out, forcing me to re-write every moment in my history while not knowing if my memory is even right. That's why I'm going around in circles.' That's why no matter where I am – in a room, a car or outside – I feel like I'm drowning in too much emptiness, yet at the same time, the space is too small.

I whisper, 'I only know who I am *not*.'

'*I* know who you are. You're Astrid Bell. A talented and gorgeous songwriter and soprano. Yes, your voice *will* end up okay. You're loyal, disciplined and hardworking. You love to help others. You're responsible. Your one downside is you're not quite as talented as me.'

'Shut up,' I murmur, suppressing a smile. Jacob doesn't miss it, and looks like the cat that got the cream.

Strains of Pink fill the car. Jacob once told me he can't stay away from Pink's lyrics and the dark rich power in her voice.

He play-punches my arm. 'You're a good person. One of the best. And if you need me to keep reminding you, then ask.'

'I could say the same of you.'

'Nah. *I'm* a lost cause.'

I lean forward and slap his leg. It's a reflex. I retract my hand. But the way he's smiling, cajoling, like he really cares . . .

'You. Are. Not,' I say. '*Ridicolo.* One day, with your good looks and incredible voice, you'll have the world at your feet.'

My pulse booms in my throat. I study my lap. He leans in and hooks my chin with his fingertips. I try to make my expression say *go away* because I can't say the words out loud, but he still touches his lips to mine. The tightness in me softens, so that I don't pull back. But I don't kiss back either. Jacob pushes his lips more firmly onto mine. He cups his hand behind my head, slides his tongue between my teeth.

I let the tension drain from me, let my body lean into his. But it doesn't last. Maestro. Mum. Harper. My voice.

Savannah. Each word is a complication, a threat, a story with no end. A story I need to make sense of before I can move forward with Jacob.

So I don't hurt his feelings, I slowly shift away then lean my forehead on the steering wheel.

'What if I told you I'm over Harper?' he says, gravelly.

'I wouldn't believe you.' My voice is a tragic whisper. 'You're too sad.'

'I'm sad because of my mates. Not Harper.'

'You can't know that. She still texts you.'

'Not very often. And we're just friends.'

'I don't think I could take it if we – if she – I like you too much.' Jacob falls silent. I hadn't meant to say those words out loud and try to bury them with logic. 'Everything's upside down and inside out. Maestro deceived me. A part of me wonders if he's still lying. I feel like he's not telling me everything – he can barely look me in the eye. Something's missing, but I can't put my finger on it. I know she was a flake of a mother but to tell us she was dead? I don't know. Maybe Mum *didn't* abandon us, but left for some other reason he won't ever tell me. He's the one person I trusted. I can't think about you – us – when all this is going on.'

I turn over the engine, suddenly too churned up inside. I need to be alone. The windscreen is fogged up and I flick on the air. The wipers swipe side to side. 'And people keep dying. Or leaving. Or lying. So no. We can't. And you're probably deceiving yourself about Harper. I can't live with more lies.'

I indicate and check my mirrors. The rain's stopped and the wipers squeak while we drive back to Jacob's house. It's better than silence.

When I pull into his driveway, he grips his jaw then bangs a flat palm on the dashboard, making me jump. 'You can't seal yourself away from everyone just to be safe. That's like you're already dead. Life is dicey. It's just like letting your songs go out into the world. It's scary and it's a risk, but if you don't do it then the songs can never live. They may as well not exist.'

I probably shouldn't exist. I get out of the car, walk around the front, and open his door.

He pulls to his feet. 'The solution's obvious. I wanted to talk to you about this but didn't know how. You should move in with me.'

'Have you heard anything I've said?'

'This is about getting you away from Maestro, not us. I'm getting my act together. I'm not drinking. I've tidied up the studio.'

'So that I move in with you?'

'Why not? I can set up a bed in the studio for you, bring you food, and you can shower up at the house. You'd have your own place away from him.'

'But with you.'

'I'd move back into my bedroom. We can sing together when we like. Find jobs. We could even move out together, because I need to leave home after the Con. Two wages are better than one.'

'You've got this all planned out, haven't you?'

'Yep. Reckon it can work.' He smiles, moves to place his hand on my arm.

I pull away. 'In case you've forgotten. I can't even sing anymore. And I need a friend, not a boyfriend. And I definitely don't need to go from being controlled by Maestro to being controlled by you.'

'I'm trying to help. Not control you.'

'I'm not your ticket out of home or your puppet.' I slam his door shut and walk around to the driver's side. 'I'm not ready to be pushed into anything. I need some solid ground to stand on before I make decisions about the future.'

'Well then I'll get you enough money so you can move out by yourself. Jeez. I want to help.'

'Then I'd owe you. I'm sick of owing people. My whole life I thought I owed Mum because my birth caused her death. I thought I owed Savannah for taking away her mother. And Maestro for taking his wife and because he never blamed me for it. Now, none of that's true and I never want to owe anyone anything. Except I'm fighting the feeling that I owe Maestro – he stayed when she didn't. And he's not even . . .' Unable to say the dad word, I get into the car and yank off the hand break.

Jacob knocks on the window. 'I'm sorry. I didn't mean to be pushy,' he shouts, as Pink sings about learning to love again. But the song's wrong. I can never learn to love Maestro again.

25

Jacob

I usually shower after 8 am to be sure Mum and Dad have left for work. Today, when I head for the kitchen, the clattering of dishes makes me wonder how Maria's back so soon. Dex had called to say the hospital was keeping her in overnight and that she was stable, but she's only been home one full day now. But it's not Maria in the kitchen.

'Jacob. How are you?' Mum air kisses me on both cheeks, hands waving on either side of me because they're sticky from the peach she's slicing. 'I'm running late, so I can't stop,' she continues. 'Maria's just delivered some bad news though.'

'Is she okay?'

'She sounded fine on the phone. But she's leaving us just before Christmas.'

I first think of Dex, and how we'll have to find another way to fit in his vocal training, and then I wonder how it'll feel without Maria in the house, eight till seven, six days a week. We may not talk much, but she's been a presence in this house more consistently than my parents have, since I was five.

An off-key note repeats inside my skull while I let that sink in.

It was Maria who made me chicken noodle soup when I was sick and home from school. Maria who cleaned up the sand I traipsed into the house after surfing so I wouldn't get in trouble. Maria who helped me search for Coda when he got lost. Maria who called my school to excuse me after finding me with a hangover – my first bender. She cleaned up the vomit next to my bed too. She never complained to the parentals. And even though she's been sick lately, in thirteen years she's always turned up, bar a handful of days. I suddenly wonder who babysat Dex when he was a little kid. While Maria taught me how to tie my shoelaces, who was feeding her toddler?

'She's not well enough to work,' adds Mum. 'I had no idea but she's had diabetes for years and it's taken a turn for the worse. She's going back to Italy.'

The glass I'm reaching for in the cupboard slips from my fingers. I save it from falling. It's hard to know if the stomach plunging to the floor feeling is because I'm sad for Dex, or for myself; I can't imagine my afternoons without him.

'It's a real pain. I don't have time for this.' Mum waves a piece of paper at me. 'But she's recommended some other people to replace her.'

'Don't s'pose being too sick to work is much fun for Maria and Dex either.'

'Who's Dex?'

I snort. Just the kid who cleans your house after school without pay to help his sick mum keep her job. But then why would she know who he is, and that Maria even has a son, when she barely knows what her own son is up to?

'I remember. Dexter her son? Anyway, we'll have someone in her shoes soon enough. Don't worry.'

Mum talks like she's replacing a lightbulb in one of her crystal chandeliers – inconvenient, a waste of her time, but easily done.

My appetite takes a hike. 'I'm not worried, Mum. It's not like I need the housekeeper to parent me anymore.'

Mum tuts and slips a slice of peach into her mouth. I slam the cupboard door and make for the garden. 'Going surfing.'

For the second time today.

♫

I get as far as the back stairs before I stop and have to sit down. I push my face into my hands.

'I've got something to tell you.'

Dex is at the gate. Instead of bounding across the lawn, he slopes, dragging his feet.

'I heard. You're going back to Italy.'

'Yep. As soon as Mamma has enough money.' Dex drops to the grass and pulls off his trainers, laces still untied. He chucks them. One. Two. 'I've tried to talk her out of it, I said I'd get a job and take care of her because she can't work here much longer. Her angina is becoming unstable, and she shouldn't exert herself. She might need an operation or she could have a heart attack. But she wants me to finish school plus her brother will help her in Italy. Except my singing –' He breaks off and blinks, then stands. 'My dreams –'

'You can carry on singing in Italy, right?' Even saying 'Italy' feels like a part of me got wrenched through the space between each bone of my rib cage.

Dex is leaving. Forever.

'Never happen.' Dex shakes his head. 'My uncles will turn me into an up-myself bishop or have me working in the bakery forever. I want to get a recording contract. I don't want flour in my hair, flour up my butt. My uncles already think I'm *anormale* and that prayer and hard work will chase the bad out of me.'

'What bad?'

He turns in a small circle, mouth pursed. 'I mean you might've guessed, and it's cool. I'm not ashamed of who I am. I just wonder if it'll stop me being a pop singer. That's why I don't talk about it.'

'If what will stop you?'

'Me being gay.' He casually lays his words between us like he's simply shaking off a beach towel; we both stare at the sand that's left behind on the floor. I meet him head on when I feel his glare on me.

'Right.' I don't feel surprised somehow, more like something had been tickling at me for a while and I'd vaguely wondered what it was, but now it suddenly stops tickling.

Hands on hips, Dex draws himself taller. 'Say something.'

'I don't know what to say. I mean, of course being gay won't stop you being a pop star.'

I assess Dex. The reality that he's gay, the reality of what hard work really looks like and what an uphill battle he has ahead of him is as in my face as someone spoiling for a fight. No wonder Dex looks at me like I'm an idiot when I complain about my life. He's fifteen and yet it's like he's lived two lifetimes, juggling school and work, caring for his mum and worrying about money, having to come out and deal with all that. He's not running from any of it. I'm blown away by how brave he is. Compared to him, I'm a complete coward.

'I came out like eight months ago. That's all behind me. It was a relief. I hated the pretending. The lying. Now I hang out with other gay kids. I have a boyfriend, even if he hasn't come out yet. I go to PROUD community meetings and hang out in gaybourhoods. I'm being me for the first time.'

'When did you realise you were gay?'

'About the time I sat on Santa's knee and asked for Barbie's Ultimate Kitchen for Christmas.' We roar with laughter so hard I have to stand too.

'You really don't want to go to Italy?' I ask.

Dex wipes away tears – of laughter, I hope. 'No way. My life will be a living death. My dreams of being a pop star will be over. But what choice do I have? Mamma has to come first. Time to put on my big-boy pants and get on with it.'

The urge to punch something rushes through me. 'What can I do? Is there a way to stay?'

Dex toes the grass. 'The demos we've been recording. Can we submit them to some labels? Like now?' His expression shouts with hope, as if I can magically make wishes come true. But will Astrid agree? I'll have to convince her. This is life or death for Dex.

'Sure.' I put my hand up for a high-five. 'And you'll be famous and then Maria can be a lady who lunches and you can buy all the insulin your mamma needs and take her to the best doctors. No need for your uncle's help.'

'Sounds perfect. Mamma wants to be "home" for Christmas. Can we make that happen before then?' Our high-five is more of a brush than a slap because Christmas is only about ten weeks away. We turn toward the studio.

I beeline for the fridge, craving a beer, then divert myself to the piano instead. Suddenly, compared to Dex's problems, keeping my promise not to drink anymore isn't exactly hard.

'And tomorrow,' I say, 'I'm gonna come help you clean up at the main house, so we have more time to practise and record stuff. No arguments.'

26

Astrid

'This sucks,' growls Jacob down the phone. He's Facetimed me from his studio and I hear him slam a chord on the piano. Even though his cast's been off awhile, he's annoyed he can't play accurately yet. 'Listen to this,' he continues.

I discard the *La Bohème* script and lie back in the cushions on my bed as he balances the phone on the piano's music rack. I'm surprised to discover he's a perfectionist.

The last couple of times we met up to work with Dex were a little awkward. But with Dex clowning around, from practising his walk down the red carpet in Hollywood to setting teabags on fire, and our joint goal of putting together something good enough to record, Jacob and I have slipped back into our friendship. Without Dex, there'd be no way I could hang out with Jacob. There'd also be no chance of getting a recording contract and being a songwriter. Even if it feels a little stilted, Jacob and Dex are all I've got. The only real family I have are thousands of miles away in London.

Today, Maestro isn't teaching at the Con so he wants to do some careful voice training with me. And Dex is late to the studio. At least Jacob called me and not Harper to pass the time.

The other day when his phone rang, I went to answer the call for him. It was Harper-with-a-love-heart-next-to-her-name. I showed him the screen, but he'd shaken his head no. I rejected the call, forcing myself to accept the reality – although Jacob's taken down the photos of Harper, she's still a part of his life.

Like Maestro is still part of my life, even though he's not my dad.

I'm angry with him for the lies and right now that's throttling my love for him. If I were a little older, I'd give more serious thought to leaving home. But even then, it's been just the two of us for so long. I have no family or friends to live with. I've never had a job. How would I support myself? But it's hard to stay, treating each other as father and daughter when we know that's not true anymore.

Jacob gives up on the piano, picks up the phone again. 'See?' He strides over to the fridge. I hear it open, then slam shut. 'I've got something to tell you,' adds Jacob, his voice now small.

Anxiety pricks at my skin like I ran through a rose bush.

'Dex –' Jacob paces around the Lego sofa. 'Something happened. I should fill you in.'

He explains about Dex leaving for Italy and about him being gay and how his family thinks he's abnormal and the bishop uncle in Italy will 'fix' him. I want to find Dex and hug him and hug him.

'The way I see it, we have ten weeks to get you and him signed with a label,' says Jacob. 'Then he would earn some money and he could convince Maria to stay.' He groans. 'There has to be a way.'

'But we're not ready. The songs aren't right yet.'

'Astrid, they are. I promise you. You have to let them go and just take that risk. What's the worst that can happen?'

Fear swarms through me. But if I don't do this, it's going to affect Dex too. 'How likely is it that he'll get signed up so fast?'

Jacob's teeth bite down on his bottom lip. 'If he doesn't, Dex goes back to Italy and never sings again – unless it's "Here I am, Lord", which is awesome, I'm sure, but it's a song for Dexter De Brun, not Dex Brown.'

'Dex Brown?'

Jacob shrugs. 'He once told me Dexter De Brun isn't his idea of a name for a pop star and his surname means Brown. His true self is Dex Brown, don't you think?'

'I love it.'

'I can't improve on Astrid Bell.' His smile, though hesitant, cradles me. A ribbon of heat curls through my body and an Instapic of our two kisses rushes at me. Jacob adds, 'This is for you as much as for Dex.'

I put aside the phone, giving him a view of my bedroom ceiling, and curl into a ball, clutching at my shins. 'It sounds as if you're going to miss Dex.'

'It's stupid, but he's become like a brother to me. He used to be this snotty little kid on the sofa who I avoided. But he's brave and talented and even though he's had to fight for everything he has, he's still cheerful and hopeful. I don't know how he does it. I totally respect him. I won't let Dex lose his dreams. Dex *needs* this.' Jacob's voice cracks. 'He hasn't got anyone else watching out for him. No-one in his corner. You and I have become his family and I can't let him down.' He flexes his jaw side to side. 'It's a question of honour.'

It's a question of who Jacob is.

'Fine. Send the demos,' I say. 'Let's see if they get to live on.'

21

Jacob

A week later, I'm coming off the high from surfing when I spot Astrid sitting alone on the beach, her knees pulled into her chest. It's nearing the end of October but she's wearing jeans and a jumper. She lays her cheek on her knees. Definitely crying not sunbaking.

More alarmed than I let on, I move to sit next to her, setting the board beside us. She turns to me and her blotchy features scrunch as she flings her arms around me, sobbing into my neck.

'Maestro's pulled me out of the festival in San Francisco,' she howls. 'My nightmares have come true. I was ungrateful for my voice and wished I didn't have it. And now it's gone.'

I stroke her hair and keep squeezing her to me, never wanting her to let go. 'It's not even five weeks since the accident.'

'I'm going to be exactly like my mum, after all. I'll never sing again.'

'That's not going to happen. It's a different medical condition. And whatever happens, you've got your songwriting.'

'No!' She struggles to her feet, her face puffy. 'I'm a singer first. Writer second. I know it now. Sometimes you need to lose something before you realise how much it means to you.'

My watch alarm goes off, reminding me Maestro's about to arrive at the studio for my lesson. 'Maestro time,' I explain. 'I can call and cancel.'

She hunts for something in my features, bottom lip trembling. But then she pulls herself up by invisible strings. 'No. Don't. I'll see you this afternoon.'

This girl's tougher than a drum claw hook.

♫

Doc and his cape whirl into the studio like he's the Phantom of the Opera. The usual calm that surrounds him has gone and I almost check behind him to confirm he's not being followed by ghouls and vampires. I get what Astrid means when she says his eccentric behaviour's getting worse. As usual, he glances around to make sure I'm keeping to rule one: a tidy studio. I suppose he's also on a quest for evidence – beer bottles, caps, used glasses.

'Why were you and Astrid at the beach earlier?' he demands. I realise he was searching for Astrid in my studio, not empty bottles.

'What, no *Good morning, Jacob*? No *buongiorno*?'

He pinches the bridge of his nose. 'Well?'

Keeping my tone smooth, I reply, 'I was surfing. We bumped into each other.'

The doc's eyes convert into thin coin slots. 'She was upset when she left the house.'

'Were you *following* her?'

'I know she won't listen to me, but I'd appreciate it if you didn't distract her.' The doc swaps his satchel from one hand to the other.

I shoot for the fridge. 'Juice?'

He slams his music satchel on the coffee table with enough force that the table moves a finger-length across the carpet. 'She's never been in a – relationship. Perhaps tell her you're busy with your rehearsals for the Con.'

'Whoa! Hold on, Doc.' It's as though my spending time with Astrid is his kryptonite. 'There's nothing going on. But don't you think she might need a friend right now? She needed to talk to someone and I was there.'

He presses his lips together. 'She's hardly talking to me at all these days.'

It's like I'm surfing into a wave that's too big to handle. I need to bail. 'We're not doing anything, promise.'

He holds up a defensive arm and grimaces. 'I need you to stop talking. I didn't want to have to remind you, but if you don't keep it platonic, our arrangement is over and you can find your own way into the Con next month.'

'You're threatening me?'

'Not at all. That was our deal, was it not? Astrid may not wish to listen to me. But you, I'm afraid, have no choice unless you don't want me as your voice coach.'

'And you think that keeping me and Astrid apart will mean you don't lose her? You know her having a boyfriend doesn't mean you lose her, right? Or is it your influence over her you're afraid of losing?'

The doc digs around in his cracked leather case. 'To become a star, she must remain focused. It's about having the right mindset.'

'We're just friends, Doc. No need to get your knickers in a twist.'

Astrid's right. The doc who wanted to help me is still there, the one who gave me extra lessons and invited me to Vienna, underneath that cloak maybe. But there's something smouldering inside him and I'm getting a strong whiff of desperation.

♫

By the end of the first week of November, we've received two rejections from music labels out of five submissions. I feel like a too-tightly strung violin. Astrid picks dejectedly at her fingernails. But Dex is taking it worst of all.

'One label even asked us to send in any new stuff,' I say, fake positive.

'There's a lot of luck involved,' adds Astrid.

'Buh. We're running out of time.' Dex is pacing the room. He punches a fist into his palm. 'Can we send out more – now?'

'We can send out another round to smaller labels,' I say.

Dex searches for his shoes. 'I gotta get out of here. I'm too pissed off to sing.'

'That's not how a star behaves.' I snag the back of his T-shirt. 'Put your feelings into your music.' Dex wrenches himself free, but trips over his own laces. I stifle a laugh and let him wrestle to his feet by himself. 'This is not all about you, Dex. I know it's important to you, but it's also about Astrid. She needs this too.'

'I know I can be uptight. But the one lesson I've learnt is no one else is gonna make my life happen how I want it. No one else is gonna watch out for me. Losing my pa, coming out, looking after Mamma, working at this –' He waves his arms around the studio, face reddening.

Seeing Dex's confidence slip, his flippant attitude crumble – it's almost too much. A ball of cottonwool lodges in my throat.

'But you're right. Like Gerry and the Pacemakers said,' adds Dex, 'I must hold my head up until the end of the storm, I have to have hope. I have to walk on.'

I swallow and turn toward the piano. 'I get it, Dex. So let's keep at it. Maybe we can post a video of you singing on YouTube. Loads of people have gained a fan base that way.'

'Great idea,' says Astrid. 'We can set it all up in Jacob's studio – special lighting, new clothes. Then your – our – demo might get more attention.'

I can't believe Astrid's finally happy to let her songs go out into the world. 'And we can use SoundCloud too.'

'Mamma would freak. The internet scares her. She thinks someone's going to come and steal me or something.'

'She would never see it,' I say. 'We'll film you and build your accounts from here.' Dex considers this and Astrid runs her fingers through his coif. He pushes his head into her palm like a pussycat. I pull up the Uber Eats app. 'We're gonna need pizza. This could take a while.'

'Nothing spicy for me thanks. Not good for the throat,' Astrid says.

'Don't worry. I'll order the slippery elm and pineapple one – with extra spinach.'

'If there's one that comes with perfect vocal cords, I'll take that.' Astrid suddenly becomes teary and the energy slips out of the room.

It's been a fortnight since she pulled out of San Francisco, and every day she's seemed more worried. I go to sling an arm around her, but she turns away.

'It'll be okay,' I say to her back, bracing for the kick of rejection.

Dex slaps his thigh. 'You're like Amish kids waiting for Rumspringa. I don't get why you don't go for it.'

'Rumspringa?' asks Astrid.

'They slammed it at my church. It's when the Amish teenagers do whatever they want – wear the clothes they like, go out and see the world, hang free, have sex, whatever, before they decide whether to be baptised. I think about it all the time, but I don't get to choose. I'm trapped in my life. But you're not. You have choices. Just kiss and get over it, already. And no vegetables on my pizza – my teeth repel them.'

I peer over Dex at Astrid. She sags into the Lego sofa and I recognise that until she works out how to trust her father again, and until she finds her voice, I'm on the back-burner.

28

Astrid

I thought my heart was already jam-packed with sad until Jacob told me some of the labels had rejected my songs. Apparently sad can become something darker and heavier and desperate. For days my stomach churns; maybe I really do want to be a songwriter. Until now, it's seemed like more of a hobby. Or perhaps that's what I told myself because I didn't think it was possible. It would give me some independence from Maestro if we got a recording contract.

Neither Maestro nor I have a clue how to exist under the same roof. When he walks into a room, I can't stay and walk out. When he speaks my body stiffens and it's all I can do not to snap back, even if he's only asking what I want for breakfast. I avoid meals with him and wait until he leaves the house before I come out of my bedroom. We're two separate instruments co-existing on opposite ends of the same orchestra. I wish I could talk to Kara about everything – Jacob's got his own parent issues and I keep thinking that at least he *has* parents.

The only part of our life we have continued is the voice training. Neither of us can let that go. Maestro carefully tests my voice every day, never pushing, and we behave like student and teacher, not father and daughter. For now, I play the role like I'm a character in an opera, but I know I won't be able to for long. And that's why I ask for his help, though he has no idea it could lead to me finding a way to leave home. I tell him how Jacob's been helping Dex. I don't say I wrote the songs, but that Dex composes and sings them.

'But now Dex needs some help getting the demo to labels,' I say, after a particularly good lesson. 'You've got connections in the music industry. Maybe not major labels, but some smaller ones. Maybe you know who to ask about broadcasting his demo online.'

'I could potentially ask colleagues for advice. They may post the demo if it's any good.'

'And you have hundreds of successful past and current students who might re-post it or host the demo on their websites or YouTube channels?'

Maestro closes the piano and stands. 'Why do you want to help this boy?'

'He's fifteen and talented. He's a nice kid. Why wouldn't I? Why wouldn't you?'

'I'd have to hear the demo first. I can't make any promises.' From the grimace on his face, I realise he isn't going to give me my ticket out of home.

♫

A week after Jacob sends the second round of demos, Maestro and I stand side by side examining the view through the floor-to-ceiling windows while we wait for Jacob to join us in the Utzon room of the Sydney Opera House. My range has improved lately, the pitch becoming steady, the sound of straining gone, but I hadn't dared to hope.

Until now: my vocal cords have healed and my voice is back.

Maestro's ecstatic, and he's in one of his impulsive moods. He called in a favour from a friend in the industry so we could have our voice lesson in this amazing room. They usually do more intimate chamber music performances here.

Once upon a time, carrying news like this, Maestro and I would've stood arm in arm, grinning at each other until our mouths ached. But almost two months after The Truth we're struggling to find our way out of the web of lies we were living in. The problem is that many of the repercussions of Maestro's lie cannot be undone. There is no fix.

However, with today's news I'm finally sure: I want to become a soprano. With the choice almost taken away from me, I've learnt it's something I want to do for *me*. Maybe now that I know I want this, I won't suffer from stage fright. Nerves scatter through me, but this time they're more like stardust than splinters.

'I have a question.' My voice is no-nonsense. This is how I talk to Maestro these days; a robot with no emotions. Maestro mostly wears his voice-coach mask, although the pleading apology is in every expression. Like me, he doesn't know what to say anymore because there's nothing left to be said except sorry. Which he's repeated often. But sorry doesn't fix anything. I've no doubt if I went to him for a hug, I'd get one, but until I do, he's letting me take the lead – which has to be a first.

'Ask away.' He squints at the Harbour Bridge.

It's a question I've been too afraid to ask; I'm not sure how much more truth I can handle. But I have to be braver now. 'Can you tell me who my – my biological father . . .'

Maestro charts the scuff marks on the floor with his foot. 'Your mother refused to tell me more than he was a renowned opera singer.'

My stomach balls in on itself. 'Did he know – about me?'

'I think so.'

'So Mum came back to you and Savannah because he didn't want me either.'

'But *I* wanted you, Astrid. I persuaded her to keep you.'

His words are a new truth that colours and lightens the old truth, like mixing white paint with black to turn it grey. None of this is black and white. Even before I was born, Maestro wanted me. And then after Mum left, he still wanted me. He didn't abandon me when Mum left, or give me up after Savannah died. He didn't go back to a stage career, but instead, stayed to bring me up even though I wasn't his blood. And he proved that he wanted me every day of our lives for seventeen years. And by the hope on his face now, he still wants me. He still loves me.

We spin round in unison at the sound of Jacob entering

the room. He's wearing boardies and a T-shirt, both of which still appear damp. He ogles the fourteen-metre tapestry along one wall, and then me. I'm wearing a new fitted red cotton dress pinched at the waist, yet he makes me feel like I'm naked. A blush steams up my neck and into my cheeks.

'Jeez. Fancy place.' Jacob steps further into the room and takes in the harbour views. 'Guess you won the lottery.'

'I said two months and I was right,' shouts Maestro, arms flung wide.

'My full range is back,' I explain.

Jacob backslaps Maestro before hugging me. 'I always knew it'd work out,' Jacob whispers. We both hold on a little too long before letting go.

'Astrid wants to sing with you today,' says Maestro. He doesn't explain that I'd refused to come here without inviting Jacob to share my lesson.

'What can I say?' quips Jacob. 'I've had to switch off my phone. All the sopranos want me as their partner.' His cheeky expression tickles my belly.

Maestro accompanies us on the grand piano in the centre of the rectangular room and has us warm-up for longer than usual, like he's afraid to push into my upper register. I start to think this is going to be a washout session when he holds up the score for *Phantom of the Opera*.

'I have a new challenge for you. It will build the foundations on your technique, Jacob, while we decide what style of singer you're to be.'

Maestro plays the intro to 'All I Ask of You' and Jacob slips into the first few lines. They're right in his safe range.

'Good,' says Maestro. 'Now focus the sound in your chest. Imagine it there. Isolate the muscle.' Jacob's voice builds. It's smooth and divine. That's the right word. And when I join him I examine how my voice shapes and holds each note, if it's transitioning without strain, and after a while I trust it's healed and let it climb higher into the upper register.

Jacob grins at me and we almost miss our next cue. Our voices tangle like they're holding hands and it's as if we're bubbled inside a snow globe and everything else remains on the outside. But I'm not prepared for the intensity in Jacob's expression when he sings to me. It's as though he's kissing me, running his fingers through my hair, up my back, from across the metre between us. And I don't want him to stop.

I've sung duets before, but my body has never tingled like his voice has entered my bloodstream. We sing the final bars and I know if I don't step away as soon as the last note ends, I'll kiss him so passionately Maestro will dig a basement under our house and lock me up forever.

Worse, I might let Jacob into my heart.

29

Jacob

Once we've finished singing 'All I Ask of You', Astrid goes home. The doc doesn't want her to overdo things and with two weeks until the Con audition, he and I have a long session planned.

I fight against how empty I feel whenever Astrid leaves, but it's worse than ever today. Singing that song – the gravitas of opera, the history behind it, again overwhelmed me. I let my emotions about the boys out, and I allowed them to weave into my voice. The memories are still tough to think about, but as I recalled each one, I thought about them in a positive way, rather than hiding from them. It felt like a release. And when I sang about sharing our love, I thought of Harper. But only for a split second; it felt okay that she's now in the past. Instead, Astrid burst into my head. I couldn't stop myself smiling at her like a lunatic.

I hadn't wanted the song to stop, but when it did, I struggled to pull myself out of my head, and out of the song. That never happened when I sang with Purple Daze.

Doc ponders Astrid's retreating figure then swivels to address me. 'Son.' He stands and rests a hand on my arm.

'Your voice is sublime. You sing from somewhere deep inside you.' His smile grows. 'And then when you add that depth of emotion it's – there are no words. You will sing and others will be unable to stop themselves from staying to listen and *feel* and get lost in the music you sing. As I do. You have a rare talent.'

I recall how people stared at me with wonder in Vienna, how I knew then that my voice had the power to affect people – make them cry with happiness, or distract them from whatever they needed rescuing from in their life, and maybe Doc just confirmed that.

'Careful, Doc. I might get a big head.'

'Funny you should say that. When you sing, you are truly humble. Vulnerable. You wear your heart on your sleeve. It's appealing. Charming. I noticed it in Vienna. How did singing the song feel today?'

'Hard to describe.' I can't expand. Because it's the one feeling that *is* forbidden – I'm in love with his daughter.

'To not nurture that talent would be against the laws of nature. It's possibly the only reason I'm still coaching you, even though you haven't severed ties with Astrid as per our agreement.'

'Come on, Doc. With everything Astrid's going through, what kind of person would push her away for self-gain?'

The doc ponders me and nods. 'You're a surprising package, Jacob Skalicky.'

For the next couple hours, the doc feels no shame in pulling apart my voice, my technique, my breathing. And then he puts it all back together again. 'Push down as if you're going to the toilet' and 'relax the soft palate'. He has me sing with a pencil between my teeth to train the sound to go in a forward direction. He breaks down musical phrases note by note, stopping to perfect every tone. By the end of the lesson we've made it through one page of music. But it's perfect.

'Great job today,' he says, 'Except I'm running late. Could you pack up my music while I go to the bathroom? And the form you need to declare your chosen music for the Con is in my briefcase.' Doc points to his case as he strides to the toilet. 'You need to sign it.'

I collect the sheet music, remembering the things I learnt. We've chosen the audition songs and it's good to have the decision made. I slide the music into his satchel and open his briefcase, rummaging for a form with the Con letterhead. I'm pretty impressed to find one with the letterhead from the Metropolitan Opera House in New York City. As I push it aside, I catch sight of my name on the letter – and Astrid's. I scan it. An unexpected opening in 'An Evening with Yolanda Gustav'. We've both been invited to sing after Yolanda was honoured to witness our magical performance in Vienna. I clench the letter, check and re-check the wording. The event's to be *televised.* Hardly able to breathe, I confirm the date on the letter – two weeks ago.

'You found it.' Doc gestures to the paper I'm holding.

'No. But I did find this.' With a rush of anger I shove the letter at him then turn and stride toward the piano.

'Jacob, did you see the date of the event? It's the same day as your Con audition. Besides, it's opera, not popera.'

I slam my fist on the piano. 'What happened to waiting to decide what sort of singer I am? You should've told me. Given me the choice.'

'I didn't think you'd – your audition. I spoke to your dad and he agreed.'

'What the hell would *he* know?' I spin around and stop myself getting right in the doc's face. 'Why would you ask *him*?'

'I have an obligation to your father. He contracted me to get you into the Con. I have to respect that commitment.'

'What about your obligation to me?'

'I *was* thinking of that. And you similarly want to get into the Con.'

'Not over something like this. I mean it's *Yolanda Gustav*. There's no better soprano alive today. You said yourself that performing live gets you places. And this is the frigging Met! *And* it's being televised – millions will see it.' I clench my fists and ram them under my armpits. 'My dad wants me in the Con because it's this set, safe path. Like getting a uni degree. He needs me to have a certificate to prove something before he'll support me. He doesn't want me wandering the globe without a goal, but he doesn't understand the music world. *You* do. This is huge. It could launch a career. How could you do this to me?'

Doc Bell rubs his forehead. 'I'm sorry, Jacob. I did what I thought was right.'

‘What about Astrid? She’ll be fuming about this.’ All I can hear are my unhinged breaths.

‘She’s going to attend,’ he finally says. ‘I accepted the invitation on her behalf. I planned to tell her this evening, now we’re sure she’s better.’

It’s like a tidal wave crashed inside my brain; I can’t take it in. Has the doc betrayed me?

‘She has no engagements and she needs to get back into the opera scene. There is no reason for her *not* to attend.’

Even though two weeks ago he couldn’t have predicted her voice would be better.

His words rattle inside my head like coins inside a tin money box.

‘No. This isn’t happening.’ I glare at the concrete beams above us. Astrid said something about them being part of the structural support beams of the Opera House. Right now, every kilo of their weight crushes me. With a final scowl at Dr Bell, I leave, determined to never see him again.

♫

It always seems to happen overnight. The Purple Woods have woken up and as the wind gusts through the trees, flowers drift in the air and paint the ground. A wave of longing for the summers of long ago washes through me.

When I get to the river I kick at the rocks and fling stones into the water until my arm aches. This time I remember my hands and don't punch anything, though the effort is like pushing back at a charging bull.

Jeez, I need a drink.

I thought Doc understood me. But he's been running my life as much as he has Astrid's.

A couple of beers.

No-one will ever find out. I'll chuck the bottles.

If I start drinking, I won't stop.

I take deep breaths of sky then park myself on a rock that juts out into the rushing river. The trees whisper. Blossoms rain from the trees. Some fall into the river and are carried downstream. That's me – drifting down a river in a direction I don't want to go. Harper once asked me if it'd be as easy to follow my musical dreams if the studio burnt down. I argued I'd find a way. But I was lying to myself. Because I'm still here, living off my parents when they're making me unhappy and forcing me to compromise my future. Does the studio have to burn down before I get off my arse and act?

I think back to Purple Daze's last gig – how the room was chock-full of screaming girls reaching out for me as I sang. How they'd overdone the stage fog. How I stood in the middle of the boards, my voice magically pairing with the instruments and the backing from the boys; the feeling of belonging and mattering to others. Maybe I'll form a new band.

But that future seems as though it's part of someone else's life.

Pushing to my feet I wander along the riverbank, in the opposite direction to the grog. Venus and Adagio, the Hunters' dogs, have sniffed me out and now jostle at me. The house-sitter must've let them out. I bend to hug them. They strain to lick me to death before scampering ahead, circling back now and again. I follow them, listing pros and cons of each of my possible futures; entering competitions like Astrid, submitting demos to music labels. Time blurs.

Each option has a complication, but everything boils down to whether I'm brave enough to chase my dreams without the advantages my parents give me. Dex doesn't have a music studio. He has no money, no support, no trained voice coach, but he's not letting that stop him. Holy coif. I need to suck it up.

Eventually, abandoned by the dogs, I return to the Mother Tree. Footsteps approach and I remember that Dex was coming over this afternoon. But it's not Dex who emerges from between the purple blooms.

It's Astrid.

A flash of rage rifles through me. 'Did he tell you?'

'He told me.'

'He stuck a knife in my back in the worst way. So did my parents.' My body heaves with fury.

'I've told him I'm not doing it either.'

'What? No! Why?'

'It's time to spell out that he can't keep controlling me. And also to show my support for you.' She walks toward the

Mother Tree. Her back to me, she adds, 'He's done it to keep us apart. And I won't let him. He needs to know that.'

I search for the right words. She can't let this opportunity go. Long seconds float away with the blossoms.

'And because I'm afraid,' she adds, turning to lean on the tree. Her face is clotted with worry. 'You won't be there to rescue me if I freeze at the Met.'

'I can't always be there. You have to confront your fear at some point.'

'But this is live at *the Met*. I'm not ready to test myself there.'

'You've always pressured yourself to live your mum's dream or please Maestro. That's where the nerves come from. Sing for yourself, rather than them, and the nerves will go. I'm sure of it.'

'I could say the same of you with Dex. You're living your dream through him.'

'It's not the same. I'm helping Dex chase his dream and it's the one pure thing I've ever done. There's no reward, no prize, no recognition. It's untainted by anything else in my life.'

'But you *are* going to the Con for your parents.' She gives me the truth as matter-of-factly as chucking stones in the river. I feel the sting of each one.

I dig my bare heel into the earth, bouncing it until a dint appears in the ground. 'And that's why I'm pulling out of the audition.'

'I didn't mean for you to pull out.' Her clipped voice softens. 'I'm simply saying we all do things to please others.'

'And you're right. I've spent my whole life trying to please my parents. It's got me nowhere. I need to be who I am, and stop walking in some fictional son's shoes. If it means everyone abandons me, I'll survive.'

I'm staggered I said that out loud. Life is like surfing a barrel: just when you think you've predicted the wave, set it up, drawn the right line, and you're gunning through it with laughter busting inside your chest, it closes down on you and you're crushed into a sandbar. The thing is, my best barrels have always been waves I thought I wasn't going to make – the ones where I all but shut my eyes and tucked in at the last minute.

'What will you do instead then?' Astrid's words break into my thoughts. She's leaning against the Mother Tree, her white cotton dress clinging to her body.

I force my attention up into the treetops. 'I'm not sure yet. But as Dex would say, it's time to put on my big-boy pants.' Having made that declaration out loud, I feel stronger. It's like I've been a sand sculpture on the beach for years now, and every day the wind, life, someone, blew pieces of me away. But now I'm solid. I'm concrete. I'm defined.

'Dex will practise by himself today,' says Astrid. 'I saw him when I arrived. He told me you might be here.'

I find a small smile. 'Thanks.' But I feel bad for letting down Dex. I'll make it up to him.

Astrid's fingers play an imaginary piano tune on the branch beside her. 'Maestro said he doesn't want you distracting me. I suspect what that really means is that he doesn't want you influencing me. He still wants to manipulate me,' she says. 'And that might've been part of the reason for his decision about the Met. I think he believes you're encouraging my songwriting, which he's dead against. Apparently, my focus is off. He's like your typical stage mum times a thousand. And he's also my voice coach, manager and agent. He manages every part of my life.'

The setting sun halos her body, giving her a nymph-like effect. A crazy need to hold her bowls through my veins. I realise that no matter how many times I get dumped by that barrel, I keep going back for more because the two seconds inside the wave, when the world slows down and muffles and the sun glints on the lip of the water, is so worth it.

I move closer to her. She pushes herself against the tree. 'What do *you* want, Astrid?'

'With my career? I'm still figuring it out.' Her long eyelashes flutter up to me and flick down to the ground again. 'Maestro said he's seen the way we look at each other. And he didn't think we'd see you again after you stormed off. I knew I couldn't bear that.'

My blood instantly heats up. She's killing me here, with her mixed signals. I've never met a girl who's this hard to read. I take a couple more steps and trail a finger from her collar bone to her elbow. The doc's out of my life as far as I'm concerned.

'I don't want to fight this anymore,' I say, shifting closer. We're inches part. I touch her cheek with the back of my fingers. She stirs, lifts her face at last. I can trace confusion, fear, longing. I move my mouth closer. 'I have no doubt I'm ready for this –' My lips brush hers as I speak and she lets her mouth open slightly. 'You have to know that now.'

I tense, knowing her next words could pin my heart to the tree behind us.

She replies by kissing me. Her arms pull me in and she presses herself against me, lets my fingertips skim down the side of her body to urge her hips into mine. Through her skimpy dress, she's so soft and open to me I have to remind myself to slow down; this is new to her.

We stay there for a long time, entwined under the Mother Tree, kissing and touching and feeling the cascading blossoms around us like silky snow. When I lift her onto the low branch to the side and sit next to her, my thighs aching from leaning into her, our rough footprints are framed in the purple floor of the woods.

I point at them and Astrid giggles and flushes, lips swollen with my kisses. I lean in and kiss them again. When I pull away she reaches up and catches a falling flower.

'Let's climb the tree,' I say. 'If you can get to the top, it's even more amazing. You've got to see it for yourself.'

She canvasses the branches above us. 'I'll give it a go.'

I guide her to the next branch up, remembering how I always tried to help Harper, to be a good guy, a gentleman, but she preferred to do it by herself. Not that she was wrong, but was there ever any space for me next to Harper?

Our progress is slow because every few branches I stop and kiss Astrid.

When we reach the final tricky part, I say, 'This is it. When you push up from this branch you'll be above the canopy. Get ready to be blown away. Not literally.'

Astrid struggles a little, but when she succeeds I hear her gasp. I push up next to her and our heads bob like buoys on a sea of purple.

'*Incroyable.* It's as if we stuck our heads inside a painting. Or we're somewhere over the rainbow. Alice stepping through the looking glass.' For the first time it's Astrid who leans in to kiss me. I smile into her mouth and kiss her back.

When the kiss ends, I don't want to spoil the mood with more talk of Maestro. I pluck some blossoms, let them dribble through my fingers. They'll shrivel away soon, their glory days brief.

Astrid's gaze sweeps across the purple haze of blossoms toward the horizon. 'Here's a truth for you.' She bites her bottom lip. 'I wish we'd made it to Cambridge. I wish I'd met my grandparents.'

A gust of wind blasts my hair behind me, and Astrid wobbles. I grip her arm to steady her and vow to get my shit together so that Astrid always has someone to rely on.

30

Astrid

Arm in arm we wander away from the Purple Woods under a sky smeared in shades of blush. Inside Jacob's studio, Dex has already left and Jacob makes cheese sandwiches because he skipped lunch and might gnaw off his leg. I play the piano and sing a new song I've written for Dex.

'He's gonna love it,' says Jacob when I swivel to him. He finishes the last of his sandwich and beckons me to sit with him on the Lego sofa. My heart curls and whirls, a renegade kite in my ribcage.

The ridiculously soft sofa pushes us into each other. My stomach pleasantly jolts. His mouth on mine, his hands on my skin, I want to let go and fall with him to wherever this is taking us.

It's as though I've been clinging to a sort of survival rule book all my life, living each day in a haze of what I should do and must do according to Maestro. Or according to my own rules of how to keep safe and not get hurt by risking anyone leaving me. I'm ready to throw away the book because what if *not* following those rules leads somewhere amazing – like when you're writing a song and play a B instead of a B flat by mistake, but discover it sounds so much better.

Jacob's mouth releases mine and moves to my neck, setting off a series of sparks through my body. With every glance and touch, I have to finally admit he wants to be with me, not Harper. I guess I already knew that after he took down her photos and started ignoring her calls and texts, but I wasn't ready to throw out the survival rule book yet.

Jacob moans and places tiny kisses across my collarbone. He pushes aside the strap of my dress. His tongue traces along where the strap was. Wanting him to never stop, but a little afraid too, my chest heaves. I arch into him, needing our skin to dissolve so I can merge into him, our bodies cupped together. When he pauses, his smile is lazy and sexy and a hot ache pulses through me. Shaking a little, I undo the top button on my dress, then the next and the next. He watches my fingers, my face, his gaze probing mine.

At the sound of three poundings on the studio door, Jacob springs off me like a sleeping cat in a sudden thunderstorm. I sit up, pulling at my dress to cover myself.

Jacob adjusts his shorts, staring at where the thuds came from. 'I locked it.'

'I'm glad.' I button my dress, suppress my panic. The pounding repeats.

'It's not going to be my parents. And Dex would've caught the bus by now.'

I swing my legs round, flatten the creases from my dress. 'It's Maestro.'

'You're ready for this?'

'Ready.'

Jacob unlocks the door and lugs it open.

'Is Astrid here?' Maestro booms. He strides into the studio and when he sees me, says, 'Astrid. I was worried.'

I smooth my hair. 'I needed to talk to Jacob.'

Maestro's expression sharpens as he inspects me, my dress.

Jacob stomps to the fridge, opens it, slams it shut, then leans on it. His leg jigs crazily.

'Why was the door locked?' demands Maestro. 'It's never locked.'

'I lock it at night,' says Jacob, pre-set.

Maestro draws tall. 'You're both lying.'

Jacob snorts. 'Coming from you?'

He points a finger at Jacob. 'Didn't I warn you what would happen if you broke the rules?'

Jacob cracks his neck. 'So what? You're no longer my voice coach.'

Maestro's glance slides from left to right. 'You're angry with me, Jacob. And I'm sorry for that. But I did what I thought was right. And to punish me by leading Astrid astray –'

'*Stop*. Jacob's not leading me astray.' My voice trembles. 'I *do* have a mind of my own. And you have to believe that if I'm with Jacob it doesn't mean I'll get distracted. You have to have more faith in me. You can't cage me forever.'

Maestro spins away. 'Trust me. I'm protecting you.' I can hear he's clenched his teeth as he speaks to the opposite wall.

'See what happened the last time you were *protecting* me. You had to lie for seventeen years. You have to stop protecting me, because it's just hurting me.'

Maestro swirls round. 'I did what I thought was best at the time. I may have made a mistake before, but I must continue to protect you now.'

I stop myself from saying he's not my real dad. 'But you're suffocating me. I have no life other than you and music. No friends. No activities outside of the house. Today I climbed a tree for the first time in forever. I want *out* of this cotton wool you've got me wrapped in.'

'The last time you climbed a tree wasn't a happy time.' His tone is low, taut. 'You were six and you jumped out of it and sprained your wrist.'

I remember the tree, the hospital, the disappointment that I had not died. 'And do you know *why* I jumped out of the tree?' I ask. Maestro is rigid as a double bass. 'Because I wanted to follow Savannah to heaven to ask Mum how she died because *you* wouldn't tell me. That's why there were all those "accidents".' I let loose my final round of ammunition. 'It's as though I'm your puppet. And you're strangling me. When I think back it all looks different now. Did you refuse invitations to rehearsal dinners because it was bad for my voice or bad for your big plan to "handle" me? Or were you hiding me from other people who might know the truth about Mum? Did you homeschool me for the same reasons? Perhaps Mum ran away because of *you*. Maybe you suffocated her. And she couldn't stand it and ran away from you. All this stuff about her being selfish and a bad mum, it could be more lies.'

He steps nearer, but I back away.

'I don't know what to think, Maestro. *Because I never got the chance to ask Mum*. You kept me in the dark because it suited you. It meant I went along with the idea of becoming an opera singer.' Finally, the words are out there.

'You have *always* wanted that too,' Maestro yells, the house fire blazing in his eyes.

I skip backwards, glance at Jacob through a puddle of tears.

Maestro looms over me. 'This is not the time to discuss every decision I've ever made. The issue is I do not want you singing together at the Met. Or anywhere else. You have a solo career, Astrid, and I do not want Jacob distracting you from it. Likewise, he cannot be distracted by you. He has his own path to follow.' Maestro turns to Jacob. 'I do want you to have a successful career, son. It'd be a tragedy for the musical world if you didn't. But Astrid is always my priority. She's relying on you too much, Jacob. She needs to learn to stand on the stage alone or her dreams of being a soprano are gone.'

'And she will.' Jacob's tone is as flat as a gravestone. 'The media in Austria loved us?'

Maestro mumbles, 'Yes. Very much.'

'I'm assuming you've rejected other offers on my behalf,' Jacob says.

Maestro swallows and contemplates the jostling storm clouds through the high windows. I get a sinking feeling and there's the discordant slide of a violin bow in my head as it screeches and descends.

Jacob kicks the fridge with the back of his heel. 'Where? When?' he demands.

'What does it matter now?' Maestro flicks his hand at Jacob.

I fold my arms. 'You've been so – manipulative. You've proved what I said. You have to let me go my own way. I need to make my own choices. It's *you* who I rely on too much. You've made sure of it. I do need to learn to stand on the stage alone, but more than that, I need to stand independently of you in life. I can't be your pawn any longer.'

'Don't be melodramatic. Of course you're not my pawn. But you are my daughter and right now you will do as you are told and meet me at home.'

'You kept other offers from Jacob.' I stare him down and don't move. 'There are things you're still not telling me about Mum, aren't there? You have to be honest, or we can never move forward.'

Maestro turns away and takes in a deep breath and I brace myself for more truths. But when he faces me again, he takes a few steps in my direction, his hand extended toward me.

I back away. 'And I'm *not* your daughter.'

My words instantly put out the fire in Maestro's eyes. They empty as he lowers them. More gently, I say, 'Go home, Maestro. I need to talk to Jacob. I need to – think. And make some decisions.'

'You are *not* staying here.' He fires up again.

‘She said to go home, *Maestro.*’ Jacob is red-faced, his lips curled into a snarl. ‘For once, do what’s right for her and not you.’

‘I *always* do what’s right for her. And Astrid, while you live under my roof –’

‘She can live under my roof,’ shouts Jacob, expression wolf-like. ‘Let her breathe without your help for *one* night. I’ll make sure she’s safe. She can sleep at the house and I’ll sleep here.’

When Maestro cuts to me, I fill my glare with ice. ‘Go home, Maestro.’

Fury slips from his face.

He wavers on the spot and rubs his eyes, like a child. It’s as though he’s jumping from one character role to another in an opera. ‘Please know that I was just protecting you from a truth that I believed was too terrible to hear. I can barely say the words. But I can see now that it’s the truth that’s important. Without it, I’ll lose you.’ Before I can say anything, Maestro adds, ‘The night Veronika left, I was performing in *La Traviata.* The nanny called in sick so Veronika had to take care of you both by herself. When I got home I found you strapped into your babyseat in the car. You were floppy and covered in vomit. And beside you was that note you found about people not being what they aren’t. Inside I discovered Savannah unconscious in her bed. Her breath smelt of wine. Veronika had a habit of letting your sister have a sip of her drinks to help Savannah go off to sleep. But this time, she’d let her drink too much. As I held you in the hospital while they tried to revive Savannah, I swore I'd never leave you alone with that monster again. I promised that if Savannah lived, I'd stop performing. You had overheated in the car and Savannah's blood pressure had dropped. She didn't have enough glucose reaching her brain. They told me you both could have died.'

Maestro reaches his arms out to me, but it's too much to take in. I step away.

'Please understand how I couldn't tell you this,' he says. 'I wanted you to feel loved by your mother. I wanted you to love her. So she had to be dead to you.'

I can't find a single word to say and drop my face into my hands.

'I'll go now, and let you decide what you want to do,' he adds. He sweeps across the room to pick up his satchel and stops to the side of Jacob. 'Look after her for me. Do the right thing by her.'

The veins of Jacob's neck protrude like tree roots under the surface of the ground. A nerve jumps in his temple. As soon as Maestro has left, Jacob's arms surround me. 'It's awful, I know. But at least you know everything now.'

I pull back. 'Do you believe him?'

Jacob takes my hand. 'Not even the doc would make that story up. I'm so sorry you had to hear it. People should have to pass a test to become parents. I don't know what to say. Except, even if he had good reason to lie to you, he still shouldn't have manipulated your life – and mine. He's tried to keep us apart, he's isolated you from friends your own age, he's made you sing when you wanted to write songs instead.'

'Plus he hid other offers you'd had, and the Met . . . And that day he said he'd told me the whole truth about Mum – he was still lying. How do I know *this* is the truth now?'

Jacob darts to the fridge for a Coke, opening the can fiercely. The tab snaps off and the drink fizzes over his fingers. He slugs it back, watching me over the can. Rage, confusion, frustration crowd each other for space.

'Neither of us can trust our parents. So we'll have to come up with our own plan.' His voice is rickety, his tone off. A misplayed chord.

I slump into the Lego sofa, let the air whoosh out of me. A terrible melancholy grips me. Maestro and I have sunk to the point where we can't even be under the same roof. I remember wandering under the Eiffel Tower together with *crepes au chocolat*; running for the Staten Island Ferry; learning to cook roast potatoes on a rainy day; waiting under an ancient bridge in Rome for the rain to pass; sharing the story of how he and Mum met and fell in love. Where did those versions of us go? Did they ever even exist?

Jacob glares through the walls. I sense the anger humming beneath his skin. 'What did you mean – you're not his daughter?'

I've not lied to Jacob, but I've kept the full truth from him. Like Maestro did to me. The thought of saying the words out loud – perhaps I understand a little what Maestro meant.

'I don't want to talk about it. But my mum had an – affair. Maestro's not – not.'

Jacob crushes the empty Coke can, discards it in a bin, then makes for the iPad. 'Time for a new soundtrack for our life. You seen the movie *Almost Famous?* Remember the scene on the bus when everyone's fed up and kinda lost and that song comes on the radio and they're all singing it and by the time they get to their destination, they're not lost.'

The intro to Elton John's 'Tiny Dancer' fills the studio.

'This is our new soundtrack?'

Jacob hurdles over the arm of the sofa, nearly landing on top of me. I giggle and his face is close, and for a few moments we gaze at each other.

He says, '*Somehow* we're going to get to the Met, we're going to sing together, and we're going to be famous.'

31

Jacob

'This has to work,' says Dex, as we watch his latest YouTube video over breakfast at a café. Breakfast is my way of making it up to him after I bailed on our session yesterday – he always seems half starved. 'We leave for Italy in five and a half weeks.'

In the video, the lights are low and Dex, wearing a red leather jacket I bought him and black nail polish I did not buy him, is doing his trick with the gas lighter and holding fire in his hand. Behind him, a line of fire seems to hover in midair thanks to a friend in the restaurant business letting Dex take apart the old gas fire from his pizzeria. The intro to 'A Forgettable Life' begins.

I check my phone, anxious to hear from Astrid. She went back home last night after we decided going home suited the plan we hatched to the beat of 'Tiny Dancer'. I nicknamed the plan Operation Rumspringa, and it's going to get us both to the Met, singing on stage together. Astrid will pretend that nothing's changed, and she and Maestro are going to the Met together, but in the meantime, we'll let Yolanda's team know that I'm able to make the performance after all, and we'll get my visa and travel stuff organised, including a new flight for Astrid. We plan to leave the day before Maestro had intended, so he can't stop her – or me – from going. And I won't tell my parents. They probably won't even notice I'm not in the country.

As if she'd read my mind, Astrid's text appears on my screen: *Never mind eggshells. Treading on broken glass over here. Told Maestro he can never ever lie to me again about anything.* Though her words are laced with humour, it can't be easy being in her shoes right now.

Dex peers at the text. 'What's she on about?'

I drop the phone into my lap and reach for the salt. 'She had a row with her dad.'

'At least she has a dad,' says Dex.

'Sometimes, parents don't make the right choices. Sometimes, we're better off without them.' I think of my own parents and renew my vow to strike out on my own, no matter how hard it might be.

We're almost finished watching the music video, where Dex is the embodiment of charm and charisma, when Astrid calls.

'How are we today?' she trills. And just as music can fill every corner of a room, the sound of her voice fills every niche in my heart.

'We're fine. Dex and I are doing Sunday brunch. But how are *you*?' I place the phone between us. 'We're at a café. You're on speaker phone.'

'We've been watching the YouTube video,' says Dex. 'Your songs are – I can't even find the words. I might fall in love with this girl, Jacob. You better claim her quick.'

'She's not some prize anyone can claim.' I decide to tease a little. 'Besides – you prefer guys.'

Dex gives a self-satisfied grin. 'True. So I think we should film my next video with me wearing nothing but shaving foam. It would go viral, right?'

I'm used to Dex's humour and chuckle, but Astrid objects.

'Kidding,' Dex says. 'Anyhow, I gotta go meet my boyfriend. You still wanna drive me, Jacob?'

I nod, switching speaker phone off before saying to Astrid, 'Not even a bishop in Italy can stop this kid.'

She replies, 'Just like Maestro can't stop us.'

32

Astrid

Every day I rehearse my solo with Maestro as though the plan for us to go to New York in ten days remains in place. He thinks he's back in the driving seat and in return, he's acting extra flexible and considerate by letting me choose the songs I want to perform at the Met. Songs chosen by me and Jacob. He thinks that's enough and I let him hang onto the idea; soon he'll learn I'm about to dance to my own tune.

I still feel like my life has been split into before and after, and I can't stop thinking about my real dad and the inevitable question – should I try to find him? There are no clues; the impossibility of it daunts me. But I want to know *someone* who has my blood in their veins.

More and more, I escape into Jacob's curtained soundproof booth where the outside world can't hear me. I can relax there and let my voice do what it knows how to do. The voice is similar to a spirit level. It can be tweaked, and the body used to support it: a muscle released, the shape of my mouth adjusted, my diaphragm modified, the chin lowered, until the voice becomes stable and, like the vial of liquid in a spirit level, balanced in exactly the right position. But in the booth, it feels like hiding inside a safe bubble and my voice somehow balances automatically, without me stressing and criticising.

Today when I come out of the booth, Jacob is sitting in the dark. Only the light from the TV and the computer stops me bumping into things. I watch from behind while he checks Dex's fire video, now ready for YouTube. As he waits for the upload he checks an Instagram profile on his phone, a guy called Mad Dog. I remember he's one of the band members. Someone has tagged a photo of a man they believe committed a hit and run to Mad Dog's profile, asking people to re-post till they find the culprit. Jacob re-posts it.

I rub his back, squinting at the pic of Mad Dog. 'Nice hair.'

Jacob rubs the back of his neck. 'The henna dye was bloody messy though.'

His response makes me stupidly happy because he's talking about the band without his eyes turning bruise-coloured, and without seeming as if the oxygen had been vacuumed out of his lungs.

My phone rings. Maestro. Checking on me. I turn off my phone.

Sometimes Jacob records me singing in the booth and I listen to myself in the dark before bedtime; it's a huge confidence boost. But it doesn't stop the sensation that the ground beneath my bed seems to whirl and swish as though life is now a raft on a surging river, and I'm a little afraid of not surviving the rapids ahead.

33

Jacob

Shadows press in on me.

I haven't switched on the lights in my parents' house, but I'd know my way to the drink cabinet in a blackout. I clutch the vodka bottle in my hands.

We loved the demo you submitted and would like to invite Purple Daze . . .

Just one drink. Anyone would after receiving that email. Just to deaden the feelings.

The grandfather clock in the corner gongs nine times.

Mum likes a contemporary style of interior design; slick clean lines preferably in the form of steel or glass, and then she adds one old piece so it stands out. Her bedroom contains one of those antique full-length mirrors. An oak hat stand lives in the marble and mirrors entrance hall. A 300-year-old writing desk impresses guests in the spare bedroom. I've always known I don't fit into any of these rooms – I'm not charming or stylish enough, and I'm not a highly desired item.

Tick. Tock.

The sound of a car makes me stand. Headlights sweep across the room. They're early. Mum had texted it'd be a late night again. My solar plexus thumps as I put away the stolen vodka, untouched, and flick on some lights. I can't escape through the side entrance of the kitchen though because that means going through the hallway and footsteps are already clattering across the tiles. The smell of takeaway Indian makes my stomach growl.

'Jacob. Nice to see you,' says Mum as I hover in the kitchen doorway, unsure how to get away without having to make up conversation. 'I hope Maria fed you. I only bought takeaway for two. We could split it though.' She pulls off her high heels, sits on the bar stool at the kitchen island bench, rubs her feet, groaning with pleasure.

'I've eaten,' I lie.

There's the clunk of keys on the hall table before Dad joins us. 'Evening, Jacob.' He drops the *Sydney Morning Herald* on the bench top, the blocked headline just three words; Rockmelon Salmonella Outbreak. Two dead. 'How are you?'

He won't listen to my answer. 'Tired. Just heading to bed.' I make for the side door to get to the studio.

'Bedroom's not that way,' says Dad, like he doesn't know I sleep in the studio. It occurs to me that maybe he actually doesn't know. 'Besides, we haven't seen you in days. Come and sit with us.' Dad surveys the curry Mum's opening. 'I haven't eaten since breakfast.'

I slump into a bar stool, trapped.

'I'll dish the food and we can talk in the dining room,' says Mum.

I make a temporary escape into the dining room, yank out a chair. I'm suddenly so, so tired. I listen to Mum moving about in the kitchen, and Dad's shoes clipping across the hallway.

Dad strides in, loosening his tie. 'I haven't had a chance to tell you, but your mum and I have accepted an invitation to use a holiday home in the Hamptons for a week. A reward from one of our satisfied clients. We haven't taken a break since last Christmas.'

'You're telling him about the Hamptons.' Mum places a plate of curry in front of Dad at the head of the table and pulls out a chair opposite me.

'The Hamptons in America,' I clarify.

Mum grinds salt onto her food. 'Eleven months since we took a holiday.'

I hope they don't want me to come too. 'When d'you leave?'

'Next week,' she says. 'It means we'll miss your audition, but we can call and say good luck. It's no different to saying it in person, is it? You're old enough –'

But I don't hear another word because I'm back to having my soul shredded. Having them here for the audition shouldn't matter, but somehow it does.

Jeez, I'm not even doing the audition.

But *they* don't know that.

Resentment simmers on the surface of my skin. I'm ready to detonate. And that never ends well for me. Dad hasn't lost a case in six years and as far as he's concerned, I'm one of his cases he's obliged to work on from time to time. He won't let a mere boy bring him down.

'Jacob.' Dad's courtroom voice booms. 'I *said* I spoke to Dr Bell a few days ago and he thinks you're in good shape and will breeze the audition. Hence, we're very confident in you.' He pushes rice and meat into his mouth, chews it and swallows.

Mum presses a serviette to her lips, says, 'Have you got any other news to tell us? What's happening in your world?' She's fishing. She knows I'm not usually hanging around the house at this time of night.

We loved the demo you submitted and would like to invite Purple Daze . . .

I pick up a knife and spin it in circles. Maybe I should tell them about the Met, partly because I want to shock them, partly to start an argument. But I can't have them getting in the way of me leaving for New York. They might block my credit card, which will cover the two flights and two hotel rooms in New York City. And I had this brilliant idea to buy two flights and two tickets to the Met for Astrid's grandparents.

I promise myself this'll be the last time I freeload off my parents. When I get back from New York I'll cut up the credit card. Besides, now Mum and Dad won't even be in the country and won't know if I turn up at the Con or not.

Wondering if they'd care if I went on a rockmelon-eating spree, I try a different defence. 'I was going to ask if we could go to dinner after the audition. To celebrate. Guess now I'll be eating alone. Again.'

'Oh, Jacob, we can go to dinner anytime,' says Mum. 'How about we go tomorrow night – not tomorrow – we have the Goldbergs' dinner. But I'll check my schedule.'

'Sure.' I get up, knowing that'll get 'forgotten', and push the chair under the table. 'I'm for bed.' Maybe I should tell them about the email, but what's the point?

'Jacob!' Dad doesn't seem to know how to lower the volume on his booming voice. 'What else is happening? You seem – not yourself. Did you have something you wanted to talk about?'

I glance toward the doorway and freedom. Dad, already bored with me, checks his beeping phone.

'I'm just dead tired,' I say. May as well *be* dead.

'You spilt some sauce,' Mum says, touching the tomato-coloured spot on my white T-shirt. I flinch, confused about why I'm wearing JW's shirt. Last night I retrieved it from its safe place in a drawer. I needed to touch it, smell it, after his Instagram page disappeared into the ether. I won't be sorry never to see the video someone shared to his page, called 'Dumb Ways to Die'.

Mum adds, 'Have you seen Harper lately? Aria?'

'Jacob!' I wince at the volume of Dad's voice. 'I'm reading an email from Dr Bell. He says you've pulled out of your lessons? What the hell is going on?'

I should've known Maestro would tell Dad our lessons were over. 'We didn't hit it off.'

'That's not good enough. We said if you failed the audition –'

It's time to spin a tale. I need to delay this conversation. 'Who said I'd fail? The audition's in a week. I don't need more lessons. It'll be fine.'

'It had better be, or –'

'Yes I know.' I stand and begin my retreat. 'And no, Mum. In case you didn't realise, Aria and Harper no longer live here.' To this day Mum doesn't know that I was with both of them, one after the other. I pretend not to have heard whatever Dad yells at me and head out via the lounge, swiping the bottle of vodka on the way.

♫

I riffle through my CDs and, switching off the lights, blast Black Fast's *Spectre of Ruin* into every brain cell. The drums, the ranting, the electric guitars, drive away the hurt, my parents and *We loved the demo you submitted and would like to invite Purple Daze . . .*

I estimate there are only about two shots of vodka left in the bottle I swiped. I take a deep breath and then slowly unscrew the top. But I stop when I think about Dex and Astrid. Even though the deal with Doc is off, Astrid liked how I made the commitment to be a better version of myself plus she has this huge hang-up about alcohol damaging my vocal cords. And I stopped drinking for Dex to make sure he wouldn't follow in my footsteps.

I'll go to the Purple Woods. They'll never find out.

I sneak back into the house and pilfer the bottle of Jack because two shots is never going to be enough. Dad's explaining some legal line of argument to Mum and speaks loudly enough that they can't hear me.

Clutching the two bottles I jog round to Harper's place. Then I'm hurling myself toward the river and the Mother Tree, along the path I've taken so often I could walk it backwards. I ache for that first moment when oblivion begins to numb my veins. I lean against the Mother Tree, a bottle in each hand, panting.

This is gonna be heaven. I savour the sweet smell of Jack Daniels. Nearly two months since I last touched alcohol. *Nearly.*

Always nearly. Like I nearly made it into the Con. Nearly got a recording contract. Nearly died on that Harley. But then I'm a lost cause.

I blink at the surrounding trees, remembering Harper's words almost a year ago. *You have to move forward. We can't be children in the woods forever.* And it hits me that I keep taking the same path whenever the going gets tough. I balance a bottle on each leg. Their labels smudge. I swipe at the tears. What would I say to Dex if he did the same thing? I have to take a new path because this one leads nowhere. I'm sort of proud I haven't messed up and broken this promise. I'm not sure I've ever done that.

I contemplate both bottles and know I won't drink either of them tonight.

I'm about to sneak the bottles back in the house, but as

my foot hits the bottom step the outside security light clicks on, making me squint, and a voice says, 'There you are. You weren't in the studio.'

Astrid steps out of the shadows. 'And you left Black Fast –' Her mouth tightens when she sees the bottles. Something imperceptible shifts, like a subtle key change in a get-it-on song to something more grave.

'I can't believe you've done this. Or haven't you been caught until now? Remember the kind of things you do when you're drunk – the Harley?'

I raise my hands as though she has a Glock to my head. The bottles dangle in plain sight. 'It's not what you think. I was going to, but I didn't.'

'I don't believe you.' Her tone's flat and disappointed and masks every bit of fury I can see in her face. Reckon a bomb's about to go off.

Swallowing my own rising anger, I say, 'Smell my breath.'

'I don't need to.'

'How else can I prove it? I was about to put them back in Dad's cabinet.'

'They're pretty much empty, Jacob. Don't you think I've had enough lies to deal with in my life?'

'Then why aren't I falling over my own feet and slurring?'

She removes her snarly expression from the bottles and puts it on me. The longer it probes, the less it snarls. Eventually, she sighs. 'Why do you make everything difficult?'

'You'd rather I *had* been drinking?'

'You scare me – sometimes. You're unpredictable.' Her stare impales me. 'Too similar to my mum.'

Ka-boom.

An air-raid siren goes off in my skull. A suitable answer forms and un-forms as words ricochet around my brain like bullets fired into an empty bathtub. I rub my knuckles against my head, then point at the studio where we'd spent some of the afternoon making out before Dex arrived. 'You weren't complaining before.'

'Stop talking. You're out of control and I'm a wreck. Maybe we shouldn't go through with this plan. I've made a mistake. I should've listened to Maestro. I should have chosen not to love you.'

It's as if she reached into me and grabbed my heart, then hurled it against the wall. It's both an ugly and beautiful moment because it hits me like a meteor shower – I really do love Astrid. And she loves me.

'Operation Rumspringa,' she continues. 'Operation Ridiculous, more like.'

The hole where my heart was aches.

This is the part where I rant and rave and tell her to go because I'm a mess-up. This is the part where I get drunk, fetch my motorbike and drive into a brick wall, or go punch a branch until I break some bones.

Stop. I'm not going down the self-pity rabbit hole.

I'm sick of treading this path, yet I can't figure out how to find a new one. But then I cotton on that I'm already on a new path – I haven't gotten drunk and I'm not pushing Astrid away before she can push me away, or letting fate decide if I die or not.

Except now I can't work out where to go from here. But I have Astrid standing there. She hasn't run away. She's waiting for me to say the right words. I bet she's got some music score going on in her head – one that's dramatic and bursting with hope. *Her* heart is on the line too.

The right words to say have to exist in a song. I plunder my memories.

Nothing fits.

The outside light times out and we're plunged into darkness.

'Explain to me why you wanted to get wasted,' Astrid says.

Using the stair railings, I pull up to my feet. 'I need to show you something.'

We walk to the studio side by side, but a metre apart. Inside, Black Fast is loud enough to vibrate objects across surfaces and the TV blares images of dust-covered people pulling survivors from the wreckage of a concrete building. I cut the music and point at my laptop. 'Read it,' I manage, before my face buckles.

Astrid steps closer to the computer as though it might explode. It whirs when she moves the mouse, waking the screen. I hold my breath while she reads, and the breath becomes a mighty storm in my chest.

'Oh,' she says. 'I'm *so* sorry.' Her sympathy makes me feel more and more like I've been unstitched and might come apart. 'It's been an awful day for you. Did you write Purple Daze's songs?'

'No way. I'm not a great writer.' I think of Callum, rocking on that chair to find his muse.

'If they were alive, we'd be celebrating right about now – Purple Daze's first recording contract. It's sick. Warped. The world's not a fair place.' The computer screen casts blue light around Astrid, making me stop to take her in. 'If they'd only met you.'

'But if they – were here, you and I would never have met.'

It's as if there's a light inside me and at the thought of never meeting her, the light switches off.

'Is this why you wanted to get drunk?' she asks.

I nod, then add how my parents are taking off for the Hamptons, so they'd have missed my audition had I been doing it.

'And despite all this shit happening, I didn't get drunk. I'm not going down that path anymore.'

'I don't know, Jacob. Everything's – messy. You must see that I have to be able to trust you?' She draws herself tall again, tough as that drum claw hook. 'Maybe we should take a break. Keep it friends only. I have to think. I better go.' She walks around the piano. *Away from me.* 'I need the bathroom before I leave.'

Normally I'd let her go, but I'm on a new path, and it's becoming clearer the further I walk down it. As she's disappearing into the bathroom I push my way inside the tiny room with her.

'Jacob. Stop.'

'I will, when I've said this.'

'Seriously, Jacob. Get out.'

I put my palm over her mouth. Her eyes widen. *Great start.*

'Yeah, I mess up.' I remove my hand. 'I'm not perfect. And you're pretty close to perfection compared to me, but you're not. I mean, you're crap at climbing trees.'

I think Astrid might smile, but she sends her smile away and inspects the floor.

'Got my soul ripped out by Harper, lost my mates, wished I could die, but I'm not using them as an excuse to push you away. You don't get to choose who you love. *It* finds you. Maybe it's a little like talent – you don't get to choose it and you shouldn't throw it away once you have it. It'd be like us deciding not to sing at the Met because we're afraid of choking.'

She folds her arms, but at least she's listening.

'And you can't throw *me* away. I love you. It's scary to love back. I get it. But you're one of the bravest people I know. After Vienna, I can't imagine how you're dealing with the thought of the Met. But you're going back onto that stage . . . because you know you *won't* break.'

As I'm speaking, Astrid pulls in a deep breath and releases it.

'I don't know why neither of us haven't broken already, but what I *do know* is if Dex can face life both sober and positive, so can I. What I know is you've helped me see I must honour Purple Daze by *not* following them to the grave. Thanks to you I believe in second chances. And now I need you to give *me* a second chance.'

I press her hands against my chest. 'I've been shit-scared of ending up in a forgettable life. I used to say to the boys before a gig, "Being forgettable is worse than never having lived at all." Kind of ironic now. But you've made me see that how you behave and the songs you sing are only part of it. Part of being unforgettable is being loved, while loving someone else with every stupid cell in your body.'

Astrid's expression softens. '"Because you love me, I am unforgettable,"' she says, quoting a lyric from her own song.

I get down on one knee, which is pretty difficult in the tiny bathroom, and cup her hands in mine. 'I vow to you, Astrid Bell, to never get blasted drunk again: if life sends me a crappy soundtrack sometimes, and I think I might stuff up, I'll come to you first before I hit the hard stuff, and together we'll work it out.'

Her posture relaxes. She kisses my knuckles. The music score in my head crescendos and I want to pick a special song that matches the moment, but I reckon Astrid's the only person capable of writing that one.

I scan every feature on her face, willing her to reply with something good.

'I'm not brave,' she finally says. 'The sole reason I'm doing the Met performance is because you're there to sing with me.'

'Good to know. Then I'll blackmail you. Kiss me or I won't sing with you.' She starts to smile, but pulls it away again.

I thread two fingers in her belt loops and tug her to me. 'Push me away if you don't like me like that, but don't push me away because you're afraid of not surviving whatever happens between us. Whatever happens, you won't break. And neither will I.'

She grips my biceps. The warmth of her seeps through my skin, and it's oxygen breathed into my airless lungs.

I whisper, 'I promise I'll try to be good enough for you.'

'You *are* good enough, Jacob.' A smile finally flickers onto her face. 'Except you really need to do some laundry.' She jabs the spot of spaghetti sauce on JW's T-shirt.

'Does that mean you're sticking around?'

'Like elevator music sticks in your head.'

I tut. 'That's going to be annoying.' We're smiling, a little shy, yet a little surer. 'Do I have to sing to you to get you to kiss me?' I ask.

Checking out the brightly lit bathroom, she giggles. 'In here?'

I break into 'What I Did For Love' without holding back. She pushes at me, tries to clap her hands over my lips, but I stand on tiptoe and turn my head, still singing.

'*Arrête.*' She jumps to reach my face, and I collar her wrist, and grab her mouth with my mouth. I cling to her, breathing through every electrical sensation darting around my body. And finally I'm inside a love song of my own.

34

Astrid

That night in Jacob's studio, after we cleared up that Jacob hadn't been getting drunk, and after we finalised the plans for Operation Rumspringa, Jacob fell asleep on the sofa. I hunted for a blanket to cover him. His parents weren't going to do it.

Something tells me he won't be needing them anymore. He's moved further away from his grief and healed so many wounds, including the ones his mother and father inflicted.

Now, back in my bedroom, I pull out my music book. But I don't write a song. I write the hardest words I've ever had to write.

Dear Maestro,

Notes are best kept short so you don't skip over the middle to get to the end. I'll make this quick.

Jacob and I have gone away for a couple of weeks to get some headspace. I don't want to go to New York with you unless I can sing with him. Jacob has pulled out of the Con because he needs to make his parents hear who he wants to be in his future.

People shouldn't try to be what they are not. It only leads to unhappiness.

I hope you hear me when I say I want to be a songwriter as well as an opera singer, and it's my choice to be who I want to be. Listen again to Dex's demo because he's singing the songs I wrote.

Astrid

35

Jacob

Mum and Dad leave for the Hamptons the day before Astrid and I leave for New York City. Then Astrid and I will fly one day before she was due to fly out with Maestro. Even if Maestro turns up in New York, which he probably will, we'll be there and he can't stop us singing together.

We'll arrive four days before the performance. The doc had planned for three days to let Astrid get over her jetlag and to rest her vocal chords. Plenty of time to let the organisers know we *are* there, despite any contradictory messages.

Before we board the plane, Harper texts me to say she's finally found a house to buy in Florida. She's out in the world being who she should be. So is Aria. Now it's my turn.

Astrid's sneaking a peek at my phone screen as we wait in the queue to board. I show her Harper's text. 'She's got her life. I've got mine – with you. Got it?'

Astrid kisses me, then says into my mouth, 'You might need to keep reminding me.'

On the flight, we watch movies, fingers entwined, listen to music with shared earbuds, lean on each other while we sleep, and play-fight over Astrid's butterfly pen to fill in our landing cards. I glance at Astrid's card. She's written 'Singer-Songwriter' in the occupation box.

It's another bittersweet moment as I'm reminded of how we're not getting very far with the submissions for her and Dex. Our meals are placed on our tray tables and I can't help thinking Dex and Maria will be on a plane to Italy soon, eating cardboard food too. By the way Astrid's staring at me, her nose wrinkling, she's clocked my change of mood. I make zigzag shapes with a plastic knife in what's supposed to be mashed potato.

'I didn't want to spoil the trip,' I say. 'But we're at a dead end with the labels. I'm so sorry. I'm pissed for you as well.'

'That's okay.' But her flippant tone doesn't match the tightness in her mouth. 'I'm disappointed, of course. Maybe I'm not good enough because it's not Dex's voice that's the problem. It has to be my songs.'

'No way. It's just a tough world to break into. It's not your songs.'

'I'm more worried for Dex than myself. I've got time to learn and improve.'

I ball my hands. 'Dex will leave for Italy. He'll have nowhere to sing and nowhere to record. I've failed him.' Dex has had an effect on me as much as Astrid has; he got me singing again and made me realise I can make it without my parents' backing. The mountain he's climbing is way steeper than mine. Mine's a hill compared to his.

'You're not his dad. I know you want to support Dex in a way your own parents have never supported you, but you can't let this become something else that eats at you.' She elbows me. 'You've done everything you can.'

'He was depending on me.' I stab my knife in the mound of potato, lean back against the headrest, wracking my brains for a way to not let Dex down. He's walking along a road to a forgettable life. If I'm to live with myself, I have to turn him around.

36

Astrid

Jetlag means we sleep through our first day in New York, and I miss Maestro's texts checking if I'm all right. I text back, asking him to give me the headspace I requested in my note, but that I'm fine.

Jacob and I emerge from our rooms the next day – we're taking things on the relationship side slow so Jacob booked two rooms – ready to attend the tour of the Metropolitan Opera House that all the performers for 'An Evening with Yolanda Gustav' are invited to. On arriving at the Met, we're given a map. We laugh at the possibility we'll need one, but it's soon apparent we do.

Most of the performers aren't rookies and the tour becomes a private one for me and Jacob. We wander along low-ceilinged cement passageways, some lined with lockers, others with ladders or coils of electrical cords.

'Why are there soap holders everywhere?' Jacob asks our guide, a sober, hunched-over man who walks slowly and doesn't appear to want to give a tour to a couple of youngsters.

'To stop the spread of germs, of course. It's recommended you use them often. To the performers here, their voice is their instrument. If they become sick, their voice can no longer work and we avoid that at all costs.'

Jacob cracks his knuckles and I wonder why the guide talks as though we wouldn't already know this; like *we're* not performers, too.

He talks of Pavarotti, Placido Domingo, Jose Carreras, Renee Flemming, Violeta Urmana, Maria Callas and the other famous singers who have graced the opera house. And how Veronika Bell gave her astonishing performance as *Carmen* right here on this stage. I could be standing in her footprint, or walking past her dressing room. Except unlike in Vienna, she's no longer this dazzling movie-star mother who was tragically taken from us; she's simply a selfish singer who abandoned her children and smoked herself into an early grave.

The guide walks us onto the set on a picture-frame stage that has to measure 100-feet wide and 100-feet deep. The cavernous theatre seats 3,800 people and contains at least five tiers of red velvety seating. The starbursts of light make the giant gold petal formation on the ceiling glow. But the stage and the theatre are a tiny part of the building and we tour past a myriad of workshops containing carpenters and scenic artists, costume designers, milliners, wig makers, even a cobbler. It's as if a whole busy town has formed right inside this building.

Below the stage are three more levels containing additional work spaces and storage for instruments and sets. I study the map to make sense of it, but give up. I hope my dressing room is near a toilet so I don't get lost and miss my call.

'Awesome,' says Jacob, throwing an arm around me as we exit through one of the revolving doors under the huge arched windows.

'*Ah, zut.* That tour made me more nervous than ever.' I pull free of him to button up my coat and wind the scarf around my neck. 'It's as though the staff are the important ones and the performers are transported in and out like we don't belong.'

'But everyone in the building is working to make our performance perfect. Make-up, set design, orchestra, lighting. And without us, all that means nothing.'

I pull on some leather gloves. 'Don't. You're not helping.'

Jacob's face falls and I feel a little guilty. He's nervous too. But when I follow his line of vision, I realise his face didn't fall because of me. Maestro is here. Maybe ten metres away. He looks different, wearing a navy single-breasted overcoat instead of his cloak.

He makes a beeline for us. I circle back, unsure if I should make a run for it, but Jacob latches onto my elbow. 'No point,' he says. 'He'll only find us another day. Back me up.'

Maestro looms, two metres away. One metre. But I don't see anger in him. His brow creases. He hugs his briefcase to him in a death grip. His watery eyes press a question into mine.

'You didn't buy Astrid's note then,' says Jacob.

'Your dress was gone, the one you'd chosen to wear for the performance.'

'You're not stopping us from singing together,' I say, clutching Jacob's arm.

Maestro shifts to survey the pedestrians and traffic opposite. He points at my scarf around my neck. 'It's cold. Breathe through your scarf. Protect your voice.' He rests his briefcase on a lifted knee and produces some sheets of paper. 'Your rehearsal times, practise room protocol, other important information. I'm here to help.'

I accept them, wordless.

'I've just heard they've had a last minute change to the programme,' he adds. 'Instead of two duets, they want one song with both of you singing, then a solo from you, Astrid.'

'What? Why?' I shout-whisper between gritted teeth. 'You're manipulating things behind the scenes again. *More lies?*'

'No! A soprano cancelled this morning. She's sick. And the programme is male heavy. You'll step in and close the evening, with Yolanda joining in on the last third of the song. It's a good thing.'

My stomach drops. Sweat prickles my head, my pulse shifts gear and revs to a hundred kays per hour. 'This is *exactly* the kind of behaviour I would expect from you. You're like some terrible Svengali from a tragic opera,' I shout, then retch onto the pavement.

'Let's go.' Jacob hails a cab and I walk unsteadily toward it.

'I promise I had nothing to do with it,' yells Maestro from behind us. He adds, 'I contacted your father, Jacob. He knew nothing about the Met or that you were missing the Con audition. They're coming to see your performance.'

His hand on my elbow, Jacob grips a little too hard for a split second then pulls me toward the waiting cab. I stumble blindly beside him.

Inside the cab, I crave the icy air and lean out the window. When I glance back at Maestro, he waves. His smile appears to hurt his face as he sticks his finger in his ear and presses his nose like it's a button. Our secret sign for *I love you*.

It's like I've tumbled over a cliff.

The taxi pulls off from the curb and the bond that has held us together tugs and stretches. But it will never break. Even if I'm not sure he's telling the whole truth about why Mum left, or about the change to the programme, the bond is indestructible. Our history is the history of a father and daughter, flawed and filled with regret and mistakes perhaps, but he is my dad.

I remember how once I was happy with the life Maestro made for me. But I've grown up and changed. As I settle back into the seat and take slow breaths, I wonder if Maestro can change.

Jacob is mute and lost in his own head. As a wave of queasiness hits, I hang out the window again. Jacob's hot palm rests on my back. *I can't do this.*

In my hotel room, Jacob settles on the edge of the bed, passes me a glass of water.

I can't bring myself to sip it. 'Later. I feel sick. I need to sleep.' I hug a pillow. 'Jacob, it never starts this early.'

'It's the shock of the doc materialising and the change in the programme.'

His phone beeps with a text. As he reads the screen his face drains of colour.

'What's wrong?' I ask.

'Dad. It's a long list of people they've invited to watch my performance. Such-and-such from some big law firm and so-and-so who Mum used to go to school with. They should book the frigging royal box. Fourteen people! Way to crank up the pressure.'

'They're not mad at you though, for skipping the Con?'

'That lecture will probably come later. The only thing they've insisted on is I keep lunch free the day after the performance. It'll probably become a discussion about my future after I sing like a strangled bird.'

Nausea swirling, I gulp at a block of air.

Jacob pinches the skin at his neck. 'They've never come to one of my performances – ever.'

'That's because this is the Met, not some bar.'

'What if I freeze? A textbook humiliation and proof for Dad that he was right all along. He'll probably make good on his threat to pull down my studio.'

'I thought you didn't care if they kicked you out. You're doing this alone now.'

'True.' Jacob rubs his jaw back and forth. 'I guess I've never admitted this to myself. But despite everything, I still want them to approve – you know – be proud. And here's my one chance. I don't want to stuff it up.' He suddenly stands. 'Sorry. I'm not helping. I'll let you sleep. Or do you want me to stay?'

After I tell him over and over that I'm fine, he slides out of the room. But I'm not fine.

I wanted to say that he's practised and ready, that he's good enough to get asked to be here, but if that's the case, why can't I tell myself the same thing? Funny how he wants his parents' approval like I wanted Mum's, even from heaven. And now it seems I was seeking the approval of a – was she crazy? Or just neglectful.

Heat pricks behind my eyes. I hate this, so why am I doing it? Certainly not for Mum.

Everything is organised though. I've booked an appointment at the hairdresser. My dress for the performance hangs on the curtain rail because it won't fit in the cupboard. It's a strapless emerald green with fitted bodice and full skirt. Maestro chose it from Mum's closet. She wore it at this very opera house.

Even the thought of wearing the dress makes it seem as though I'm breathing through a straw. I make a run for the bathroom. This is going to be the worst performance yet.

37

Jacob

The next morning, Astrid and I are freezing our arses off at a near deserted café in Central Park. The cold helps with her queasiness. She's sipping on peppermint tea and I'm downing a double espresso when my phone rings. I almost don't answer, but when I pull it from my pocket, it's my home number, back in Sydney.

'Hello?'

'Yo. Dude.'

'Dex.' I give Astrid a thumbs up as she nibbles on a ginger biscuit.

'Got it in one. I'm at your house, bro.' The grandfather clock in our hall gongs.

'I can hear that. What can I do for you, kid? I'm not sure I can help with your carpet-ironing technique.'

'When's the big night?' he asks.

'Two more days, dude.'

'You got access to YouTube?'

'Sure. What's happening?'

'Check out my account.' I put him on speaker and open the YouTube app while Astrid sips on ginger ale. Dex's face jumps onto the screen, a puff of fire on his palm. Astrid leans in.

'What am I looking for?' I ask.

'Check out the numbers, dipstick. And the comments.'

Astrid points at the thumbs-up icon by the recording of 'A Forgettable Life'. At first, I think it says 34 but then I see the 'k' at the end of the number.

'Thirty-four *thousand*. And 667,000 views. Jesus, Dex.'

'Nah, just Dex will do. Thanks though.'

'You have over ten thousand subscribers,' adds Astrid.

'Reckon your dad sent out my stuff to his hotshot mates,' says Dex. 'It's gone viral!'

'Are you telling me this came from my dad?' asks Astrid. She gapes and slaps the table. 'Maestro must've done it before he left for New York, after he read my note and so *after* he knew I wrote the songs.'

'Your dad's ace,' adds Dex. 'And you might want to check out the comment from Angel Records.'

I scroll until the pink angel wings logo shows up, read it out loud. 'Your music speaks the truth, Dex Firebender. Get in touch if you're interested in signing with us. Your writer, too.'

Jumping out of my chair, I punch the air. 'Yes. We got this.'

Astrid shouts, 'Knew you could do it, Dex.'

'Couldn't have done it without ya both. That song is immense.'

'Thanks Miss Scusami,' said Astrid

'We have to get this sealed fast,' I say. 'So your mamma doesn't take you to Italy.'

'Lucky for us she can't get the money together with the Christmas flights being three times the normal cost. She thought they'd come down the closer we got to Christmas, but they're going up and up. Plus the PROUD group are doing a fundraiser for us in January. Get this – a charity *drag* show. So we have more time to get this deal sealed and to convince her to stay.'

Astrid's ginger biscuits pushed aside, we talk non-stop about meeting the talent scouts at Angel until Dex has to hang up. Afterwards, Astrid and I wander through the park toward the Met where we plan to take silly selfies. I've only ever seen Central Park in movies. It's weird to see it's not always green and summery, or full of trees heavy with golden autumn leaves that twirl in the air and carpet the ground. They must have to wait for the right season before they film.

We walk along a black path, shiny with rain from earlier today. The morning is misty, making the spindly twigs that intertwine and weave above us look like spider webs on the end of each dark bough.

'Bit bigger than the Purple Woods.' I chuckle.

Astrid gazes at the bare trees on either side of us. 'So Maestro must like my songs, to have sent them out to his friends.'

'Yep. Seems like he's coming around to you being a songwriter.'

'I can be both. A soprano and a songwriter, can't I?'

'Of course you can.' We link fingers and cross the roads toward the Met.

'I can't believe Maestro did that. It was his way of saying he's okay with me choosing my own future, don't you think?'

'He's done the right thing by you this time. Has he tried to get in touch since yesterday?'

'We've exchanged a few texts. I've asked him to give me some space. And he is.' Astrid steps around a squashed hotdog on the pavement.

'He's changing then. For the better.' I lean down and kiss the top of her head.

We climb the steps toward the square in front of the Met and watch the fountain dance. It's programmed to change its heights and rhythms like it's making music of its own. We're leaning in to take a selfie, the impressive Met building in the background, when an elderly couple approaches us. The woman, petite and wearing a simple black dress, her light grey hair clipped short around her neck and ears, steps forward. A kind of desperate joy dances over his face.

'Astrid?' she asks.

38

Astrid

When the slight woman who resembles my mum says my name, her voice is light and sing-song, and how I once imagined my mother's voice would sound when she said, 'Astrid'. I somehow don't need to ask who she is.

'We're Veronika's parents,' says the man with her, stumbling over the words and stepping forward to support the woman by her elbow. 'I'm John Miller and this is my wife, Esmeralda.'

Blood whooshes into my ears.

'I should explain, everyone,' says Jacob, his grip around my waist tightening. 'I sent the flight tickets. Astrid didn't know.'

'What?' I turn to Jacob, feeling as though my body is flickering, like in the old silent movies. It's as if everyone here used up all the oxygen before I could suck any of it in.

'I didn't want you to regret not meeting them,' he says into my ear. 'They're your blood.'

The old anger I've nursed for my grandparents most of my life wakes. I look over their heads toward the Met.

'And you're a singer just like your mum,' says Esmeralda. 'When we got the tickets and a photo Jacob sent, we had to come and hear you sing. And at the *Met*. We're very proud.'

'And we're so happy to meet you,' adds John.

There's a delay between my mouth opening and the words coming out: 'You flew here from England to hear me sing?' They nod in unison. 'But you didn't agree with singing as a profession and it's why Mum fell out with you. It's why you abandoned her.' I start to weep. 'You hate music. You wanted nothing to do with your *own daughter*.' Somewhere inside me I've felt that because Mum's parents didn't want her, that's why Mum didn't want me.

I can't stop shaking. The man wipes the sweat from his forehead with a hanky from his inside jacket pocket. The woman's face crushes as she leans into him.

'I don't wish to speak ill of your mother,' says John, breathy with emotion, 'but that's not exactly the truth.'

'Let's sit,' Jacob says, gesturing to the circular ring structure that surrounds the fountain. I'm grateful because my legs are buckling like a collapsing music stand.

'I'm afraid your mum told some fibs,' John eventually says. 'We did fall out, but not over her music. Her singing was an immense joy in our lives. We're both singing teachers after all.'

I examine his face. It doesn't seem like the kind of face that would lie. He seems wholesome and normal and not an ogre at all. But I need to understand.

'Why did she say you threw her out then?'

'I can understand she didn't want to tell you what happened. But it's best you ask her. It's not my story to tell.'

'No!' I'm on my feet, sick of the lies, the mysterious history of my family. 'I'd like the truth, now. Please.' I'm not ready to tell them that their daughter has taken her secrets to the grave.

John glances sideways toward Esmeralda.

'It's not possible to ask her now.' I tear up. 'I'm nearly eighteen. I deserve to know. I *need* to know. Before I perform. It may help. I get performance anxiety, and Mum's part of the reason why. Please.' I've never admitted that out loud before.

Esmeralda nods to John. He clears his throat. 'Your mother was spirited and wonderful and inspiring, but she got herself into trouble when she was eighteen.'

'He means she got into the family way,' says Esmeralda, her voice stretched.

'We pushed her to keep it, but it was the worst thing we could've done. There was a lot of arguing. That, along with her dreams of a more glamorous life. Well she –' He swallows hard and glances at Esmeralda before continuing. 'She . . . lost the baby. Then disowned us. She told us never to contact her.'

'Lost the baby? You mean she got rid of it.' By the way he shuffles and averts his glance, I know I've nailed the truth.

'We wrote to her at all the venues we knew she was performing at,' continues John. 'But the letters came back unopened. Then when we learnt through the musical press that she married your father we were thrilled. He was an amazing and respected tenor. We wrote to her via the Sydney Conservatorium of Music because we knew he had ties there. But the letters came back telling us to stop writing.' Esmeralda sobs, strapping a hand over her mouth. John leans forward to pat her arm. 'And then the letters stopped coming back. Eventually, we stopped writing.'

'You could've come to visit,' I say.

'We are not moneyed people, dear. We knew Veronika would reject us. We needed to build a bridge first, then we would've come. But she didn't want that.' His expression roils with the pain he's felt all these years, puncturing a hole in my anger. 'And then it was like she disappeared after you were born. We have worried about her ever since.'

'She left me, too,' I whisper, more to myself. Everything they're saying fits with what I now know about my mum. It seems she made a habit of abandoning the people who loved her most. For some reason, they made her feel trapped.

'Where's Veronika now? Is she in New York with you?' asks John.

I blink at them, glance at Jacob.

'I think we'd better find a café, don't you?' he mumbles to me.

I turn back to my grandparents. 'It's a very long story. Do you have time for coffee?'

39

Jacob

The day before the concert we're allocated orchestra time. We also walk through the staging, learning our entrances and exits. As we're leaving the stage, none other than Yolanda Gustav enters the wings. She's wearing a huge faux fur hat and four-inch heels.

'Ah, Miss Bell. Mind the stairs on your entrance,' she says, air kissing first one of Astrid's cheeks, then the other. 'Lift your dress or you could end up on your knees. I have seen it happen.' She chortles as though it's a hilarious thing to have happen to you at your debut at the Met. She pats Astrid's arm. 'Good luck. And I'm slightly sorry we changed the programme. Ah, when people are sick. But I hope the idea of closing the evening with me is a teensy bit tantalising.'

Astrid makes sounds that seem as if she's agreeing with her while Yolanda shifts her attention to me. '*Meine Güte.* You are even more beautiful close up, Mr Skalicky.' She extends a limp-wristed hand and I go to shake it, awkward because her hand is palm down. She pulls it away. 'You are meant to *kiss* a lady's hand, darling. It's how we do it in the theatre.' I try to laugh, and this time when she extends her hand, I kiss it.

'I am excited to entertain the audience with you both. Vienna was extraordinary. You have a special bond and watching you – it made my chi sing. Many duets, they sing in isolation. But not you two.' She beckons Astrid with a crooked index finger. 'Come, child, we have a quick rehearsal now, me and you.'

They're singing a few bars together to finish the performance, so it's over pretty fast and Yolanda hugs Astrid goodbye. 'I must go. But you are both under my wing,' she says. 'See you tomorrow.'

The moment she disappears backstage, Astrid makes wow eyes at me. 'Seems like Maestro didn't interfere with the programme – it *was* due to a drop out.'

Unable to get Yolanda's warning out of my head, I ask, 'Is your dress long?'

'Yep. The longest. I'm shorter than Mum was.'

'It's one of your mum's?'

She shrugs. 'Maestro kept all her dresses – her jewellery, shoes, hats. He said she wore this one right here on this stage.'

Wincing, I say, 'Tell me you're not wearing her shoes.'

'They were made to match the dress. We have the same size feet.'

No way. I take her hand, and glancing at the map, I lead her along several narrow passageways and into one of the workrooms. It's packed with about twenty people going about their tasks; ironing fabric, pinning outfits on mannequins, sewing on machines, storing rolls of material. I approach a woman who's ironing a men's dress shirt. The iron has the electrical cord coming from the ceiling and puffs enough steam to start a locomotive.

'Excuse me,' I say. 'I'm hoping you can help. This is Astrid Bell and she's performing tomorrow night, but the airline lost her dress. I thought maybe you could help locate one.' I gesture to the room around us. 'From the costume department.'

The pale woman, her fair hair pulled into a ponytail and her top lip covered in sweat beads, inspects Astrid up and down, then nods. 'I don't see why not.' She flicks a switch and disappears down the other end of the room.

Astrid pulls at my shirt and shout-whispers, 'What are you doing? I haven't lost my dress.'

'How can you *not* feel overwhelmed wearing your famous dead mum's outfit? Talk about literally treading in someone's shoes.'

Evelyn, the woman who's helping us, pins and fits Astrid into a full-skirted aqua blue dress. It has a beaded strap over one shoulder and reaches her mid-calf. 'I don't think Mum ever owned an aqua-coloured dress, never mind one that didn't touch the floor,' says Astrid.

'It's a new arrival and it's young and fresh,' says Evelyn. 'And yours will be the first name sewn into it.'

'It's traditional to sew the soprano's name onto a tag on the costume department dresses,' explains Astrid. 'Maybe one day someone will slip on this dress and be excited about wearing a dress Astrid Bell wore.'

'You look like Cinderella,' I say. 'Now I need to find you some glass slippers – by tomorrow night.'

Evelyn raises a finger. 'We might have some if –'

'Thanks a lot.' I cut her off. 'But Astrid needs her own shoes this time.' I bend to whisper in Astrid's ear. 'No more walking in someone else's shoes.'

Evelyn rummages in a drawer and gives me a business card. 'This shop is nearby.' I skim the picture of the diamante sandals on the card. Evelyn adds, 'They make fairytales come true.'

'I might need a fairytale,' Astrid says.

'The dress will be finished for you by tomorrow,' says Evelyn, shooing us away.

We exit the Met, and I punch the address of the shoe shop into my phone. I link arms with Astrid, and sing 'These Boots Are Made For Walkin'' as we march down the road.

'People are staring. Stop it,' says Astrid. But I don't stop. 'You need to wash your T-shirt, you nut,' she adds, pointing at the spot of tomato sauce.

'It won't come out.' I chuckle as if this is the best news I've heard in a while. 'I *have* washed it.' By accident, but the stain didn't come out.

'New York suits you,' Astrid says. 'It's as if you've left behind everything that pulled you down in Sydney.'

I stop on the pavement and pull her against me. 'It's not New York that suits me. It's you.'

40

Astrid

When I'm led into my changing room the day of the Met performance, the first thing I do is ask where the toilet is. Despite not having eaten since last night, I'm soon holding back my newly styled hair as I dry heave into the toilet. My eyeballs roll into the back of my head, beads of sweat break out over my skin.

Here we go again.

Back in my changing room I scan the small space and my aqua dress, which is hanging on a hook. The shelves are lined with skin creams and Vaseline, old make-up and paperbacks. The sound of other singers rehearsing in their dressing rooms seeps through the paper-thin walls. I click on a humidifier for white noise, unpack my new translucent shoes, then check the time. I'm due in make-up in fifteen minutes. Inside the shoe box I've stored a plain black jewellery box. I check inside for the diamond ring Mum bequeathed me, snap the box shut. Someone knocks at the door and I pack the ring away again. When I answer, the huge bouquet of pink and white flowers hides the person carrying them.

'Miss Astrid,' states someone from inside the flowers.

I accept the delivery and search for a card. It reads *Number One.* Five minutes later the same guy knocks, this time carrying pink gerberas with white daisies from Maestro and red roses from Jacob. Maestro's card reads, *I'm holding on too tight, and instead of keeping you close, I'm pushing you away. I'm sorry. I love you.* I miss that he's not standing beside me now, but it also feels sort of good. I like being in charge of myself. Jacob's note reads, *There's only one Astrid Bell and she's amazing.*

I arrange the flowers in the small room; they overpower the smell of old make-up and sweat. Still in my jeans and T-shirt, I fetch my map. As I'm leaving for make-up, the flower guy returns with another bouquet.

'I owe you a big tip,' I say, thanking him. This card reads *Number Two.*

Intrigued by who the numbered flowers could be from, I walk down a low-ceilinged concrete corridor lit with fluorescent lights, its dark red carpet worn down by the footsteps of thousands of performers over the last 146 years. I block out the sound of other singers vocalising on scales and practising their songs. A loudspeaker crackles and calls 'time' for Yolanda. A vice squeezes around my neck and my belly feels dizzy. I push forward anyway, my legs feeling boneless, until I find another bathroom.

When I get to make-up, Jacob is already there, but the clock tells me I'm not late after all. The room is an open space with mirrors and vivid lighting and numerous stations to cater for multiple performers. I go to Jacob and air kiss both his cheeks. 'Thanks for the roses.'

He catches my fingers. 'You didn't dye your hair. Or straighten it.'

'Au naturelle tonight.' I missed my appointment when we went shoe shopping, so I went for a quick looped-up curled style instead.

'I dig it.'

I move on to my make-up station, still trying to figure out who the flowers are from. While I breathe slowly and deeply, a woman applies my foundation, chattering about how she did Renee's make-up earlier. She sorts through little boxes until she finds one labelled A. Bell and inside are the pair of false eyelashes I chose the day before. A necessary evil on stage. After she's applied them I notice my little box is mixed in with boxes labelled R. Fleming, Y. Gustav and V. Urmana and the idea that my falsies were there, mixed in with theirs, makes me feel as if I belong here a little more.

Jacob joins us when he's done, his eyeliner darkening his eyes and making them appear more intense. His smile shakes my heart. When I'm done he's in no rush to get dressed and we chat to the make-up woman, then one of the other male singers. It's a change to the usual pre-performance routine Maestro has me follow, but I decide to go with it.

'How many people work here every day?' Jacob asks a stagehand on the way back to our changing rooms. Jacob's is next to mine.

‘’Bout fifteen hundred of us,’ answers the Irishman. He adjusts his grip on a lamp he’s holding. ‘Sometimes there’re two hundred of us backstage on one performance. Tonight’s queer easy – only three set changes. Plenty of time to wet the tea.’

Jacob corners another stagehand and I join in with the discussion about how many sets they’re storing under the stage, the cost of the average opera, the fact his missus works in wardrobe and reckons she irons at least a mile of fabric per opera and there are twenty-eight operas a year. The next person we chat to also works in wardrobe. She estimates that the most costumes she’s worked on in one opera is 700. Everyone is friendly and happy to talk about their jobs. They wish us all the luck in the world and I truly feel as though I belong here.

‘You’re Mr Social tonight,’ I say, when we get to our dressing rooms. Inside are three more bouquets of flowers. I pick out the note attached to a dozen white roses. It reads, *Break a Leg. Love from your adoring grandparents*. Happiness splashes through me, knowing they’re here for me, but then I realise it’s more pressure to overcome, more reason to get stage fright. Nerves scuttle through my chest. Nausea claws at me. I should run to the toilet, but Jacob hands me the cards from the two other bouquets. They’re numbered three and four.

‘Is this you, or Maestro’s doing?’ I ask.

Jacob’s grinning like a ventriloquist’s puppet. ‘It’s not me.

I'm happy for you, but jeez, I should be jealous. You have a *few* secret admirers.' He fakes a frown.

'I doubt it. Maybe it's Dex.'

'He wouldn't have the cash.' Jacob examines the latest card then kisses me on the top of my head to avoid smudging my make-up. He adds, 'I'm going to get dressed and warm-up.'

After he leaves, I step around the flowers, now taking up floor space, re-check the time on a wall clock with missing roman numerals, and get dressed while doing my vocal exercises. I unzip the aqua dress with shaking fingers and catch sight of the tag: Astrid Bell. As it slides over my skin, a gazillion goosebumps prick across my skin. My belly tickles, but I think more out of excitement than nerves. Another knock with bouquet number five interrupts me. They must be from Jacob, but he seemed genuine when he denied it, and it's not Maestro's style. Jacob's parents wouldn't send so many. I've never even met them.

I'm warming up my voice and trawling through possible admirers when another bouquet arrives, followed by another. I barely have a moment to slip on my new shoes when Jacob knocks a rhythm which keeps going until I open up. He's handsome in a tux, his golden hair framing his face.

'Wow!' he says, stepping back to admire me. 'That dress with your hair all loopy and long – stunning.'

Tonight, I feel like a princess, but not one who's locked in a tower.

Even though we must be twenty minutes early, I follow

Jacob past the waiting area where others pace while listening for the loudspeaker to call them. We walk down a low-lit corridor toward the stage. People with clipboards and headsets skirt around us, others talk on mobile phones and ignore us, guys wearing black T-shirts and jeans carry scaffolding and props and boxes of tools. I get the urge to run for the toilet again.

'I heard more knocking. You didn't get more flowers, did you?' Jacob asks.

'Another two. It's you, isn't it?'

'Not me. I sent the red roses.'

'It's a mystery.' I'm aware we're nearing the stage. My guts knot.

A guy with a grey beard beckons to us. 'You're late.' Jacob nods and steps up his pace.

'How is it we're late?' I ask. 'We haven't even had our call.'

'I changed the clock in your dressing room,' says Jacob. 'And cancelled our call. No time to be afraid. This is it. Ready?'

'Right now?'

He squeezes my hand and before I can say 'toilet', we're walking onto the stage.

41

Jacob

The lights in the auditorium are like groups of exploding fireworks frozen in time. They dim as Astrid and I near the centre of the stage. Although the size of the Met is cosmic, seats stretching four or five tiers up into the sky, I don't let myself focus on the thousands of people watching – only two people matter anyway: Mum and Dad.

Worrying I might freeze like Astrid did in Vienna means I've barely slept. Worse, what if she freezes too and we're standing here, two petrified statues, the music playing and our mouths silently framing the first note.

'The Phantom of The Opera' music starts. *Breathe. You'll be fine. Breathe.* This is a job. Do your job. Butterflies are good. They're releasing more awesomeness into me, more oxygen with every flap of their wings so I have perfect breath.

I'm terrified and in awe at the same time.

When I'm surfing, I take one wave at a time. Now I need to take one phrase at a time. And I'm not the only one performing tonight. We're all in this together, even the make-up people and the stagehands. It's similar to a sport team. *Trust my voice and be myself.*

I check in with Astrid. Her smile slaps at her face as she scans the rows of faceless people that seem to stretch into the horizon. She cuts to me with terror in her eyes. My stomach lurches into my throat with every note played.

I watch the conductor for my counts.

Do your job. Breathe.

The first line is pure as I sing about forgetting the darkness and my wide-eyed fears and how nothing can harm me. The words couldn't be truer. Astrid's gaze wallows in mine; she reins in her breathing.

The start is soft and I tame the need to unleash the lyrics rather than control my voice. But by the fifth bar I figure I've got this; the fluttering of the butterflies melts away. My voice knows what it's doing. I shove all my confidence into my expression and sing to Astrid. She needs to join me in three.

Two. One.

She's on time with her first lyric. She does it. We map each other's faces.

I relax a bit more and sing the building melody, engaging with the audience and remembering to not appear wooden, to allow the emotion to enter my voice, and to put drama and character into the music. I think of the boys, wondering if they can hear me. I think about staying alone in a hotel room for the last two nights and never even opening the minibar fridge. I think about Mad Dog's Instagram page, the only one left, but maybe it's better someone takes it down; he'll be staring at nothing and nobody forever. And I think of taking a risk and leaving home now, because home isn't always the place you currently live.

We move to the crescendo. Astrid has switched her focus to the audience. She's in her zone, letting her body and voice do what they have practised for years. We turn to each other for the finale. I sing to her with every ounce of love I feel for her. The orchestra swells and we rise to the final notes and Astrid hits the highest note in the show – an E6.

It's flawless.

Before the music fades, the audience explodes onto their feet. I pull Astrid into a hug, which is probably not the right etiquette, but I don't care. Laughter rumbles around the auditorium. We approach the front of the stage and can appreciate the sea of people – because of the spotlights it's impossible to make out specific faces, but there are thousands of heads. I bow and step back to watch Astrid execute her deep curtsey. The thunderous clapping increases when I take her hand and we bow and curtsey in harmony. Then we leave stage left.

Yolanda is waiting in the wings. She braces Astrid and kisses her forehead, then squeezes my cheeks. The audience hasn't sat down and their applause isn't easing, but the Met has a strict policy against encores.

'Go,' Yolanda says, ushering us back onto the stage. 'You deserve their love.'

We hurry back into the spotlights. The clapping builds. Cheering and bellowed messages make the rounds of the theatre. We curtsey and bow, and as we leave the stage, they shout for more. Yolanda catches Astrid's hand, then mine, and walks us back onstage, raising both our hands to the sky. Another ripple of cheers and escalating applause.

Finally, we are released. In the wings, I pick up Astrid and spin her. She's laughing and crying at the same time, and telling me Purple Daze would be proud.

And I believe her.

♫

We trot down to our changing rooms. I'm shimmering from the inside out; if I took a selfie now it'd seem like I had a bunch of glow sticks under my skin. When we arrive another bouquet is being delivered for Astrid. This time they're from my parents. Astrid smells them and scans inside her changing room, now filled with flowers.

She rubs the lipstick she's left behind on my lips. '*Zut.* What's the real time, Mr Clock-Changer? I have to get to hair and make-up.'

'You have over an hour before your call. Don't panic.'

But at the mention of the panic word, that's exactly what she does.

Her eyes bulge, chin trembling. 'What if I can't do it without you?'

'No *what ifs.* Let's get out of here – focus on something else.'

Jeez, I figured after she'd performed once, she'd stop freaking. I cajole her out the dressing room and search for people to talk to, to distract her. But she's like a wooden doll lagging behind me, unable to join in. When I next check in, she's gone. Rushing to the nearest bathroom I find Astrid on her knees, her dress bunched around her waist, her head in the toilet. I capture her loose hair, but on the next gag, realise she has nothing to vomit. She hasn't eaten anyhow. I dab at her damp neck.

'Take deep breaths.'

'Thanks, Jacob. It's okay. You better go. Someone might complain.'

'I'm not leaving you,' I say, as someone enters the restroom. We listen to the someone wee and wash her hands. Astrid breathes through her nausea, as pale as sheet music. The someone starts to sing a scale. Astrid stifles a giggle. The singer launches into several warm-up exercises, her voice echoing in the tiny room. We work to squash down our laughter. Astrid's hair sticks to her sweaty skull and she has panda eyes from crying. Her palms in mine are clammy. But she's smiling.

'I need to get to hair and make-up,' she says, after the woman leaves. I'm amazed there's never a hint of her *not* performing. She's simply going to push herself through this. I hope she doesn't repeat what happened in Vienna, because the song she's singing is in Italian – it's not as if I can step in on this one.

42

Astrid

I push aside thoughts of omens; it's a different make-up lady and station than earlier. Maestro has warned me against superstition, often reminding me of the time Savannah lost the toy kitten whose nose she would kiss before each audition, and how it meant she got spooked and couldn't sing that one time.

'Good evening,' I say, then check in with Jacob behind me. He's handsome in his penguin suit, his bow tie now hanging loose around his neck.

'Hello, Miss Bell. You were exceptional, tonight. As were you, Mr Skalicky. Remarkable,' says the make-up lady in the precise accent of the English and with the air of a strict school teacher. With her small, grey-streaked hair bun she's older than most of the make-up artists here, possibly mid-fifties. She stands with her feet in a neat turn-out like Mary Poppins. 'My name's Poppy.'

We air kiss.

'Take a seat, Pamina, dear.' She steps aside to let me sit.

'Pamina. The princess from *The Magic Flute*?' I'm aware of her inspecting my blotchy skin and running mascara.

'Mozart. My favourite.' She pulls at a wad of cotton wool and uses long strokes to remove my make-up. 'It means "little honey".'

'You're obviously an opera fan. Do you get to watch sometimes?'

'Yes. I've been an opera buff for thirty years. I particularly requested a break over your performance. I met your mother a few times, you see. I even got to do her make-up.'

My stomach sinks through the three levels of storage below.

Poppy indicates I should close my eyes so she can remove my old make-up. 'Your mother was remarkable. But *you* will surpass her.'

'I doubt it.' I manage. 'She was amazing.'

'She was. And yes, you have a few years to go before you can fully control your voice. But the cleanliness and purity already there, alongside the lyricism, sounds wholly unique. Your dynamic control, the cascades of coloratura – and you have a grace and dignity on stage your mother never possessed. You always got the feeling she couldn't wait to get off the stage to attend a more important event.'

'I don't think it's a good idea to talk about this right now,' says Jacob, a palm on my back.

'Goodness. I didn't mean to speak ill of your mother.' Poppy winces. 'I'm sorry, Pamina dear. I meant it as a compliment. I can get carried away sometimes. I apologise.'

I touch her arm. 'Thank you. You didn't offend me. It's nice to meet someone who knew her. What was she like?'

Poppy hoots. 'Miss Bell could always make me laugh.' She selects a foundation and begins to apply it. 'And she always dominated a room. She walked in and the air got sucked out of the room and replaced with her energy. It oozed from her.' She points to a mirror on the wall, unusable because of the many photos stuck to it. 'Top right. Pride of place. Would you fetch it, young man? It was taken in the bar upstairs.'

Jacob unsticks the photo from the mirror, passes it to me.

I scrutinise the face of my mother. I've seen photos of her before, but somehow it seems like I'm seeing her for the first time; unposed, here at the opera where she sang. From what I've heard, the photo seems more true, more *her*, than the newspaper clippings or the portrait above the fireplace, or any of the photos of her with Savannah. For a start she seems genuinely happy. She's propped on a stool wearing a green cocktail dress, a glass of champagne raised in the air. An after-party perhaps. She's in her mid-twenties, her straight auburn hair loose and flowing over her shoulders, her eye make-up smoky, lips an astonishing red.

'But she was always late.' Poppy's words startle me out of the photo.

'Did she suffer from stage fright?' I ask, and touch my finger to Mum's forehead.

'Goodness, no. Once she arrived twenty-five minutes before a concert, and while someone fastened about a hundred buttons on her dress I applied her make-up, and then she flew onstage and gave an impeccable performance. I don't think she had time for nerves. She was always rushing off somewhere – I doubt she ever slept much. A bit of a flibbertigibbet, but a loveable one.'

So I don't get this affliction from her.

'Judging from the state of your make-up when you came in, you do,' says Poppy. 'Suffer from nerves, that is.'

Nausea rises and falls inside me. 'I'm pretty much falling apart inside right now.'

'Where focus goes, energy flows.' She stops applying make-up, studies me like I'm an oil painting. 'It must be hard, living up to someone as larger than life as Veronika Bell. But you don't need to become a carbon copy of her. I've learnt a lot over the years, with famous opera singers sitting opposite me every night. Each lamented their fears, their bad habits, their weaknesses. You're not alone.' She uncaps an eyeliner pen. 'Close.' I obey and note her words echo what Jacob's told me in the past. She adds, 'And sing only for your audience. I'm sure the nerves will ease then.' Poppy tidies my hair with the end of a comb.

Staring at the photo, a glow of happiness for my mum warms me – because she experienced this joyful moment. It's occurred to me lately that she didn't seem to be a very happy person, in general. I wonder how the rest of that night from the photo unfolded for her; if Maestro came with her, or perhaps he was in another country singing on another stage.

'I've met a lot of singers, often right before they perform,' adds Poppy. 'And the nerves always dominate the ones who have unrealistic expectations. Be yourself.'

'I like to think of it as a job. I'm out there working,' jumps in Jacob.

'Exactly,' says Poppy. 'But love it. Be grateful for having the best job in the world.'

I agree I have the best job in the world. *This is just a job. That's all.*

The clench of my gut loosens. As I breathe out, the queasiness eases.

It comes to me, at first like the twitching of theatre curtains, and then in a smooth rush, similar to when the curtains swish wide open to reveal the stage set. All my life, emulating my perfect mum was my dream, one that sometimes seemed unattainable. But thinking of performing as a job instead of a dream, *work* to be done to entertain the paying audience, takes away the possibility, or responsibility, of losing something as huge as a dream.

And I don't have to be perfect; my mother certainly never was.

The dream I was trying to reach vanishes. All that's left is me, my voice, the Met. Jacob.

Poppy applies my lipstick then pats my arm. 'You're done, Pamina.'

I hug her, careful not to wreck my make-up, then go to attach the photo back on the mirror.

'You should keep it,' says Poppy from behind me. 'She's your mum after all.'

Pausing, I examine the photo again. 'No,' I say, wistful

and feeling a little like I'm saying goodbye to Mum. 'She belongs here.'

Here she lives eternally, remembered by all who walk through these rooms.

'*In bocca al lupo*,' says Poppy. She hugs us both.

On the way back to our changing rooms, Jacob asks what she said in Italian.

'It means "in the mouth of the wolf". Similar to "break a leg". You can never say g-o-o-d l-u-c-k to any performer.'

'Yes, I know.' He tickles me. 'We should get out of here for a bit. It'll help you forget the performance. Focus on something else.'

'We can't leave. I'll be even more worried we won't make it back in time.'

Jacob raises one finger, a light bulb moment bright all over his features. He checks the map. 'This way.'

We wind through the building and I recall how Poppy said my mum was a bit of a flibbertigibbet. That, added to what my grandparents revealed about her, matches what Maestro's told me. Suddenly we round a corner and come toe-to-toe with Maestro himself. I freeze.

'I keep making the wrong choices for you,' he says before I can speak. 'But it's because I'm afraid of losing you. And I understand it's wrong that you are my whole world, but you are. It's made me a bit crazy. I'm sorry.'

A sob clumps in my gullet and a realise I don't want to grab hold of my dreams if it means letting go of my dad – because that's what he'll always be. Maestro has always been my dad. He didn't have to *try*. It's just who he is.

I throw my arms around him. He's shaking and rests his chin on my head. His body relaxes into mine and he clings to me. For once, I'm the parent and he is the child. After a moment, I step away, blinking back tears. Maestro's face is rumpled and wet, a craggy rock in the rain. 'You won't lose me,' I say. 'No matter what I do with my life, I'll always be your daughter.'

Maestro squashes me against him again. 'I told you she'd died because I was afraid you'd decide to find her and discover I wasn't your biological father. I couldn't risk you going to live with her – I didn't trust her to keep you safe after that final night. And your singing. You are so talented, the thought of that being wasted . . . then when I learnt your mother was actually dead, I felt utterly guilty and so terribly fearful of losing you because of the choice I'd taken from you. The instinct to keep you safe and closer than ever took over. It governed my every thought.' He loosens his hold. Our cheeks brushing against each other as he speaks. 'It felt as though I was metamorphosing into someone else. Someone I didn't recognise.'

'I thought my singing helped you get over Mum. But she wasn't even dead. Were you trying to turn me into Mum?'

He straightens and studies me. 'Your singing did help me. I confess that. But not to get over Veronika. It brought joy back into my life. I became possessed by the idea that together we could tour the world's opera venues. Maybe I could start performing again. I got caught up in this ideal future for us. But it was selfish of me. I'm so terribly sorry.'

'I do understand. We only have each other in this world. But you've been holding on too tight. I can't breathe anymore. I'm asking you to loosen your grip. I don't want to run away from you.'

'I realise that now. And to show you how sorry I am, and that I'm paying attention and can change, I listened to the songs you wrote and sent Dex's demo to all the right people.'

'Dex told me. Thank you.'

His puckered face smiles. 'You were amazing tonight. The best ever. Jacob is obviously good for you.' He turns his attention onto Jacob. 'I owe you an apology, Jacob. You're old enough to have made the decision about the Met. And I was being manipulative. I don't want you to think you're not important to me, though. You are. That became part of the problem. I wanted to be a part of your amazing future, to help you reach the heights I know you will, yet the fear that you'd distract or influence Astrid tortured me, especially with the nerves affecting her so badly. It was a quandary. It was easier to blame you for everything that was happening between us. But you've become a big part of our lives and I don't want that to change.'

Jacob shrugs, grinds his jaw.

'And congratulations on tonight, young man,' adds Maestro. 'You were as extraordinary as I knew you could be. Your parents will be proud and perhaps won't doubt you anymore.'

Jacob's smile slices at his face. 'Who knows.'

'When I told your father you were in New York, he was furious. He hung up and I called him back. I owed you. Revealing the Met performance was to be televised helped – and the fact you intended to sing opera.' Maestro studies his feet. 'I may have glossed over those points when I first discussed the Met with him. It's unforgiveable. But I'm laying out the truth here. I want us to start again. Can you forgive me?'

Jacob lugs his serious gaze to me, then grins and jigs his eyebrows up and down. 'I believe in second chances.'

He and Maestro shake on it and Jacob pulls the three of us into a group hug.

'Thanks for doing that for him, Maestro.' I stand on tiptoe and kiss his cheek.

'Can I ask you a favour?' asks Maestro. We break apart and Maestro taps the floor with his shoe for a couple of beats. 'Can you start calling me Dad again?'

I take his hands. 'Of course. I don't remember why I stopped. Dad.'

His eyes crinkle above his shaky smile.

♫

'What are you up to, Jacob Skalicky? I'm usually going over my lines by now.' Having said our byes to Dad, Jacob's still on a mission to distract me before my final performance.

'You've learnt your lines.' Jacob marches ahead of me. I can't keep up in my heels and stop to pull them off, chasing after him in my nylons. I have spares. I can't guess where we're going, but I trust him.

We step into an elevator and take a flight of stairs, then another, until he pushes open a heavy fire door. We're on the roof of the Met.

The building isn't high. All around us skyscrapers stand tall, their lights blinking. I wrap my arms around myself against the frosty night air, taking in the city view and the sight of Central Park through a gap between two buildings. The low moon appears to perch on a distant skyscraper as if it fell out of the sky.

Jacob sits on the housing over an air vent. When I join him, he slips his jacket around my shoulders, tugs me against him. 'The sky is huge.' He lifts his face to the heavens. 'We could be up the Mother Tree.'

'Except there aren't as many stars here.' There are so few, it's as though someone individually press-studded them onto the sky.

'And we're surrounded by skyscrapers.'

'You sent me all the numbered flowers, didn't you?'

'A plot to distract you. I read that if you can change focus from worrying about the things that can go wrong, you can keep the nerves at bay. And I thought hanging with the back-stage workers who come here daily and think nothing of it would help.'

'Thank you. Where focus goes, energy flows . . .' I nudge his leg with mine. I'm shivering with the cold, but this is the only place I want to be right now. 'You were incredible tonight, by the way. They loved you.'

'And you. It was as close to perfection as life can get.'

'Life.' I let out a sigh that creates a cloud of fog in the nippy air.

'Yes, life. Why?'

I rake over the night sky, light-headed. 'I don't want to die anymore. I used to want to. To see my mum and Savannah.'

'I wanted to as well. Except not to see your mum or sister.'

I elbow him, then remember the first day I met him properly. 'Like when you went surfing with a broken hand in the storm.'

'Sort of. I was leaving it to fate.'

'Maybe the world doesn't want us to die yet.'

Jacob frowns at the skyline. 'I'm afraid of messing up though, ending up in the gutter or something. Alone and forgotten.'

'Stop it. That's never going to happen. We're going to fight fate together.' I pull back to show him how deadly serious I am. His arm falls from around me. Doubt crouches in his features, but I watch him process this new reality, that someone truly cares about him, and add, 'I love you *enough*.'

His eyes begin to sparkle, then roar with something unspoken. They cradle me. 'I want to kiss you,' he says, 'but your lipstick.'

I kiss my fingertip, press it to his lips. Then, shoulder to shoulder, we fill our eyes with stars.

For a moment, I feel euphoric; it's as if I'm a bird flying across the night sky. Jacob may have opened the songbird's cage door, but this songbird has finally flown from the cage.

'I'm loosening the grip on – whatever it is I've been clinging to,' I say. 'A promise. A dream. Someone else's future? I feel – free.' Jacob threads his freezing fingers through mine and I lose myself in the muffled clatter and beat of the city below.

After a while, Jacob brings my hand to his mouth, kisses my knuckles. 'Check you out.' He grins down at me. 'You are Astrid Bell. A star on the rise. You're strong, brave, hard-working and responsible. Not a single piece of – what was it? – flibbertigibbet inside you.'

I dwell on the low moon that's gradually rising into the heavens. Then I inspect the translucent shoes I'm holding in my lap. 'Yes. I think I know who I am now.'

♫

Back in my dressing room I begin my warm-up vocal exercises and when the call comes to go on stage, I tell Jacob I need to do this by myself. He doesn't argue, but his expression is dark with concern.

When the music for *La Traviata's* 'Violetta' aria begins, I straighten my back, lift my head and glide onto the stage. I am as brave as Alice stepping through the looking glass into an exciting and unpredictable world. And I'm simply doing a job, like a plumber fixes a sink or a salesman sells a guitar. Except I have the best job in the world – to make people forget the real world, where sickness and death and terrorism exist. And I get to make people *feel.*

Silently, I shout out to my biological dad: *This is me. This is what you missed out on. I don't need you because I have everything I need.* And I hope my real dad, formerly known as Maestro, sees the smile I send out into the audience just for him.

My voice balances with the orchestra, my tone buoyant, the transitions smooth. I'm an angel granted a magical gift to sing holy and miraculous sounds. Because music is the only thing in this world that's pure. Music is the truth. And when Yolanda joins me in the final third, our voices have perfect parity and the theatre whirls with enchanted music. It lifts me outside of myself.

As we hold our final notes, I know that I'm in heaven at last.

43

Jacob

As dawn bleaches away the night, the sun water-colours the New York skyline with lilac. We meet the doc for breakfast halfway between our hotels. On the walk there, I think about how Maestro is changing, as are Astrid and I.

'I reckon people have seasons,' I say.

Astrid squeezes my hand. 'Like opera seasons.'

'No. Like nature. Sometimes people have rough patches when life is empty and dark like winter. Then other times life's crammed with possibility and inspiration, and that's similar to spring – like when the Purple Woods bloom. The trick is to remember that seasons pass, so you have to hang in there.'

'You're a poet. Ever thought of songwriting?' She shoulder-bumps me.

At the café, Astrid talks to Doc honestly about her love of songwriting and he applauds us on our work with Dex. He's excited to tell us about the offers coming in for Astrid, and us – to perform all over the world.

'This is the start of your career, Astrid,' he says. 'And I think it's time I passed on the roles of manager and talent agent to someone new. Someone with updated knowledge and skills.

With the Angel Records contract, you'll need a whole team to support you.'

Astrid looks at him doubtfully.

'Time to dump that Svengali cape, eh, Doc?' I quip.

Maestro bows his head at me. 'I already have. Besides. It seems I might be quite busy this year. You'll need to travel alone at times. I've been asked to sing at the Paris Opera. I'm considering doing it, now that you're nearly eighteen.'

Astrid lets out an unladylike squeak, which makes us all laugh. 'Dad! You *have* to do it.'

'I will drop everything if you ever need me to.' He stares at the diamond ring she's wearing – the one her mother left her.

'Thanks, Dad. You'll always be the best dad in the world, but I need to do this for myself. It's time.' She catches the doc studying her ring again. 'I'll stop wearing it if it upsets you.'

'No, don't. It's all you have of her.'

'It feels good to have her taking up less space in my heart, and merely a small part of my finger.'

'You have a brave heart, Buttercup. Unlike me. You will never run away from the things that challenge you.' The pride spilling from him is something I will never see in my own parents.

He turns to me. 'And you, Jacob? Were your parents proud?'

'Hard to say.' I move the juice glass a quarter rotation. I'm starting to understand that my parents' negative view of me is wrong. Just as Veronika leaving Astrid doesn't make Astrid a bad daughter, I'm not a bad son. 'At the after party, they were more concerned with introducing their debuting son to their friends than congratulating me. The first thing Dad said was, "You haven't forgotten the luncheon tomorrow?" No doubt, fifty influential people will be there. But it's not about me. It's about them. I'm finally that highly desired item they can approve of, but I'm an object for them to bring out and display, like an antique hat stand. I've raised their social status, now that I'm at the Met and not the Bridge View Inn.' I try to laugh.

'And it seems as though performing opera at the Met, and being televised for all their friends to drool over, makes up for the fact he's not going to the Con,' adds Astrid. 'It's as if the Con was never on the table.'

'Which is why I told my father I wouldn't be at his luncheon.'

He'd not been able to make a scene with so many people around us. Before I left, I broke my dad-funded credit card into four pieces and passed them to him as we shook hands goodbye. The look on his face was mostly shock with a tinge of realisation.

'The sooner I earn my own money and break away from them, the better.'

'That'll happen, son,' says Doc. 'With these offers, you'll both be earning your own money now.'

Except I will never cut off my parents as Veronika did. I don't want to live with the kind of lies Astrid's family have.

My phone rings. It's my home number again. Dex. I put him on speaker.

'Jacob. When you dudes getting back? I'm lonely here.'

'A week or so, kid. Hang in there.'

'I'm sick of vacuuming. I'm practically a professional at it now. My new life needs to begin. I'm not going to walk on anything but ironed red carpet from now on. My fans are waiting for me and I'd hate them to die holding their breath.' I laugh at his banter, as do Astrid and Doc, while Dex continues to tease, adding, 'What? What I say?'

Maybe Dex Firebender Brown has hit the nail on the head. He's learnt what he needs to from this season of his life. As have Astrid and I. Now it's time to move into the next season. That's how life can begin again. That's how we can walk on.

Acknowledgements

The acknowledgements page is the hardest page to write. I've already poured my heart and soul into writing this novel, yet when I think about everyone who has been there, through the doubt, hard work and long hours, it really is a case of going subterranean: from the deepest part of my humble heart and soul, thank you to these people who held my hand along the way . . .

Thank you to my agent Tara Wynne who continues to be my rock, and to my agent in New York Katelyn Detweiler who continues to be my sun.

I can't express enough thanks to the team at Pan Macmillan: Claire Craig for your wisdom and gentle guidance, Georgia Douglas for your thoughtful edits and uncanny ability to understand what I want to say, even if it's not on the page. Also Brianne Collins and Sam Sainsbury for your enthusiastic feedback and for helping me write a better book, and Kylie Mason for your meticulous eagle eye. And as for the cover? Thank you to Astred Hicks who nailed it first time; I love it so much I'll sleep with this book as I did with Enid Blyton's *The Magic Faraway Tree* when I was four. Thank you also to my publicist Hannah Membrey, and to the people who work behind the scenes to get my book on the shelves. Your efforts and enthusiasm are very much appreciated.

Enormous hugs and thanks to Ella and Eric for understanding how important writing is to me and for helping with the dishes, washing, cooking and cleaning as a way of giving me more time to write. Like Jacob and Astrid, you are still young and striving for that unforgettable life, but you should know this: you will always be unforgettable.

Thanks to Mum and Dad who bought me my first typewriter when I was thirteen. And Mum, you're an awesome editor. You should consider a career change! Thank you to Mark for his continued support and faith in me. The same goes for the rest of my family, most of whom are sprinkled far and wide around the globe, but I know you have my back.

There's always a writing group, isn't there? And there should be. An essential part of my writing world is the Stiff Wigs Writing Group (SWWiG), though we continue to swig mostly tea with the occasional gin and tonic. Alison Quigley, Debbie Smith, Brenda Kelly and Sara Hutchinson – we've been on quite the journey and there's more to come! Thank you for reading numerous drafts, especially that last one in which you were embroiled in my publishing deadline and had a week to read. Hanging out with you is a highlight in my life.

And what would a young adult author do without the Society of Children's Book Writers & Illustrators? I thank you for your support and encouragement, from the bottom of my heart. Even when I toured across the USA, oodles of you came to support me, never having met me. SCBWI rocks!

There's more! Thank you to Shelley Davidow, Annah Faulkner, Paul Williams, Cass Moriarty, Rose Allan, Emma Middleton, Tina Clark, Terry Quinn, Kate Foster, Susanne Gervay, Kat Colmer, Ellie Royce and the Electric Eighteens who continue to cheer me on, to believe in me, and to inspire me. Your friendship and support means everything.

And finally to my readers. You have no idea how much you make my day, my month, my year when you message me about how my writing has affected you in a positive way. You motivate me to write more books. Thank you.

Taryn Bashford

The Harper Effect

Harper Hunter doesn't know how it came to this.

Her tennis dreams are collapsing: her coach says she doesn't have what it takes to make it in the world of professional tennis.

Her new doubles partner is moody, mysterious and angry at the world. What is he hiding?

She is in love with Jacob, but he is her sister's boyfriend. Or, he was. Harper could never betray Aria with Jacob . . . could she?

As Harper's heart and dreams pull her in different directions, she has to figure out exactly what she wants. And just how hard she's willing to fight to get it.

'An exciting peek inside the world of professional tennis, this adorable young adult romance will leave you wanting to hit fireballs at your opponent across the court and snuggling up to your doubles partner after the match!' Kristine Asselin, author of *Any Way You Slice It*

'Details about tennis and the struggles of teens on the cusp of adulthood are nicely balanced. Harper is well-characterized, and the secondary characters, including coaches and parents, ring true. Colt and his backstory are compelling, and the revelations are skilfully handled. The match action is pitch-perfect . . . A layered romance in a unique setting.' *Kirkus Reviews*

'Debut author Bashford captures the conflicting emotions of a teen facing more than her share of dilemmas. Harper's struggle to sort out priorities, understand the meaning of love, and emerge a winner will be strongly felt.' *Publishers Weekly*